Bees that hae honey in their mouths,
hae stings in their tails.

—Scottish Proverb

LOVE'S A MYSTERY

LOVE'S A MYSTERY

in

GNAW BONE IN

JOHNNIE ALEXANDER & DANA LYNN

Love's a Mystery is a trademark of Guideposts.

Published by Guideposts
100 Reserve Road, Suite E200
Danbury, CT 06810
Guideposts.org

Cover and interior design by Müllerhaus.
Cover illustration by Dan Burr at Illustration Online LLC.
Typeset by Aptara, Inc.

ISBN 978-1-961441-44-6 (hardcover)
ISBN 978-1-961441-45-3 (softcover)
ISBN 978-1-959633-23-5 (epub)

Printed and bound in the United States of America

THE THISTLE RINGS

by

JOHNNIE ALEXANDER

*Rest in the L*ORD*, and wait patiently for him:*
fret not thyself because of him who prospereth in his way,
because of the man who bringeth wicked devices to pass.

—PSALM 37:7 (KJV)

ᴖᴖ Chapter One ᴖᴖ

The old man stirred in his sleep, muttering the words Kenna Calhoun had heard him say whenever the dark days of his past especially troubled his soul. *Cor nobile, cor immobile.* A noble heart is an immovable heart.

"I'm here, *Seanair*," Kenna said, using the Gaelic term for grandfather. She rested the back of her hand on his forehead and breathed a sigh of relief that although his pale skin warmed her fingers, the burning heat was gone. At least for now.

"My lovely Kenna," he murmured, his eyes half opening, his mind confused. *"Mo chridhe."* My heart.

The endearment meant his thoughts weren't on Kenna but on *Seanmhair*, the grandmother who'd died a few days before Kenna's birth. In those dreaded dark days, the grieving widower found comfort only in the sweet innocence of his precious granddaughter. As if she'd been born to restore his joy and his purpose.

"I'm here," Kenna murmured, not caring if he believed her to be the wife he'd adored. He loved Kenna too. At this moment, only that mattered. "Are you thirsty?"

Without waiting for an answer, she poured a glass of water from the pewter pitcher on the washstand and held the glass to his lips. He managed only a sip or two before drifting again into sleep while mouthing the Latin words.

Cor nobile, cor immobile.

The once great Granvilles, who had amassed lands and power long, long ago and had been given their title during the reign of Queen Anne, had taken the Latin phrase as their motto. From their beginning, the mighty Granvilles never failed to have a Calhoun by their side. At first as trusted warriors and bodyguards, later as stewards of their great estate.

Until those dark days, when a boating accident took the lives of the sixth duke, the duke's heir, and Seanair's chridhe. Steward Calhoun almost died himself in his attempts to save his wife, his best friend, and the young man born to take his father's place.

Kenna returned to the old wooden rocker made more comfortable by cushions she'd stitched herself. Her rocking soon adjusted to the rhythmic rise and fall of Seanair's chest. A few more months, the doctor had said. Beyond that...

She dozed, falling into a dreamless sleep, then jerked awake to her grandfather's shout.

"I must find him," he bellowed as he fought a losing battle with the blankets. "Where is he? Where did she take him?"

Kenna rushed to his side. "Shh, Seanair. You must sleep."

"He's lost." Tears swam in her grandfather's pale blue eyes, and his arthritic fingers dug into her skin with more strength than she expected him to have. "His grandson is lost."

"Not lost, Seanair. He's safe. You've always told me his mother took him away to protect him."

Her grandfather shook his head, and spittle ran down his chin. "He must claim what is his. It's only right. We must find him."

Kenna cleaned his chin with a soft cloth, her mind overflowing with Seanair's wondrous stories of his years on the estate, first as the companion to the future sixth duke then as his steward when the title became his.

The glory days of grand balls, rousing hunting parties, and bountiful harvests, Seanair always insisted, would never return. Not because the world changed after being caught in a horrific war, but because a pretender claimed the title that did not belong to him.

Kenna smoothed the blankets, and her grandfather drifted into a restless sleep. His long fingers twitched, as if grasping at something only he could see. She longed to find the words to put his mind at ease. Instead, Seanair would go to his grave carrying the weight of a burden he couldn't put down.

She kissed Seanair's soft cheek then wandered to the leaded-glass window. Dawn was still hours away, and the moon hid behind heavy clouds. For as long as she could remember, the story of the lost Granville heir had played in her imagination.

On warm summer days, Kenna would climb high into her favorite tree, a graceful rowan whose berries were gathered each autumn and made into jam. Perched on her favorite limb, her back resting against the trunk, she imagined fantastical stories where she traveled to distant lands seeking the sixth duke's lost grandson.

In her childish stories, she found him in brutal poverty, working his fingers to the bone for a master as despicable as any who inhabited Charles Dickens's thrilling novels. As heroine of her own tale, Kenna whisked the boy away from the cruelty and restored him to his true home.

As she got older, romance entered her stories. She revealed to the missing heir his true identity, and he asked for her hand in marriage. Together they returned to Granville Hall to live happily ever after. During those years, Kenna was never quite sure if she was more in love with the mysterious heir or the prospects of living on the grand estate.

She smiled now, remembering those silly imaginings. Though in the quiet of the predawn hours and affected by her grandfather's pleas, she dreamed again of being the heroine of the story. The one who found the sixth duke's grandson, the true and legal seventh duke. The one who took away Seanair's burden.

If only… Her gaze shifted to the narrow desk pushed into a corner of the spacious room. Until a few years ago, Seanair occasionally received letters all the way from America, which he read in private and hid away. He'd answer no questions about them but was withdrawn and moody for days after receiving one.

Were the letters in that desk? Could they give her the clue she needed to fulfill her quest?

Gnaw Bone, Indiana
Two Weeks Later

Only a few coins clinked in Liam McIver's pocket as he followed the path across tree-thick hills from the artist colony to the post office in Gnaw Bone.

Liam knew from painful experience during his stays in prior years that the colony manager never allowed unpaid extensions. Penniless artists with more hopes than cents had burned him once too often. "Unkept promises don't put food on the table or fresh linens on the bed," the man was fond of saying.

If the commission check wasn't in today's post, Liam would have to beg Miss Alice, the cheerless landlady at the town's boardinghouse, to take mercy on him. Maybe he could offer to do chores around the place to earn his room and board. He wouldn't mind the manual labor. Maybe he needed hard work to shake him from this dry spell.

It was the nature of art. Multiple commissions then nothing. His latest sculpture, an Indianapolis sportsman's favorite retriever, was received with such admiration that Liam had counted on his client to recommend him to friends, neighbors, and business associates.

With his expectations high, Liam whiled away too many hours at the Liars' Bench on the town square, either listening to the old-timers' tall tales and gossip or playing an occasional game of horseshoes. But over three weeks had gone by and the promised references, like the promised check, had yet to arrive.

Turned out the frugal manager was right about unkept promises.

Now, needing money and unable to appeal to his parents, Liam was drained of creativity and desperate for that mysterious spark to speak to him. The desperation led to fear.

What if the spark never touched him again?

Liam couldn't bear for his artistic dreams to die, but his more immediate concern was his lodging fee. At the Whippoorwill Glen Artist Colony—a sprawling house with rooms to let to working artists, well-tended gardens, and a rustic simplicity beyond the manicured lawns—Liam had learned to trust his artistic sensibilities and gained experience. He'd been coming to the colony for a few weeks each spring since he was eighteen.

Five years. And yet, if he didn't pay his bill, he'd be out the door.

Liam fingered the gold ring he wore on a chain around his neck and briefly wondered what the proprietor of the Gnaw Bone pawn shop would give him for the old thing with its strange Latin inscription.

Better to go hungry and sleep under Miss Alice's front porch, though, than risk Mother's wrath if he couldn't redeem it. The ring meant something to her—a secret she promised to tell him someday. He doubted it was anything worth knowing. Mother loved mystery novels, especially ones written by that English woman, Agatha Christie. Liam supposed his mother needed a mystery of her own to add excitement to her routine life.

If the check didn't come, Liam could pawn something else. His art supplies. His sculpting tools. The clothes off his back. He shook his head, knowing he couldn't do it. The ridiculous ring would go before he gave up the tools of his trade or dug secondhand clothes out of the missionary barrel.

He breathed a prayer as he opened the post office door that today would be the day his trust in the sportsman was reborn. He hoped the Almighty God paid attention to informal prayers said outside of church and when Liam wasn't on his knees. It seemed Jesus had also done a lot of His praying outdoors. Liam should talk to the reverend about that sometime.

"Good morning, Mr. McIver." The postmaster pulled an envelope from a slot in the shelves behind him. "If you'd allow us to deliver your mail to Whippoorwill Glen, you wouldn't need to come to town to retrieve it."

"I enjoy the walk." Besides, Liam would crawl through the woods rather than risk his mail getting lost after it left the post office. Or even worse, stolen.

The postmaster's dour expression didn't change, and his tone dripped with condescension. "Here you are then, sir." He handed over the envelope then stepped away from the counter.

Relief swooshed through Liam when he read the return address, but he refrained from ripping open the envelope. His mother expected him to behave like an Old World gentleman even though he wasn't one. "One doesn't need a silver spoon in one's mouth to eat like one does," was one of her frequent aphorisms.

Liam didn't think the saying made sense nor did he know why she ignored the typical "born with a silver spoon" phrase. But Mother wouldn't be Mother if she didn't put on airs as if she were royalty.

He thanked the postmaster then stepped outside. Unable to wait a moment longer, he leaned against the outer wall, slit open the envelope, and stared at the unexpected dollar amount on the check. The accompanying note from the sportsman apologized for the delay and confirmed the amount was intended as a bonus.

Liam uttered a prayer of thanks as he tucked the envelope into his pocket. Next stop the bank then the general store. Maybe he'd even treat himself to a meal at the hotel restaurant. The cook at Whippoorwill Glen fed the guests well, but the menu at the hotel would be a nice change.

As Liam pushed away from the wall, Old Jim, a local jack-of-all trades, passed by on a farm wagon pulled by his swayback mare. A young woman of about Liam's age perched on the seat beside Old Jim. Red curls fell beneath a dark blue bonnet that framed a pale face. Her head turned as her gaze darted from one side of the street to the other then landed on him. She stared, her mouth set in a determined line.

If they'd met before, he would have remembered such a beauty. But just in case, he smiled and bowed his head. She stared a moment longer then turned to Old Jim. It was impossible to hear what she said, but Old Jim responded with a shake of his head. She grabbed his arm, seemingly insistent, and he pulled back on the reins. The team had barely stopped before the woman climbed down from the wagon without waiting for Jim to assist her. The old man glared at her as if she had two heads.

Liam headed toward her, but then a horse's neighing caught his attention. The rider of a glossy black thoroughbred with a flowing mane circled in the wide street behind the wagon instead of passing on the other side. He too glared at the girl.

Liam picked up his pace, reaching her as she slid past the wheel and twisted to face him with a huge smile.

"I wasn't sure you'd be here to meet me." Her accented voice quavered, but her gaze and smile held steady. "How nice of you to do so. Perhaps you will be so kind as to escort me to my lodgings, and we can talk along the way." She tucked her gloved hand in the crook of his arm.

"I'm sorry, miss," Liam began, "but I don't know—"

"Is there a hotel nearby? Or perhaps a boardinghouse?" She darted a glance to the rider on the black horse. The smile faded, and the grip of her hand tightened on his arm.

She turned to him and lowered her voice. "Please, I am in need of an escort. Will you help me?"

Liam gazed into those large eyes and knew he could refuse her nothing. "Of course I'm here," he said loudly. "I've been counting the hours until your arrival."

Her smile, as bright as a ray of sunshine on a rainy day, returned. "You are too kind. Would you mind carrying my bag?"

"Why else am I here?" Liam said lightly. As he took the carpet-bag from Old Jim, he avoided eye contact with the rider on the black gelding. But the hair standing up on the back of his neck and the tingling down his spine told him the rider now glared at him.

Hopefully, the lass with the red curls could tell Liam why.

✑ Chapter Two ✑

Kenna clutched the young man's arm as they strolled along the boardwalk past a dress shop and what appeared to be a tearoom. What she wouldn't give for a decent cup of tea. Alas, she'd had not a one since departing the ship that carried her from Glasgow to bustling, crowded, thrilling New York City.

A young couple with a rambunctious toddler had taken Kenna under their wing on that first day at sea. Later, Kenna delighted in entertaining the two-year-old when both his parents succumbed to seasickness. They'd been grateful enough for her help to invite her to their Dayton, Ohio, home, which had brought her closer to her final destination.

"Do you mind if we stop at the bank?" the man asked. "I have business to attend to, and it shouldn't take long."

Kenna swept her gaze along both sides of the street, but her menacing specter had disappeared. What possessed her to accost the stranger walking beside her as if he were her beau, she couldn't say. But the ploy seemed to have worked.

"I can go on alone," she said, letting go of his arm and taking a step away to put a more respectable distance between them. "If you could point me in the right direction. I am in need of some refreshment."

The stranger's brown eyes danced as he shook his head. "I have questions. And I'd say you owe me answers."

"All I have to do is walk away. I'm sure one of the shopkeepers will provide me direction." Kenna eyed her carpetbag, and he immediately positioned it behind him.

"You took the train from Indianapolis, didn't you?"

"How did you know?" Kenna did her best to hide her alarm but feared she hadn't succeeded when he laughed.

"I've made that trip enough times to know that unless you have a larder in this bag—which I doubt—you've not had a decent meal in hours. I ate breakfast not that long ago. But I'm starving, and I guess you are too. I'll take care of my business at the bank, and then we can dine in style."

"You have me at a disadvantage." Not a feeling Kenna enjoyed, but one she'd become accustomed to since leaving home. Too often lately she'd been uncertain of what to do, who to trust. It might be prudent to stay with her rescuer until she found a place to stay. The unwelcome appearance of the *Sgàilean Dubh* or Black Shadow, as she'd come to think of him, unsettled her more than she wanted to admit.

Today was the first time he'd openly followed her.

"Since you won't release my bag," she said, "I shall accept your offer."

"A wise decision." The man held out his arm. "Liam McIver, at your service."

A Scottish name? Could he be the one, living under an assumed name?

"I'm Kenna Calhoun." She eyed him closely for any sign that he recognized her surname. But if he did, he hid his reaction well. He only smiled as she tucked her gloved hand in the crook of his arm.

"Welcome to Gnaw Bone, Miss Calhoun. It is *miss*, isn't it? Is this your first visit to our fair village?"

"*Miss* is correct, and no, I've not been here before. It's very different here than Indianapolis."

Liam laughed, a pleasant and hearty sound. "Don't say that too loudly. The locals won't appreciate it."

"Aren't you a local?"

"I'm here often enough to be one." He paused in front of a brick building with a sign beside the door that read GNAW BONE SAVINGS BANK. "Will you come inside?"

Her eyes flickered to her carpetbag, and he grinned. "Since you insist on holding my bag hostage," she said, "and my grandfather would be mortified if I attempted a tug-of-war on a public street, I suppose I must."

Obviously amused, he opened the door, and she preceded him inside. A teller cage and two desks were arranged between a closed vault and the lobby. While Liam tended to whatever business he needed to transact, Kenna peered through a frosted-glass window.

If the Sgàilean Dubh was still in town, she wanted to see him before he saw her.

The practical side of her, the side that chose to stay in Scotland with her grandfather when her parents emigrated to Australia and that efficiently managed his household and organized the seasonal chores and obligations of a well-to-do manor house, admonished her for being foolish.

The Black Shadow wasn't a mysterious stranger intent on doing her harm. He was simply a traveler, like herself. That their paths had crossed more than once was a mere coincidence. An explanation she could accept...except when that same practicality argued against it.

A mere coincidence to see the same person again and again in a city, aye. In a country the size of Scotland, unlikely. In the vast spaces of the United States, impossible.

A cold finger raced down her spine, sending fearful tingles through her limbs.

Kenna had first noticed the man in the New York hotel lobby where she and her hosts, the young couple with the two-year-old, were staying. He appeared to be reading a newspaper yet never turned the pages. Instead, his eyes, near slits beneath dark bushy brows, scanned the lobby as if searching for something. Or someone.

When he caught Kenna's notice of him, he folded his paper and made his way toward the exit. Despite a slight limp, he had a long stride.

She thought no more about him until a few days later. Along with her host family, she traveled by train from New York to Philadelphia to Pittsburgh to Columbus to Dayton. There he was— the same man—outside the station, as if waiting for her arrival. His expression, stiff and unreadable, softened, as if relieved to see her.

Kenna's attention had been diverted by the toddler for no more than two seconds. That was all it took for the man to disappear.

If he was on the train from Dayton to Indianapolis, he'd hidden himself from her view. But only a few cars made up the train that traveled fifty miles south from Indianapolis to Nashville, Indiana, and back again. The Sgàilean Dubh definitely hadn't been at the tiny station.

"All done." Liam appeared behind her and peered out the window. "Enjoying the view?"

"It seems a charming town." Even if somewhat rustic with its log buildings and dusty main street.

"That it is." He lowered his voice. "When I step off the train at the Nashville station, I always feel as if I've left the present behind and stepped into the past. That feeling is even stronger here in Gnaw Bone."

"Such a strange name for a town."

"Is he out there? The rider on the black horse?"

"Does he live here?"

"It's possible." Liam took her elbow and guided her toward the door. "But I've never seen him before."

When they were outside, he gestured to the hotel across the street. "The food is good there. The best in town, which may not sound like high praise, but it is. Traveling salesmen stay there, and they grumble if they're not well-fed."

Traveling salesmen? That wasn't a phrase Kenna was familiar with, but she didn't want to show her ignorance by asking about a self-explanatory term. Why, though, did salesmen need to travel when it seemed every town she'd seen, no matter how small, had a general store that sold a variety of goods? Perhaps "traveling salesmen" was a fancy name for peddlers who went from place to place with their wagons of used items to sell and trade.

Was it possible that was why she'd seen the Sgàilean Dubh in more than one part of the country? She dismissed the notion immediately, since he was riding a horse instead of driving a wagon when he came galloping up behind her and Old Joe as if he were being chased by a band of renegades.

She and Old Joe had heard the sound of hooves and turned around in the wagon seat, but the curving track hid the horse and rider from view. When he came around the bend and saw them, he pulled back on the reins, causing the horse to rear on its hind legs.

"Crazy fool," Old Joe had muttered as he faced the front again and tapped his mare's rump with the long reins even though she had neither slowed down nor sped up during the distraction.

The Black Shadow had followed them into town, keeping his distance until they reached the outskirts. Then he narrowed the gap.

Kenna was unnerved by his presence behind her. So, she did what any sensible Scottish lass would do. She enlisted reinforcements, calling on the first suitable man she found to rally to her side.

She stole a glance at Liam as he led the way to a quiet table near a corner window. He was about her age, she guessed, twenty-three or twenty-four, and wore tailored pants of a quality fabric that was no longer new. Some might call him handsome with his dark hair that curled at the nape of his neck and brown eyes that seemed perpetually amused.

He'd certainly taken her plea in stride, quickly taking up the pretense. In fact, he'd taken the pretense too far by not relinquishing her carpetbag. What if it turned out *he* was the rightful Duke of Granville? Their first meeting would no doubt be told and retold, recorded in both the Granville and Calhoun chronicles, delighting all those who heard it.

If he was the lost heir, could she talk him into coming home?

They sat across from each other at the linen-covered table and were given the choice of baked chicken with mashed potatoes and gravy or roast beef with potatoes, carrots, and gravy. Both options made Kenna's mouth water.

"What is your preference, Miss Calhoun?" he asked.

"The baked chicken, please."

Liam ordered the same. When the waitress was gone, he gazed at Kenna with a curious glint in his eyes. Or was that mischief?

"Since we are old acquaintances, may I call you Kenna?"

The rules of familiarity, she'd quickly discovered, were less formal in America than in Scotland. She determined to adapt to the easier manners, since the relaxed formality could benefit her quest. Casual strangers might divulge more information than formal friends.

"You may. And I will call you Liam."

"Please do…Kenna." He pronounced her name as if he took pleasure in the sound of it. "May I ask you a question? Or two or three?"

"We shall barter questions," she replied. "One for one."

"Agreed. You may go first."

She didn't hesitate. He'd indicated earlier that he wasn't a local. "Where is your home?"

"My parents live in Cincinnati."

If both his parents were alive, then Liam couldn't be the man she sought. The heir's father had drowned, and his mother had apparently died while fleeing with her infant.

"My turn." Liam leaned forward. "Who is that man who was following you? A highwayman after your jewels? Or perhaps a spurned suitor?"

She flashed a quick smile. "You asked three questions."

"Only the first one matters."

She glanced out the window, half expecting to see the Black Shadow staring back at her, then shrugged. "Perhaps he is…what did you say, a traveling salesman. Like a peddler, aye?"

Liam scoffed. "That man is no traveling salesman. They don't ride fine horses, and they don't frighten young women."

"I wasn't afraid." As Kenna's voice rose in volume, the other diners turned to stare. Her cheeks warmed. She might not be a proper lady, but she'd been raised to behave like one.

She lowered her voice. "I only admit that a little subterfuge seemed warranted."

Liam tilted his head then smiled warmly. "I am grateful to have been chosen for the role. Your turn again."

Kenna thought a moment. She didn't expect the first man she met to be the Granville heir, but she needed to be sure. "Where were you born?"

"In New York City. My parents moved from there when I was a baby." He lifted one shoulder. "I hear it's an exciting, cosmopolitan city. But I don't remember it and haven't been back."

His answer confirmed her supposition. She needed to look elsewhere in Gnaw Bone for the lost heir. Her disappointment distressed her more than she'd expected.

"The same question to you." Liam gave her a lazy grin. "From your accent, I'd guess somewhere in Scotland."

"Aye, near the village of Lowry."

"Where is Lowry?"

Kenna shook her head. "My turn again."

Before she could ask another question, their food arrived and they agreed to postpone the questions game until later. Though *later* might never come. Not when Kenna needed to stay focused on her quest. If she couldn't find the heir in Gnaw Bone, she'd be devastated. If she didn't make it home in time to make amends with her grandfather before he died, she'd be heartbroken.

CHAPTER THREE

Kenna stood in the parlor of the Whippoorwill Glen house, her carpet-bag by her feet, and silently practiced the cover story she'd devised during the long voyage to explain her presence in a small country town thousands of miles from her homeland. If she stayed as truthful as possible, without revealing her true quest and adding only a little embroidery to her story, then no one should suspect her of being anything other than what she claimed.

Despite the tireless efforts of the art instructor her grandfather had brought to the manor house, Kenna did not have the skill to pose as an artist. If she'd known about the photographers who frequented the colony, she could have brought a camera. Although it wouldn't have been much more than a prop for her ruse, she would have enjoyed taking pictures to show to her grandfather when she returned home. But she didn't learn about the photographers until Liam mentioned them during their meal.

Afterward, he'd invited her to go with him to Whippoorwill Glen to see if she could lodge there instead of at the hotel or Miss Alice's boardinghouse. Kenna eagerly agreed, and they'd found Old Joe at the stables. Kenna's trunk was still in his wagon, so Liam arranged for him to drive them to the artist colony for a small fee. All along the bumpy journey from Gnaw Bone to Whippoorwill Glen, Kenna prayed God was leading her, despite the meager clues, to the right place.

The few letters that Kenna had found in Seanair's desk were signed *Pen*, which she guessed was short for Penelope, the name of the companion who'd fled Scotland with the infant heir and Isabella, his frightened mother, during those dark days. None had a return address.

The last letter in the tiny stack, mailed over a year ago, provided the only clue to the heir's possible whereabouts. It read:

> *T returns to the artist colony, as he does every spring, to pursue his gift. He has the talent denied his father. His parents would be very proud to see him now. As would you, my dear and faithful friend.*
>
> *Such a funny name. Gnaw Bone. I have found many of the towns here have odd names, though I suppose Americans think the same of our Scottish ones.*

The initial *T* must stand for Tavish, the name given to the eldest son in the Granville line of succession. And the only town by the name of Gnaw Bone she could find, with the help of a research librarian in Inverness, was located in Brown County, Indiana.

Despite her grandfather's objection, Kenna had set off on her own to live the stories she'd made up as a child when she pretended to be a dragon slayer, a feminine knight in shining armor, a romantic heroine.

Now she was here, at the same artist colony Pen mentioned in her letter, and eager to discover if Tavish, the rightful duke, was here too.

Liam returned to the parlor with a middle-aged man who wore round spectacles on the tip of his nose. His hawkish eyes looked over the rims, sizing Kenna up as if she were a rabbit he meant to devour. So this was Calvin Harrison, the colony's manager, and the one who'd decide if she could stay. Even if he refused, he might be able to help her identify Tavish.

She gave him her most gracious smile as Liam made the introductions. She sat primly on the edge of a velvet settee, hands folded in her lap.

"I'm not sure I understand why you're here," he said, taking a seat across from her. "Perhaps you could explain it to me."

Kenna gave him a gracious smile. "As I told Mr. McIver, my grandfather was for many years the steward for an avid art collector. Now he has a small estate of his own, and he has entrusted me to act as curator on his behalf."

"That seems like a huge responsibility for one so young," Calvin replied.

"Perhaps." Kenna chuckled. "Except that I've been my grandfather's companion since I was a girl. I've been to Paris. Madrid. Rome." All true, as the entire family had often spent holidays on the continent before her parents moved to Australia. Seanair had insisted his only grandchild be given the same advantages he'd had as a boy.

"We planned to come together to America," Kenna continued. "But my grandfather's health prohibits him from traveling. So I have come alone."

Calvin pushed his spectacles higher on his nose. "Why not stay in New York? Or visit the museums in any of our major cities?"

"I may before I return home. But Seanair is intrigued by your vast country. He sent me here to be his eyes. To see beyond the culture of New York into the, what do you call it? The heartland?"

"I suppose we do call it that, yes. Notable work is being produced by our guests here. Our landscape artists and photographers are being recognized for their achievements." Calvin gestured to Liam, who stood near the fireplace. "Mr. McIver here is making a name for himself as a talented sculptor."

"I look forward to seeing Mr. McIver's work."

"We seldom accommodate a woman alone, although exceptions are sometimes made." He narrowed his gaze, but Kenna refused to flinch under the intensity of his stare. After all, she was Kenna Calhoun, the granddaughter of Graeme Calhoun, descendent of a long line of Granville stewards. Calvin Harrison's hawkish eyes did not intimidate her. In fact, her calm demeanor seemed to impress him.

"A ground floor suite is available that may suit," he finally said. "But you may consider it small compared to your customary accommodations."

Kenna's smile widened. "I'm sure it will suit me just fine."

"You need not fear you're the only woman here at Whippoorwill Glen. My wife is out for the moment, but she will be happy to welcome you when she returns. Mrs. Green, our housekeeper and cook, and her husband have a cottage on the premises, and a live-in girl from town has a room here in the main house." Calvin stood, indicating the interview was coming to an end. "Lodging fees must be paid upfront, either on a weekly or monthly basis."

"I do thank you, Mr. Harrison. I may stay longer than a week, but I'm not sure of my plans." If Tavish wasn't here, or if she couldn't find anyone who could identify him, then she'd be going home in defeat. Even if she did locate him, she didn't dare stay away from home too long. Not if she wanted to see Seanair again.

With the details settled, Kenna left Liam in the parlor to go meet Mrs. Green and settle into her new accommodations. As Calvin had indicated, the small room had few furnishings beyond the basics—a bed, table and chair, a washstand, and chest of drawers.

The view outside her window was nothing like the views from Seanair's manor house. At home, her windows opened onto manicured lawns, formal gardens, and even the replica of a Grecian temple. But here the cut grass abruptly ended where woods began. The designs of the colorful flower beds were simple, yet beautiful in their simplicity. A stream, bounded by flat rocks, cut across the lawn and flowed into a nearby pond where tall grasses waved above the bank.

Although eager to explore the grounds, Kenna took her time freshening up. She changed from her traveling suit into a sage-green dress with a floral print then brushed her shoulder-length hair. Once she was pleased with her appearance, she returned to the parlor. Not finding Liam there, she exited through the front double doors and followed a well-worn path that meandered around the back of the house. As she neared the pond, a dark-haired man, head bent as if deep in thought, emerged from the woods.

"Liam," Kenna called out, veering toward him.

The man startled, stopping in his tracks to stare in her direction.

You're not Liam. Kenna stood still and placed her hand over her mouth.

The man's surprised expression eased into a smile as he came her way. "Liam went into town this morning. He may not have returned yet. May I assist you?"

His smile deepened, revealing matching dimples on either side of his mouth. Seanair had a miniature of the sixth duke, painted when they were both young men. Didn't he have dimples? Could this stranger be his grandson?

"Liam and I met in town, and he brought me here. I was hoping to find him again."

"Perhaps we can find him together. I'm Travis Franklin, your willing servant." He bowed so low that Kenna feared he'd fall over. But he managed to stand upright again. "And who are you, fair maiden, who has come to grace our home with your beauty? No, no. Allow me to guess. Thou art a bonnie lass who hails from across the seas."

Kenna laughed with delight. "My accent gives me away. Though I never knew I had an accent until I boarded the ship that carried me across the seas." She purposely repeated his phrase then laughed again.

"I've always had an affinity for Scotland," Travis said, placing his hand over his heart. "It's not anything I could ever explain. Please tell me you're staying here."

"I am."

"Aw, how blessed am I. My fervent prayer is that you will not tire of my company too quickly."

"I don't see how that could be possible." *Especially if you're the man I seek.*

Liam had settled his account with Calvin Harrison, paying for another month's stay at Whippoorwill Glen, before he introduced the manager to Kenna. The rest of the money from the generous commission check, except for a bit of pocket money, had been deposited in the bank for safekeeping. He wasn't sure anything was safe in his room.

Or maybe he was going crazy.

Alone in the parlor after Kenna and Calvin left, Liam sprawled on the velvet settee, arm behind his head. The events of the day, beginning with his prayer outside the post office being answered, had lifted his spirits and pulled him out of the creative doldrums that had him spiraling into despair.

The generous check and encouraging note from the sportsman gave him hope that more commissions would soon come his way. Though he would never compare himself to the great Frederic Remington, the renowned sculptor of Western American art, Liam had spent long hours working to capture in clay a sense of the retriever's movement as it trotted across a stubbled field with a limp bird in its soft mouth. The final piece accomplished exactly what he wanted.

Now, even with no specific commission, he was ready—eager even—to mold shapeless clay into a meaningful work of art. Even without clay between his hands, his fingers moved to shape a project he'd set aside while loafing at the Liars' Bench and practicing his horseshoe aim.

But his change in outlook wasn't only due to the increase in his financial balance.

From the first moment he set eyes on Kenna Calhoun, his heart had been smitten by the red-haired Scottish lass. Demonstrating both confidence and vulnerability, she brought a joy into his life he hadn't known was missing. He still couldn't get over how she'd climbed from that wagon, graceful even in the clumsiness of getting past the wheel, and approached him with such boldness.

Especially since she had indicated in other ways that she had old-fashioned notions. Or maybe she wasn't old-fashioned as much as Old Worldly.

Amazing too that she was unaccompanied on this trip despite the close relationship she appeared to have with her grandfather. The man was apparently gravely ill, which made it even stranger that she made the trip away from him. He suspected there was more to that story—much more—but he'd have to wait for her to confide in him. If he asked her many more questions, she might shy away from him.

All he knew was that he could listen to that delightful Scottish accent every day for the rest of his life and never tire of it.

When Kenna didn't immediately return to the parlor, Liam climbed the stairs to his room, which was located at the end of a long corridor. Each year, he reserved the same one far in advance of his visit because the location provided more privacy.

And yet...

He unlocked the door, took a step across the threshold, and glanced around. Everything seemed to be as he had left it before he went into town. Yet there was something in the air itself, perhaps a scent he couldn't quite detect, that put all his nerves on high alert.

Something strange was going on, and he was certain someone at Whippoorwill Glen was responsible. Expected mail wasn't delivered though the senders insisted the letters had been sent. A dollar here and there seemed to go missing from his stash. Sketches disappeared only to reappear later—sometimes in places other than where he'd left them.

Unfortunately, none of these strange occurrences were concrete enough or obvious enough for him to tell Calvin about them, let alone confront the other lodgers.

The post carrier, a good-hearted fellow with a strong sense of responsibility, may have somehow misplaced the letters. Or they might have been lost after they were delivered to the house. Each resident had a small cubby, but mishaps sometimes occurred. Which was why, even though the local postmaster's sense of dignity considered it a personal slight, Liam now insisted on having his mail remain at the post office until he personally retrieved it.

The missing money might have been spent on something he'd forgotten or perhaps been given to the church donation box. But he was never a frivolous spender. The past few years had brought economic hardship to many, what with the stock market crash less than five years ago. But even before that, Liam had worked hard at a multitude of odd jobs to earn the money for his art supplies and travels. He knew from experience the truth that a penny saved was a penny earned.

His father was a generous man—as generous as he could be given his mother's lack of financial acumen, which at times created tension between them. Thankfully, though, those moments were few and far between. All in all, Liam had experienced a happy and blessed childhood. He'd never gone hungry or worried about having a roof over his head or clothes to wear.

But Father expected him to go into a profession, not waste his life on pursuing a dream that might never come true. He refused to finance Liam's annual stays at the Glen. Liam didn't mind the need to work. He'd learned all kinds of skills working odd jobs over the years.

Then there were the sketches. He thought he'd left them in the top drawer of his bureau, but one day they were gone. Later he found them on the floor beneath his bed. Perhaps he'd dropped them there. But he didn't think that likely.

The only rational explanation—if Liam wasn't going crazy—was that someone was playing practical jokes or was a thief. But who?

Calvin Harrison? Hardly. Mrs. Green or her husband, who performed all the general maintenance and gardening chores? Unlikely. The live-in girl who seemed afraid of her own shadow and rarely spoke to the guests for fear of saying the wrong thing and losing her place? Doubtful.

That left a very small pool of suspects—one of the other artists staying at the house. For various reasons, from friendship to personal reputation to lack of motive, Liam couldn't bring himself to suspect any of them even as he could not doubt his own sanity. Yet he hadn't received the mailed letters, the money was missing, and the sketches had been moved.

He heaved a sigh then wandered to the window where movement near the pond caught his attention.

Was that...it was! Kenna with Travis Franklin. Strolling along the bank, laughing and talking. Enjoying each other's company.

A giant fist gripped his heart, giving him a sensation he'd never experienced before.

Could he be...jealous? Absolutely not. But it sure would be funny if Travis fell into the pond.

Liam leaned against the window frame, peering at the scene below while staying out of sight in case Kenna or Travis should look toward the house. Maybe he was wrong about Travis. He was a so-so painter, a dabbler who enjoyed the prestige of calling himself an artist more than the art itself. Liam had never held that against him.

Until now.

Maybe Travis was the thief of letters and cash, the practical joker who moved sketches from one place to another. Liam needed to keep a closer eye on the shifty fellow. For Kenna's sake, if not his own.

CHAPTER FOUR

The owners of Whippoorwill Glen, a semiretired portrait painter and his wife who lived most of each year in the more temperate climate found along the Georgia coast, had renovated the carriage house into separate studios at about the time Liam first started coming to the colony.

Two of the stalls at one end of the long building housed a buggy and a wagon, but the others were equipped with overhead lighting, shelves, cupboards, and worktables. Each had double doors in the front and large windows in the back to let in as much natural light as possible. The portraitists and *plein air* painters—those who painted outdoors—primarily used their stalls as storage space for their finished canvases and supplies.

The last stall, at the opposite end of the building, belonged to Liam during his stays. A second large window provided an additional view. When the weather was fine, and sometimes even when it wasn't, he opened the barn-like double doors so he could see the tree-covered hills rising to tall ridges that hemmed in the valley.

No matter what he was working on, a sketch for a potential sculpture or the sculpture itself, it refreshed his spirit to be surrounded by nature's beauty. Indianapolis's elite society considered this place of tree-covered ridges and steep valleys, sometimes called the "Little Smokies," as charmingly stuck in the nineteenth century.

In some ways, they were right.

But Liam, along with many others, found a peace and a strength in this small county that eluded him elsewhere. That steadfast tranquility drew him back year after year.

That and the daffodils that sprouted each spring in glorious fields of yellow.

As he stood in the stall's doorway the following afternoon, a coil of wire in his hands, a mental image emerged from deep within him. Kenna sitting near a stream, surrounded by daffodils, sunlight burnishing the red of her uncovered hair. He closed his eyes to capture the details of the vivid image.

The depth of the colors spoke to him, but he was a sculptor not a painter. How would the image appear without the gold of flowers and sun, the red of Kenna's hair, the pale beauty of her cheeks? Could he still create the masterpiece he saw in his mind if it was in bronze?

Before the image could fade, he laid the wire he'd been absent-mindedly twisting onto a nearby worktable and took his sketchpad to a wide stump, sanded as smooth as he could get it to provide a suitable stool.

He'd been here a couple of years ago when lightning struck the massive tree, cracking the trunk almost to its present height. Liam and one of the other lodgers had spent the following day assisting Mr. Green in cutting it down. That spring, whenever Liam had needed a break from sculpting, he split wood from the tree trunk and piled it in the woodshed. It was probably cured by now, dry enough to be used for the house's many fireplaces come winter.

As he sketched, making broad strokes on the pad with charcoal, the outline of the image he envisioned came quickly. Clumps of daffodils surrounded an undefined figure who rested in the midst of the charcoal blooms.

He flipped to a blank page to focus on the woman's face. She resembled Kenna, yet something was wrong. Even though he could recall her various expressions with amazing clarity, the memories didn't speak to his fingers.

He flipped to a new page and tried again. He substituted a pencil for the charcoal, but the features still weren't right.

To give life to this sculpture, he needed her before him while he sketched the directness of her eyes, the tilt of her chin, the slope of her shoulders. His hands itched to get into the clay, to mold and form the shapeless mass into something—or, in this case, someone—recognizable. After that, he'd carefully pinch, poke, and prod to capture her essence and spirit. To give the clay life.

He desperately wanted to turn his image into a three-dimensional bronze sculpture. But would Kenna agree to sit for him? She'd disappeared with Travis after breakfast, her eyes shining with joy, and hadn't returned for the noon meal. Apparently, Travis had made quite an impression on the Scottish lass, though Liam didn't understand why.

"Mr. Harrison said you might be out here."

At the sound of Kenna's voice behind him, Liam quickly closed the pad and rose to his feet. As he turned toward her, the sun shone brighter and the spring breezes became more fragrant. Amazing what the unexpected presence of a lovely woman could do to a man's spirits.

"And so I am." Liam prayed the loud beating of his heart didn't betray him. "I'd offer you a seat…" He glanced at the stump. It was fine enough for his purposes but not clean enough for Kenna's polka-dotted dress.

Kenna's gaze took in the stump, the sketchbook, and the open doors of his workshop before returning to him. "I dinnae wish to disturb you."

"After the way we met yesterday…" Liam tilted his head and gave her a mischievous grin. "Isn't it obvious I don't mind being disturbed?"

Kenna's cheeks flushed, and he feared he'd been too forward. If a Scotsman wanted to flirt with her, how would he go about it? Perhaps it was better he didn't know. For now, Kenna only planned to stay a week, so a romantic entanglement would be foolish. With him or with Travis. Especially with Travis.

"Do you mind visitors to your workshop?" she asked. "I'm curious as to how a sculptor sculpts."

"It begins here." Liam held up his sketchbook then immediately regretted doing so. He didn't want her seeing his unsuccessful attempts at capturing her features on paper. If she did, she'd think him a hack and would never agree to sit for him.

"These are only ideas though," he said quickly as he placed the sketchbook behind his back. "The work takes place in here." He made a sweeping gesture toward the stall.

"May I go inside?"

"Please."

At the doorway, he moved aside so she could precede him. As she scanned the interior, he tried seeing it as she did. The sketches from his last commission still hung above the long table where he had worked to create the wire armature that formed the retriever's skeleton. The armatures and practice sculptures, both larger and smaller than the final bronze, were arranged on a nearby shelf.

He told her about his hunting trip with the sportsman and how he had hastily drawn different features of the dog while it worked the field. One sketch showed the retriever's head in profile while another his neck and shoulder. She was interested in every detail, peering closely at the sketches and handling the armature pieces he'd created then discarded in the process of making the perfect one.

She picked up the twisted wire he'd been playing with earlier. "Will this be another dog?"

"It's a surprise for Miss Molly, the local laundrywoman," he said. "Her dog—his name is Clyde—is ailing. I doubt he'll live through another winter. She loves that old hound, so I want to make her a keepsake of him." A twinge of guilt squeezed his conscience. The sculpture would have already been finished if he hadn't given in to the doldrums. Not only did he wish Miss Molly already had the finished sculpture, he regretted not having it—or at least a practice one—to show Kenna.

"That's such a kindness. I am sure Miss Molly will be glad for your gift."

"I hope so." He gave a sheepish shrug. "As long as it looks like Clyde when I'm finished."

"Is there any doubt?" Her radiant smile did as much to warm his heart as her encouraging words.

He took a deep breath then flipped through the pages of his sketchpad until he found the one he'd sketched weeks before, when he was still exuberant about his work. Hopefully, Kenna would only see the pages in the pad he wanted her to see and not the ones he didn't.

In the sketch, Clyde sprawled on the front porch of the boardinghouse, his long ears hanging almost to the ground.

"Here he is."

Kenna held the book closer. "What a sweet expression he has. And look at those long ears." She smiled at Liam. "I almost feel like I could touch him and he'd be real. You have a true talent."

"Thank you," Liam said, touched by her words. He'd been praised for his work before, enough to know that his dream of pursuing sculpting as a career could come true. But her praise somehow made him feel humble instead of proud. She believed in him. If he was ever going to ask her, now was the time. He opened his mouth, but Kenna spoke first.

"I'd like to meet Clyde. And Miss Molly."

Liam smiled at this unexpected opportunity to spend time with Kenna. "I'll be taking my laundry to her someday soon. You can accompany me if you'd like. Her sister, Miss Alice, runs the boardinghouse."

"I'd like that very much." The pleased excitement in her voice bolstered his courage.

"May I ask a favor of you?"

Her expression was dubious, but her eyes shone with curiosity. "You may ask. Though I may say no."

His disappointment would be deep if she did. But his fear might be greater if she agreed. What if he couldn't capture her the way he wanted to? Then she'd see her belief in his talent was misplaced.

"Well?" she prompted. "What is this favor?"

"Will you allow me to make a sculpture of you?"

She stared at him, her green eyes wide. "I don't know what to say." Her gaze darted around the workshop as if she wanted to look at anything but him.

"I didn't mean to offend—"

"You haven't." She stared at him, seemingly desperate for him to believe her. "I promise you haven't. I am honored. And touched."

"So you agree?"

"I don't know." She let out a nervous laugh. "What would my grandfather say?"

"I hope he'd be glad to see his lovely granddaughter memorialized in such a way."

"I think he would." Her smile, so sweet and eager, reached deep into Liam's soul. "Aye. I think he would. When can we start?"

"Now? I need to make a few sketches first."

"Are you certain you were born in New York City?"

The odd question took Liam by surprise. Why would she ask such a thing? "I don't remember the specifics of that event," he joked to cover his awkwardness. "But that's what my mother tells me. I'm fairly certain she was there."

Kenna's cheeks flamed almost as red as her hair. "Never mind me." She folded her hands primly in front of her and let out a deep breath as she smiled. "What do you need me to do?"

While Liam scanned their surroundings, trying to decide the best place for a sitting, Kenna's question trailed a discomfiting thought through his mind. First, a strange rider followed her into Gnaw Bone. Now she questioned where he was born.

Why had Kenna Calhoun come the long distance from Scotland to this out-of-the-way county? Perhaps on behalf of her grandfather, as she said. But Liam suspected another reason, a darker reason, for her journey. What could it be?

CHAPTER FIVE

Kenna tried to sit still but found it nigh impossible. Her posture was impeccable, as she'd been trained in maintaining a straight back since she was a girl. But her mind felt heavy with conflicting thoughts. When her mind wandered, her posture collapsed. Thankfully, Liam's patience was comparable to Job's.

They soon fell into a routine. Kenna fidgeted until Liam quirked his mouth one way and his jaw the other, then she straightened again. Liam's adorable gesture plucked Kenna's heartstrings, another complication she tried—and failed—to ignore. She'd been horrified to hear herself questioning where he'd been born. She couldn't imagine why she'd done such a thing.

Her cheeks flushed. In truth, she could imagine quite well. She suspected Travis Franklin could be the rightful duke, but she didn't want him to be. They'd spent hours together, riding horses throughout the picturesque valley. And although she'd enjoyed exploring the countryside, she'd spent more than enough time with Travis to know he wasn't the heir she'd imagined in her daydreams.

If only Liam could be the one. A horrible thought to think, but she couldn't help herself.

She flicked her gaze his way while keeping her facial muscles still. "How do you suppose they did it?"

Liam looked up from his sketchpad. "How who did what?"

"All those lords and ladies who had their portraits painted by the masters." She stretched her fingers then immediately folded them again in her lap before Liam could make his quirky face.

"I'm only doing a sketch," he reminded her. "And I doubt you've been sitting there more than ten minutes."

"Are you sure?" That seemed unbelievable. Surely at least an hour had passed. She refrained from looking at the time on the delicate watch pinned to her dress.

Liam peered at the sun, and Kenna did too. At least as much as she could without turning her head. A quarter of the golden sphere was below the tops of the trees on the farthest ridgeline.

The day seemed to have flown by, and she'd benefitted from most of it. During her ride with Travis, she'd learned he was adopted and often came to Whippoorwill Glen. Unlike Liam, though, he was too modest to show her any of his work.

A strange refusal, considering she'd given him the same embroidered story she'd given Liam and Calvin Harrison. She'd been disappointed, since Grandfather's correspondent had specifically mentioned the lost heir's talent.

But perhaps Pen saw Travis—if he was indeed Tavish—through the lens of love. Perhaps he returned to the artist colony each year because he couldn't accept his limitations.

"It was brave of you to go riding with Travis," Liam said, interrupting her musings.

"Why is that?"

"Weren't you afraid of that man following you again?"

"The thought crossed my mind." Often, in fact. Despite herself, she shivered. "I suppose he could have been near, but I never saw him."

Liam stopped sketching to stare at her, but she managed to maintain her composure instead of avoiding his gaze. "Did you tell Travis about him?"

Kenna shook her head. "It's too foolish, really. Perhaps he was simply riding to town yesterday. He wasn't in a hurry, so he didn't pass the wagon but followed behind us."

"I'd like to believe that."

"But you don't." It was a statement, not a question. She didn't believe it either. The horse would have needed to be held back to not go past Old Joe's slowpoke mare.

Liam closed his sketchbook and lowered himself to the ground beside her. He left a respectable space between them and rested a forearm on his knee. Leaning closer, he gazed into her eyes with an intensity that went deep into her soul. When he spoke, his tone was soft. "Why did you leave Scotland?"

Kenna hesitated, surprised at the unexpected question. But what had she expected him to ask? Something more personal? Aye, that is what she'd hoped. Despite only meeting him yesterday, for reasons she couldn't explain she felt like she'd been looking for him all her life. She apparently had yet to outgrow her childish imaginings.

If he'd asked her why she'd gone with Travis, would she have told him the truth? She hadn't even been honest with herself. On the surface, she'd seen it as an opportunity to find out more about him.

But beyond that was another reason—to avoid Liam. Even though soon after her return, she'd gone looking for him. How did that make any sense? It didn't, which only added to her confusion.

Liam couldn't be the heir. Both his parents were alive, and he'd been born in this country. She could not allow her heart to be enchanted with him when her quest was so important.

"I told you yesterday why I was here," she said. "To seek the work of promising American artists on behalf of my grandfather."

"True. You did." He leaned away and shifted his gaze toward the hills.

Perhaps she should tell him the entire story. It would be nice to have someone to confide in. Maybe he'd even help her in her search. But the secret had been a secret for so long, she couldn't bring herself to do so.

The gong sounded, summoning those on the grounds to dinner, its clang echoing throughout the valley. It had startled Kenna yesterday, and it startled her again today. "I dinnae ken if I'll get used to that clangor."

"I 'dinnae ken' if you will either." Liam chuckled. "But it's the best way *not* to get so preoccupied you miss dinner."

"Does that happen to you?"

"It has." Liam shrugged. "If I've got the mind to, I ignore it. But there have been times when I didn't even hear it."

Kenna arched an eyebrow. "How could you not?"

"I can't explain it." He stood then helped Kenna to her feet. "We don't want to be late."

They returned to the house and separated to go to their rooms. After freshening up and changing her dress, Kenna made her way to the parlor where the lodgers gathered until Mrs. Green opened the dining room door. Kenna must have taken longer to get ready than she realized, because the door stood open and the others were headed inside.

As she had the evening before, Kenna took her place to Mr. Harrison's right and across from Mrs. Harrison. Liam sat on her other side and Travis across from him. Travis gave her a knowing smile as she took her seat, which caused her cheeks to warm though she didn't know why. Perhaps because Liam must have noticed it too, and she wished he hadn't. Even more, she wished Travis hadn't taken such a liberty, as if he wanted everyone to believe the two of them shared a secret. Which they definitely did not.

Another lodger Kenna had met the evening before, a landscape artist whose work had been exhibited at galleries in Indianapolis, Cincinnati, and even Chicago, greeted her warmly. To give more credence to her cover story, Kenna had spent time with him yesterday, listening to his stories and viewing his canvases. She'd loved every minute even though he was too old to be the lost heir.

As she did so often, she wished Seanair could have made the trip with her. He too would have appreciated how the landscapes captured the beauty of the rural Indiana county. The visit with the artist had been a nice distraction from her quest.

Not that it was ever far from her mind. She fervently prayed every morning and every night that she'd return home with the news that would bring Seanair the peace he craved. That she'd found the lost heir and he was ready to take his rightful place at Granville Hall.

Even if that heir turned out to be Travis Franklin.

Mr. Harrison said grace, and the serving platters, piled high with slices of baked ham, creamy mashed potatoes, and succotash were passed around. As Kenna spread freshly churned butter on a slice of bread still warm from the oven, a young man appeared in the doorway of the dining room.

Dark hair framed handsome features, and his piercing gaze appeared to notice everything around him. As he stood before them, his bearing reminded Kenna of the young nobles she occasionally met at certain social events back home.

"I see I'm late," he said. "May I still join you?"

Mr. Harrison rose. "Come in, come in. Everyone, this is Angus Lennox, our newest lodger. Please, Mr. Lennox, take the seat there." He gestured to an empty chair next to Travis and made introductions.

As the newcomer moved toward the table, he let his gaze linger on Kenna. She politely nodded then attempted to resume the conversation she was having with Liam. But he appeared more interested in Mr. Lennox's arrival.

"I made Mr. Franklin's acquaintance yesterday evening," Angus said, directing the statement to Kenna though she couldn't think why he would. "He recommended me to Mr. Harrison."

"How very kind of Mr. Franklin," Kenna replied. "Is this your first time here?"

Angus took a sip of water. "To this particular establishment, yes. But I visit Gnaw Bone often." He pronounced his words with a strange cadence, as if intent on saying them correctly. Perhaps English wasn't his native language.

"I'm surprised our paths haven't crossed before," Liam said. Something in his tone caught Kenna's attention. Did Liam think Angus was lying? But why would anyone lie about a thing that could be easily disproven?

"Are you here year-round?" Angus's tone contained a slight challenge.

"I'm here often enough."

Not wishing the argument to escalate, Kenna jumped in. "I am astounded by all the talent sitting around this table. What is yours, Mr. Lennox?"

He fixed his gaze on hers again as if, as her grandfather would say, to test her mettle. She didn't avert her eyes. Did he truly think he could intimidate Kenna Katherine Calhoun with a brazen look? If anything, his arrogance only added to her resolve to return his audacity. And to show her amusement at his failed attempt.

"I come to this fine land as a humble photographer," he finally said.

"Before long, the photographers will outnumber the artists," Travis said with an annoyed laugh. "Although an artistic eye is needed, I suppose, to frame a subject in the best light, how much skill does it take to point the lens and press a button? True, the result is more immediate than a painting, which requires a knowledge of pigments, shading, and perspective. And takes much longer to complete."

"Technical skills are needed for both pursuits," Calvin said diplomatically. "I'm not sure we can compare one to the other."

The meal continued with lively agreements and disagreements that swirled around Kenna and had her head spinning. Although she could contribute little to the conversation, she found the differing viewpoints fascinating. However, Calvin must have feared she was being ignored. He made a point of asking her questions about the museums she'd visited and spoke of his desire to someday "do the Grand Tour."

As they ate dessert, Angus caught Kenna's gaze. "Would you do me the honor, Miss Calhoun, of joining me for a walk in the rose garden? There is a matter I wish to discuss with you."

Kenna didn't bother to hide her surprise or her curiosity at the invitation. She couldn't imagine what the stranger would have to discuss with her. Beside her, Liam stiffened. In her peripheral vision, she noted the hard set of his jaw. If she didn't want to talk to Angus, here was her excuse. Liam had played along to get her away from a situation before—though she now believed it wasn't a situation at all but only her overactive imagination. He would do so again, of that she was certain.

If only Liam had asked her for an evening walk first.

Curiosity won over her desire to spend the evening with Liam. "I'd be pleased to accompany you," she said.

Liam could kick himself for not making after-dinner plans with Kenna when he'd had the chance. He'd made a grave error in judgment, taking for granted that she'd want to spend the rest of the evening with him as much as he did with her. A mistake he wouldn't make again.

When Calvin asked him to play chess, he agreed even though his heart wasn't in the game. Still, the mental prowess required to compete against Calvin would be a welcome distraction. Perhaps he could find out more about this Angus Lennox who had the disgraceful ability to tell an obvious falsehood with no fear of repercussion. Liam wouldn't be surprised to discover that Lennox had never set foot in Indiana before, let alone Gnaw Bone.

Although Liam did his best to focus on the game, he wasn't surprised when Calvin announced checkmate.

"Shall we play another?" Calvin asked.

Liam glanced at the grandfather clock that stood sentinel between two doorways. Almost an hour had passed, yet Kenna and Angus had not returned from their walk. "Another time. I have letters to write."

Mrs. Harrison, who sat nearby, lowered the book she was reading. "If you write to your mother, please give her my regards. I hope she'll come for a visit while you're here."

"I'll tell her," Liam promised. After helping Calvin move the game table to its usual place and reposition the pieces on the board, he said good night and returned to his room.

As soon as he entered, the now-familiar sensation that someone had been there swept over him. This time, he had proof that his instinct was right. The curtains had been open when he left, he was certain. While buttoning the shirt he'd changed into for dinner, he'd stood by the window and been thankful that Kenna wasn't at the pond again with Travis. Now the curtains were closed.

The door to his wardrobe stood ajar, but he'd closed it tight. The latch was tricky, so he always did. He checked inside to find his clothes and shoes as neatly arranged as always. If someone had searched through his belongings, they'd done so with exceptional care.

He collapsed into his desk chair and opened the drawer where he'd put his sketchpad. He didn't know what to do about his mysterious intruder, but at least he could dream of Kenna's sculpture. Despite her fidgets, he was pleased with the sketches he'd made. He flipped through the pad but must have somehow missed the pages. He flipped through it again, slower this time, past the sketches of Clyde and other bits and pieces he'd doodled.

The sketches of Kenna were gone, carelessly torn from the pad.

He closed the pad and tossed it on his desk as a smoldering fire burned within him. Who could have taken them? And why?

Travis was the most likely suspect. He obviously enjoyed Kenna's company. Perhaps he hoped for a more permanent relationship. Liam jumped to his feet, intent on confronting his rival. But as he placed his hand on the doorknob, he hesitated. Travis might be jealous that Kenna spent much of the afternoon with Liam. But Liam had been jealous that she'd spent the morning with Travis. Jealousy didn't make Travis guilty.

But if not Travis, then who? Another answer came to mind, but reason argued against it.

Angus Lennox could have broken into Liam's room before he came downstairs to dinner. However, he wasn't at the colony until today. Besides, what possible motive could he have except, like Travis and Liam himself, he also seemed smitten by Kenna's charm?

Despite the practical reason for dismissing Lennox as a suspect, Liam didn't trust the man. He'd lied about spending time in Gnaw Bone in such a brazen way that not even Calvin, who knew all the artists who visited the area, had questioned him.

There was something else too. An odd feeling that played on the edges of Liam's mind—he'd seen Lennox somewhere before. Or someone who resembled Lennox. Not in Gnaw Bone, of that he was certain. But where?

He kicked off his shoes so he could sprawl on the bed and think. A folded sheet of paper from the sketchpad lay on his pillow. Opening it, he read words that sent a chill up his spine.

Leave now. Or else.

CHAPTER SIX

Kenna purposely decided to forgo breakfast the next morning, at least until the others had finished. Mrs. Green opened the dining room door at seven thirty and shut it at nine o'clock, giving the lodgers plenty of time to serve themselves from the chafing dishes set out on the buffet.

The walk with Angus the evening before had unnerved her, though she had trouble pinpointing why. Perhaps it was because all the questions he asked her—his curiosity about her home, her family, even their history—had gone beyond polite conversation. Her own questions were mostly deflected or ignored. All she knew was that he'd been born in Scotland but lived most of his life with relatives in Virginia. Who those relatives were, he never quite said.

When they were alone, the earlier hesitation in his cadence disappeared. His natural speech revealed a slight Scottish accent that he must have been trying to hide before. But hide from who? Obviously not her.

They'd returned to the house to find Travis in the parlor. Kenna sensed he'd been waiting for them, and the obvious tension between the two men compelled her to tell them both good night and head for her room. Though if Liam had been waiting in the parlor too, she would have stayed.

She'd known him only a short time, yet her heart was pulled to him in a way she didn't understand. It pained her to know that she'd hurt him by accepting Angus's invitation yesterday evening. She'd said yes because of her quest, not because of any romantic interest in him.

Her only interest in Angus was to discover if he could be the heir she sought. If he was—what a disappointment. In all her childhood imaginings, it had never occurred to her that the rightful seventh duke was anything less than the same noble, brave, wonderful man as his father, someone her grandfather had risked his life trying to save.

But, she had to remember, his father did not raise his son. His mother ran away with him, but she died soon after. Pen, her companion and lady's maid, raised the lost heir. Perhaps she married. Perhaps she pretended to be Tavish's mother.

Tavish. Travis.

Did the similarity of the names have any significance? Kenna didn't know, and she didn't know what to think about him. Or if she even wanted to think about him.

For good or ill, out of the three young men who were currently lodging at Whippoorwill Glen, Liam was the one who consumed her thoughts. Yet he was the one who most assuredly could not be the heir.

As soon as the hands on the mantel clock pointed to nine o'clock, Kenna slipped from her room and made her way to the kitchen. Mrs. Green appeared a few moments later, her arms loaded with breakfast dishes.

"There you are." She greeted Kenna with a cheerful smile. "I had to shoo the Three Musketeers out of the house this morning. I'm guessing they were hoping you'd join them eventually."

"They're hardly the Three Musketeers." Kenna stood behind a kitchen chair, her hands gripping the spindle posts on each side. "I don't think they're even friends."

Mrs. Green's smile became sympathetic. "I suppose not." She set the dishes on the counter and wiped her hands. "No need for you to go hungry because of them. You sit yourself right down, and I'll fix you a plate. Just don't tell the others."

Kenna grinned as she took a seat. "I never will."

Mrs. Green bustled at the stove then set a plate of scrambled eggs, bacon, and hash browns in front of Kenna. "Careful now, that's hot."

"It looks delicious. Thank you."

"You're most welcome."

Kenna pushed a bite of egg onto her fork with her knife. "Did Liam say if he had plans today?"

"So it's Mr. McIver you're interested in, is it?" Mrs. Green poured coffee into two mugs and brought them to the table. "I'll join you if you don't mind. The dishes won't run away if I let them sit a spell."

Ignoring the comment about Liam, Kenna chuckled. "The kitchen is your domain. I'm the interloper here."

"With all these menfolk around, you're a most welcome one." Mrs. Green took a seat near Kenna and stirred sugar into her coffee. "I agree that Mr. McIver is the best of the bunch. He's a fine and talented young man. Though I should not compare him to Mr. Lennox, as he only arrived yesterday afternoon."

"Angus said he's been coming to Gnaw Bone for years."

"Did he say that? Hmm." Mrs. Green sipped her coffee but didn't comment further.

Although the silence wasn't uncomfortable, Kenna searched for something to fill it. "Liam wants to do a sculpture of me," she finally said. "He did sketches yesterday."

"That's quite the compliment."

"I'm not sure what my grandfather would say. He's very proper."

"I hear from Mr. Harrison that he is also a collector of art."

"That's true. That's why I'm here." Kenna stumbled over the words, wishing she could spill her secret quest to Mrs. Green. To anyone who could help her sort out the clues and make them make sense. Instead, her heart took her in a different direction.

"Liam seemed upset when I went with Angus after dinner. I wish I hadn't. Though maybe I only imagined it. Maybe he didn't care at all."

"I'm not a confidante of Mr. McIver's," Mrs. Green said thoughtfully. "But he's been here often enough for me to know his moods. It might not be right for me to say it, but I don't believe you imagined his feelings."

Kenna hoped the housekeeper was right. Though what did it matter? She'd be leaving soon, and Liam would not be returning with her as the rightful duke of Granville Hall. That role might be played by Travis or Angus, and neither of them were worthy of it in her eyes.

"I do hope we can part as friends, Liam and I. That there was something I could do…"

Mrs. Green's eyes twinkled. "In my experience, a man's heart often follows his stomach. I doubt Mr. McIver is an exception."

CHAPTER SEVEN

Practically trembling with excitement, Kenna carried the basket with the special dessert Mrs. Green helped her bake to Liam's studio. Before he noticed her standing in the door, she studied him.

He perched on a stool at a worktable littered with strands of wire and pieces of pipe. His entire focus seemed to be on attaching the pipes in a certain way and shaping the wire around them. The sketches that hung on the wall were of Clyde, the favored hound dog that Liam feared would not see another spring.

Kenna had crossed an ocean to fulfill the dreams of her childhood, to be the heroine that saved the once-great Granville Hall from ruin. Instead of finding the lost heir, she'd lost her heart to a man with dreams of his own.

Liam suddenly looked up, as if sensing her presence. A spontaneous smile lit his features then quickly disappeared. "What are you doing here?"

"I brought you something." Kenna held out the basket. "A traditional Scottish orange marmalade cake that I baked myself." She gave a sheepish grin. "With Mrs. Green's help. I have little experience in the kitchen."

The smile reappeared, and this time it stayed. Liam wiped his hands on a nearby cloth and came toward her. "You baked a cake for me?"

"I thought of making you haggis, and I might have if we had a freshly butchered sheep. Though perhaps you wouldn't have liked it, not being a Scotsman."

Liam's smile widened. "It might surprise you to know that I have eaten haggis many times."

"I find that unusual," Kenna responded in surprise. "People I've met in my travels turn up their noses at the very idea of putting such ingredients as sheep's offal and suet together."

"My mother had a close friend who was from Scotland. She made it at least once a year to give me a touch of home, she'd always say. You remind me of Pippa, the way she pronounced certain words." He shifted his gaze away. "She died last year."

Kenna's impulse was to express her sympathies, but she held back. Travis had told her a similar story on their drive together. In a land of immigrants, she supposed it wasn't impossible for both their mothers to have Scottish friends. But the similarities unsettled her.

Liam reached for the basket, and his tone lightened. "Pippa never made a marmalade cake though."

"I hope you'll like this one." They went together to a nearby stack of hay bales. "Mrs. Green also gave us plates and a mason jar of lemonade."

"She must like you."

"I like her too. We had such fun this morning."

Once they were settled on the bales with the basket between them, Kenna lifted out the dense cake. "All the way back in 1797, a fierce storm forced a Spanish ship into the harbor near Dundee. A man named Keiller bought much of the cargo of oranges for a cheap price. He took them home to his wife, who turned them into marmalade. Thanks to her ingenuity and Mrs. Green's fondness for preserving fruit, we now have a marmalade cake."

She placed slices on the plates and handed him one. Mrs. Green had assured her that the batter tasted delicious so the cake should too. But what if Liam hated it? Her stomach in knots, Kenna waited for his reaction.

"This is delicious," he said, taking another huge bite. "I think you're a wiz in the kitchen."

A wiz? Liam's tone and smile as he devoured the cake assured her it was a compliment.

"Thank you. But I rarely step foot in one."

"Is that because you're actually a duchess, traveling incognito?" he teased.

"A duchess? *Ach*, no! Only a simple lass."

"There's nothing simple about you, Kenna." Liam set down his empty plate and shifted to face her. "I think you have secrets, and I want to know what they are."

"You're right. I do have a secret." One she'd come close to telling Mrs. Green more than once as they baked together. But the story seemed too big to share with someone who knew nothing of Kenna's world. Liam, though—maybe it was time to confide in him. "I could use a friend."

"I'm your friend. At least I want to be."

She believed him. Her heart believed him. "You're the only one here I trust." Still, she wavered. "But it's a hard secret. One I've kept for so long, it's difficult to talk about."

"Are you in trouble? Is it that man, the one who followed you?" Liam took her hand. "If you're in danger, allow me to keep you safe."

The touch of his hand set her pulse racing and melted away the last of her hesitancy.

"I am not a duchess, nor even a lady. But my grandfather was the steward to the Sixth Duke of Granville, a mighty duke with a grand estate. And his father was the steward to the fifth duke and so on back into the mists of history. The Granvilles and Calhouns working side by side."

Unexpected tears sprang to Kenna's eyes. She let go of Liam's hand to swipe them away, surprised that the familiar story would so affect her at this moment. It was more than the story though. She missed her grandfather. She worried about him. And as much as she was enjoying her adventure, she missed home.

"Kenna?" Liam leaned closer. "What's wrong? Please tell me."

"Many years ago, shortly before I was born, there was a boating accident. And everything changed." Somehow she managed to find the words to describe the horrific scene, piecing together the stories she'd heard from her grandfather, who had given only bits and pieces at a time. He spoke of it when he mourned for the sixth duke and his eldest son on their birthdays. When he mourned their deaths on that tragic anniversary. When he mourned for his *heart*, Kenna's grandmother, always.

Others who'd been present during those dark days had filled in a few blanks, not aware that young Kenna was eavesdropping. From them she learned how her grandfather had dived into the water again and again to rescue those who'd fallen into the depths of the loch. How he'd almost died himself and might have if he hadn't been restrained. How he'd been pulled out of the loch against his will, fighting those who rescued him.

"What a horrible thing to happen," Liam said.

"It was horrible. But the story doesn't end there." Kenna took a deep breath. "Both the sixth duke and his son, Tavish II, died that day. Tavish's son, Tavish III, and the one who became the rightful duke on the death of his grandfather and father, was only a few weeks old. That's why he and his mother weren't on the boat with the others."

"What do you mean, 'rightful'?"

"Tavish II had a twin brother, Thomas, who wasn't content with being a guardian and then losing control of the estate when his nephew came of age. My grandfather was made aware of a plot to—" She couldn't bring herself to finish the sentence. The mere thought that anyone would plot to take the life of an infant was too horrid. She closed her eyes and shivered.

"He wanted to kill his own nephew?" Liam asked in disbelief.

"My grandfather secretly helped Tavish II's wife and child get away. But Thomas suspected my grandfather's involvement. When the child could not be found and Thomas was officially named the seventh duke, the long connection between the Granvilles and Calhouns came to an ignoble end."

"Surely your grandfather wouldn't have wanted to stay under those circumstances."

"He didn't want to work with Thomas, no. But he wanted to safeguard the estate for his childhood friend's grandson. He hoped he'd return someday to claim what is rightfully his."

"But he hasn't?"

Kenna shook her head.

"Can't this Thomas be arrested for...I don't know, the threats he made?"

"I don't think Grandfather has any proof he was involved. He confronted Thomas, but by then Tavish II's wife and baby had disappeared. With them gone, Thomas had every legal right to claim the title and the lands. But none of it belongs to him as long as the true heir still lives."

"You came here to find him." His expression switched from realization to skepticism. "In Gnaw Bone?"

"It does seem an unlikely place," Kenna agreed, twisting her fingers together. "Grandfather received letters sometimes, from America. The last one was written over a year ago, but it said, 'T returns to the artist colony, as he does every spring, to pursue his gift.'" The line had stayed with Kenna since she first read it. "An artist colony in Gnaw Bone."

"T is for Tavish? The baby."

"He's a man now. It's possible he lives under a different name." Kenna bit her lip and stared at the hill of trees beyond the pond. "My grandfather is gravely ill. He longs to see Tavish take over the estate again. I want that for him."

For a few moments, neither of them spoke. Liam gently broke the silence. "That day we met, did you think I was the lost heir?"

Kenna hesitated to answer. Her feelings were so convoluted where Liam was involved. "I hoped so," she finally said. "But it seems you are not." She broke into a grin. "Despite your love of haggis."

"And marmalade cake," Liam teased. Then he grew serious again. "From everything you've said, I'm guessing your grandfather left Granville Hall."

"Thomas would not allow him to stay after the confrontation they had. Fortunately, by then Grandfather had the means to buy his own property. My parents and a few others from Granville moved there with him. My father and Tavish II were close friends, and eventually he'd have been his steward if not for the untimely deaths. But he never liked Thomas, not even when they were boys."

Liam appeared deep in thought, as if he needed to consider everything Kenna had told him. She knew it was confusing, since the grandfather and the father who died and the baby son who was now a man were all named Tavish. Then add in Thomas claiming the title—a title that belonged to his nephew.

"I'm almost sorry it isn't me," Liam finally said. "I wouldn't mind traveling to Scotland with you and meeting your grandfather. But since it's not me, then I'll do what I can to help you find this missing heir. I suppose you've talked to Travis."

"I've asked him questions about his past." Should she tell Liam that Travis had a similar Scottish story to his own? "He could be the one. I'm not sure enough to tell him the story."

"How can you be sure about anyone without telling them you know their secret?"

"I don't know that I can." Kenna's cheeks flushed. "I suppose I always thought I'd just *know*. But I was wrong about that." If only Liam had been the one.

"There's also Angus," she continued, frowning. "He was born in Scotland. He's secretive, which may mean he knows he is the heir and doesn't trust anyone asking questions. Perhaps he still fears for his life. I don't know what Thomas would do if he discovered his nephew's whereabouts."

"Is he that ruthless?"

"My grandfather suspects he sabotaged the boat somehow. I'm not sure if that's true or how far he'd go to keep his title. Nor do I want to find out, but for Grandfather's sake, I'm determined to find Tavish."

"Perhaps I can ferret something out about Angus," Liam offered. "Though, to be honest, there's something I don't trust about him."

"Bees that hae honey in their mouths, hae stings in their tails."

Liam gave her a strange look, and Kenna laughed. "An old Scottish saying."

"Say it again. In English this time."

Kenna giggled then took a deep breath. "Bees that have honey in their mouths have stings in their tails."

"That's what you think of Angus?"

"Of him and Travis both."

A rustling noise at the side of the workshop caught their attention. Liam held his finger to his lips and headed that way. Kenna followed after him, keeping her steps as quiet as his. As she peered around the building, someone disappeared into a thick stand of trees.

"Who was that?" she asked.

"I couldn't tell." Liam faced her. "Someone else has learned your secret."

Kenna shivered. What if the Sgàilean Dubh, the Black Shadow, worked for Thomas and had followed her from Scotland? Had she unwittingly led Thomas to his nephew?

Chapter Eight

Liam mused over Kenna's strange story as he harnessed the colony's chestnut mare to the gig, a lightweight two-wheeled carriage. The sixth duke and his adult son drowned on the same day. The son's wife, fearful that Thomas would resort to anything, including murder, to gain the title he coveted, fled to America with her baby son.

Kenna had added more details as they strolled through the grounds. The young mother died during the Atlantic crossing, leaving her companion to protect and raise the lost heir. The companion wrote the infrequent letters to Kenna's grandfather, signing them only as "Pen."

With the horse harnessed, Liam led her around to the front of the house while keeping a sharp eye out for whoever had been eavesdropping on them earlier. Kenna worried that the man she called the Black Shadow had followed her from Scotland. She could be right. Or perhaps the intrusion on their privacy was simply Angus or Travis, both of whom Liam considered rivals for Kenna's attention, being nosy.

He could accept that explanation more easily if not for the threatening note left on his bed the night before. Someone—the eavesdropper, perhaps?—hoped to frighten him. But he didn't scare that easily, and he had no intention of going anywhere.

LOVE'S A MYSTERY

Except to Miss Alice's boardinghouse to drop off his laundry to Miss Molly.

Even better, when he'd invited Kenna to accompany him, the sadness that enveloped her from talking about her grandfather's illness had dissipated. Her entire demeanor brightened at the chance to meet the two elderly sisters who'd lived their entire lives in Gnaw Bone.

Kenna was waiting for him on the front veranda, and it didn't take them long to load the canvas bag of Liam's laundry and the basket with generous slices of marmalade cake inside.

"Did neither of the sisters ever marry?" Kenna asked once they were on their way.

"Miss Alice did. But her husband died a long time ago. Some kind of farming accident, I think." He chuckled. "Miss Alice and Miss Molly couldn't be less alike. Miss Alice is gloomy as a rainy day, and Miss Molly is all sunshine. Miss Molly never married, but to my mind she'd have been the better catch."

"Perhaps Miss Alice is the better cook," Kenna said. "Mrs. Green told me that a man's heart often—" She clapped her hands over her mouth, and her cheeks flushed bright red.

"A man's heart often what?"

She murmured something, and he leaned closer. "Say that again."

She gave him an exasperated look. "She said that a man's heart often follows his stomach."

"That's probably true," he replied. The he realized the implication of what she'd said. He faced the road while shifting his eyes toward her. She stared straight ahead, sure that spots of pink still highlighted her cheeks.

"Is that why you baked me a cake?" he asked, his tone half-teasing, half-serious. Maybe a romance wasn't as far-fetched as he imagined.

Kenna smoothed her skirt over her knees and primly folded her gloved hands in her lap. "Mrs. Green thought you might like it."

They rode for a few moments in silence, a strange tension building between them until Liam felt as if he'd burst. If there was even the slightest chance Kenna cared for him as he cared for her, he needed to know.

"Do you like America enough to make it your home?" he asked.

"Perhaps. Someday." She paused then sighed. "I won't leave Grandfather again. I shouldn't have left him now."

Liam's heart clenched, but he understood. If his mother were ill, he wouldn't leave her either. "I know it's hard to be away. But I'm glad you came."

"If you moved to Scotland, you could eat haggis whenever you wanted." Her playful tone seemed to cloak the deeper meaning of her words. "And marmalade cake."

"I might do that," he said, matching her tone, "if I were the lost heir." Since he wasn't, how could he possibly move across the ocean, even for love? He had prospects here, opportunities to pursue his dreams.

In a new country, he'd have nothing.

He could offer Kenna, the granddaughter of a man who owned an estate, nothing.

Only his heart. And that wasn't enough.

"We're here." He guided the mare into the short driveway in front of the two-story wood building on the outskirts of Gnaw Bone. A large sign near the road read:

ROOMS TO LET
BY THE DAY, WEEK, OR MONTH
CLEAN SHEETS, HEARTY MEALS
MISS ALICE MATTHEWS, PROPRIETRESS

A couple of Model A Fords, one green and one blue, were parked beside a covered cart, a buggy, and a farm wagon. Beyond the parking space, a few horses milled around in a corral near the stables.

Since they weren't staying long, Liam maneuvered the gig alongside the long porch where the two women sat in rockers handmade by their father.

"Hello, Miss Alice. Miss Molly," Liam called as he hopped from the gig.

Molly laid down her knitting as she returned his smile and gazed curiously at Kenna. "Welcome, Mr. McIver. How good to see you, and what a nice surprise. Who have you brought with you this fine day?"

Alice, who was snapping green beans, stood and wiped her hands on her apron. "You are welcome indeed, Mr. McIver," she said a little less warmly. "And so is your guest."

Liam lifted Kenna from the gig, smiling as his hands fitted around her waist. He set her feet on the ground then reached for the basket.

"Ladies, may I introduce Miss Kenna Calhoun, who is visiting us at Whippoorwill Glen all the way from the Scottish Highlands."

Alice snorted. "You are a long way from home, Miss Calhoun. What brings you to our county? A wish to stare at the backwoods country folk?"

"Now stop that, Allie," Molly scolded. "Never you mind her," she said to them. "She's got her knickers in a knot because of what came out in the *Indianapolis News* the other day. Those highfalutin folks enjoy a bit of fun at our expense, and Allie takes it much too seriously, if you want my opinion."

"I don't blame her," Liam said, shooting a smile at Miss Alice. Not that his taking her side or his smile would increase her opinion of him. Thankfully, he was already on her good side—not that she'd let him know it—because she appreciated his willingness to help with the odd chore now and then. Even the slightest praise from Miss Alice was high praise indeed.

He sided with her because he agreed with her. The city tourists who came to Gnaw Bone too often treated the locals as if they were relics from the past when the truth was they were good-hearted, hardworking people who stayed in this beautiful area when others with less gumption and grit moved on to finer pastures.

"Miss Kenna isn't here to gawk or poke fun," Liam continued. "She is interested in our local artists."

"Oh my, how wonderful," Miss Molly gushed. "Are you an artist too?"

"I'm not," Kenna replied. "I only have an eye to appreciate it, not to create it."

Alice motioned them toward the porch steps. "Let's not keep our guests standing here in the dirt, Molly. We have lemonade to offer you if you've time for a glass."

"That would be very kind," Kenna said as she preceded Liam onto the porch. "We brought Scottish marmalade cake. Liam thought you might enjoy a taste."

"How lovely." Molly lifted the cloth covering the basket to peek inside. "I've never had marmalade cake. You two take a seat, and we'll be right out to join you."

While Molly was talking, Miss Alice had already headed into the house. Both sisters reappeared soon after. Once they and Kenna were settled in the various chairs on the porch, Liam took his glass of lemonade and lowered himself to the wooden floor, his back against a post. A moment later, the hound dog lumbered up the stairs and sprawled beside him.

"This must be Clyde," Kenna said with delight in her voice as she shifted her gaze to Liam. "He looks exactly as you sketched him." Immediately she covered her mouth with her hand, her eyes filled with remorse.

"You sketched my Clyde?" Molly clapped her hands. "How wonderful. May I see?" She gave him a searching look, as if she expected him to produce his sketchpad out of thin air. "But you didn't bring it, did you?"

"Not today." Liam pretended to shoot Kenna an annoyed look. "But someday soon I will, I promise."

"I am sorry," Kenna said. "I didn't mean to ruin the surprise."

Liam waved off the apology. He didn't mind her mentioning the sketch but was glad she hadn't said anything about the sculpture. If it didn't turn out the way he wanted, Miss Molly need never know he'd tried.

"The way you make over that dog." Alice gave her sister a withering look that Molly ignored. "I'm sure Mr. McIver has better use for his talents than drawing that old hound."

"I could always sketch you, Miss Alice," he teased.

Alice snorted. "Now, you and I both know that would be a waste of good paper."

"It wouldn't be to me." Liam's gaze focused on the sisters as he imagined a bronze of the two of them, perhaps sitting on a porch as they did now. Maybe this was the niche he was looking for, the inspiration that drew him to this place again and again as Mr. Remington had been drawn to the American West. Accomplished landscape artists were gaining fame for their scenic paintings of the rural county. His sculptures reflecting the area could spark similar interest.

"We've already been photographed by that newspaper man," Alice said. "Why he thinks anyone would be interested in a picture of me standing by my mailbox, I don't have a clue. But there we were, out by the road, with him telling me to look this way and that way while he stared into that box of his."

"Oh, Allie, don't fuss so." Molly rolled her eyes which, in typical Molly fashion, included the rolling of her entire head. "She loved all that attention. She only pretends to be annoyed."

"I'd like to see the photographs," Kenna said. "I wish I had a camera so I could take photographs of everyone I've met to show my grandfather when I return home."

Liam scratched Clyde behind the ears as the conversation swirled around him. Both sisters were interested in their foreign visitor, and Kenna was just as interested in their lives here. She had a way about her that encouraged others to open up to her.

Even Miss Alice laughed a time or two. It might have helped that they enjoyed Kenna's cake and that she was gracious to offer to share the recipe.

While the women talked, Liam let his thoughts roam, first by bringing into sharper focus the mental image of the two sisters in his mind, how he'd pose them and how much of the porch he'd add to give context to the piece. Not much, and maybe not the porch at all but a porch swing. Or a bench. In a finished piece, the focus needed to be on the sisters themselves.

From there his attention wandered to Kenna as he half listened to the conversation. She was poised without being arrogant, congenial without being patronizing. Given her upbringing as the granddaughter of the gentry, even without a noble title to call their own, she must be used to a vastly different social circle than what was available here in rural Indiana.

Liam imagined that even the social elite in Indianapolis, who considered themselves so high and mighty, would probably stand out as rubes in Kenna's usual sphere.

What would he be like in that world? His mother expected gentlemanly manners and taught him the finer points of etiquette. But was it enough? Would Kenna be proud to introduce him to her grandfather?

He certainly wouldn't mind introducing her to his parents. He'd already posted a letter to his mother telling her about the commission check he'd received and the Scottish lass who'd traveled so far to come to the colony. He'd left out the little detail that Kenna had crossed the ocean unchaperoned. Mother would be horrified when she discovered that. If she ever did.

"I asked Liam," Kenna said, "about the origins. But he didn't answer me."

At the sound of his name, Liam returned his attention to the conversation.

"I didn't what?" he asked.

"How could you come back to Gnaw Bone again and again," Molly scolded him, "and not know where the name came from?"

Alice let out her usual *humph.* "No one knows for sure where that name comes from. Though there are theories."

"My favorite," Molly said, "is the one connected to the French. What was the name of that settlement? I can never remember exactly how to pronounce it."

"I'd forgotten that," Liam said, acting offended by Molly's pretended scolding. It was one of the things he loved about her. How she treated him like a favored nephew, and he could treat her as a favorite aunt.

His mother's Scottish companion had been like an aunt to him too, especially since he had no other relatives except for his parents. He missed Pippa and their relationship desperately. Molly and Alice couldn't replace her, of course, but Molly's warmth and even Alice's standoffish ways eased his heartache a little.

"There was a French settlement around here," Liam explained to Kenna. "If I'm remembering right, it was called Narbonne after a city in southern France. Over time, the name became Gnaw Bone."

"I like that explanation," Kenna said. "Don't you, Miss Alice?"

"It's not a question of liking," Alice said. "But is it true? Our grandfather tells a different story that's not nearly as genteel."

"I'd like to hear it." Kenna leaned forward in expectation.

"It's not much more than a rumor now, I suppose," Alice explained. "One man was talking about another, and he said of that man, 'I seed him over at the Hawkins place a' gnawin' on a bone.'

The name may have nothing to do with France but only one man talking about another."

"That one is so funny," Molly said with her characteristically cheerful laugh. "And no one tells it better than you, Allie."

When they were ready to leave, Kenna thanked both women for their hospitality and Miss Molly invited her to come back anytime. She seemed especially pleased when Kenna patted Clyde, who managed to get to his feet to escort them to the buggy.

When they arrived at Whippoorwill Glen, Kenna went inside while Liam unharnessed and brushed the mare. As he slid the brush over the chestnut coat, he mulled over the future.

His father thought he had the brains and acumen to go into law. The art of sculpture, to him, was a hobby, not a profession. Though his parents were well-suited to one another, one issue divided them—Liam's economic instability.

In this, his mother's will had prevailed. Father hadn't liked it, and he showed his disapproval by refusing to discuss the subject at all.

But Mother was always proud of his artistic achievements, no matter how small.

He was pleased with himself, he mused, as he made the way up the stairs to his room. He had gone from having only one project in mind—the sculpture of Clyde—to having three. The primary one, of course, was Kenna. And not only because she might leave at any time, but because he wanted a sculpture of her for himself. Something tangible to always remind him of her.

Now he also had the potential idea of Miss Molly and Miss Alice together. Someone had once called them Sunlight and Shadow, and he hoped to capture the different essences of their personalities while neither offending nor patronizing Miss Alice. She wouldn't want to be depicted differently than she knew herself to be, but neither would she want to be seen as worse.

He shook his head at that potential challenge as he put his key into the lock. Then he hesitated. What would he find amiss when he opened his door this time? More missing sketches? Another threatening note?

He braced himself and opened the door.

His bedding and mattress hung off the bed frame, and the contents of his drawers were scattered on the floor. The wardrobe doors stood open, his shirts pulled from the hangers and his shoes all akilter.

Liam picked up his pillow from the floor and sighed. Either someone was trying to intimidate him, which wasn't going to work, or he was looking for something. If so, what had he hoped to find?

CHAPTER NINE

The hand-drawn map Kenna found in her room after breakfast the next day depicted the side of the house and a path that led from the back of the kitchen garden into the woods and ended at a stone circle. A note written on the map read:

Meet me here, at the old wishing well. A surprise awaits.

It was signed only with a flourished *L*.

An *L* for Liam.

He'd told her he was going to Nashville, the town where the train station was located, to meet with the owner of an art gallery, when all along he was planning...what? Kenna couldn't wait to find out.

She pressed the map to her heart. It was a keepsake she'd treasure forever. Especially since once she left Gnaw Bone it was doubtful she'd ever see Liam again. She must return to her home in Scotland. He must fulfill his dreams in America.

A compromise would be an island in the middle of the Atlantic where, as far as she knew, no island existed. Even if it did, such a compromise wouldn't help either of them.

Kenna changed into a fresh dress, a golden cotton print that suited her complexion, and arranged her hair into a classic twist. The front sections were rolled away from her face and pinned while the rest of her curls flowed free. Taking a deep breath, she stared at her reflection in the grainy mirror.

Though she didn't dare hope that Liam had changed his mind about traveling to Scotland, the hope, as tenacious as a wildflower whose long roots had wrapped around buried stones, refused to go away.

Her heart pounded as she left the house and made her way to the wooded path. She found it difficult to maintain a ladylike walk when her feet wanted to fly.

To her surprise, she found the well in a small clearing near an abandoned log cabin. A wooden platform in front of the slanted door was bordered by vines, a broken tree limb lay across a corner of the roof, and shards of broken glass jutted from the window frame.

A picket fence stretched a few feet from one side of the cabin, but the weathered posts seemed to be held up only by the brush that grew around them. On the other side of the cabin, an overgrown lane wide enough for a horse-drawn wagon stretched into the woods.

Although the morning sun's slanted beams lit the clearing, the pathway and the surrounding woods were in shadow. A desolate eeriness surrounded Kenna, as if whoever once lived in the cabin had known great sadness. Even the birds were silent.

Despite herself, she shivered and looked around for Liam.

Perhaps he was inside the cabin, though she didn't know why anyone would want to venture past that door, which appeared to be hanging ajar on one hinge, into the darkness.

"Liam," she called then listened for a reply. Nothing. "Liam, it's me, Kenna. Where are you?"

"You're calling for the wrong man." The voice came from a nearby oak.

Kenna backed away and stared as Angus dropped from a low branch and returned her gaze with sharp eyes that seemed to see everything yet revealed nothing.

"L can also stand for Lennox." He faked a sheepish shrug. "Sorry if I disappoint."

Disappoint? She was much more than disappointed. But he didn't need to know that, and she didn't need to pretend she wasn't aware of his deceit.

"You signed with an *L* on purpose, knowing I would think it was Liam who drew the map."

"I needed to be sure you'd come." He wandered to the well and peered over the side. "Do you think if I drop a coin into the water, my wish will come true?"

"Whether a wish comes true depends on what we wish for and the sacrifices we're willing to make."

"Is that so?"

Irked by his mocking tone, Kenna didn't respond. He laughed as if her disdain amused him.

"Would you like to hear my wish?" he asked as he leaned against the stone wall of the well.

"Is that why you lured me here?"

His eyebrows raised as he chuckled at her choice of words. When he spoke, he made no effort to hide his native accent. "You came of your own free will, my dear Kenna. I dinnae force you. You canna lie and say I did."

"I don't lie."

"Neither do you tell the truth. At least not all of it." He narrowed his eyes, pinning her with his dark stare so she felt small and vulnerable. She straightened her shoulders and held her arms stiff at her sides, her hands balled into fists.

"I know why you came to Whippoorwill Glen," he said. "I know who you hoped to find here."

She started to ask him how he knew but realized the answer before she could speak the words.

"You're the eavesdropper," she said instead.

Bees that hae honey in their mouths, hae stings in their tails. Angus had proved the truth of that axiom once again.

Still, she was relieved to learn he'd been the one lurking around the workshop. That it hadn't been the Sgàilean Dubh. The man and his huge black horse seemed to have disappeared. Or perhaps he'd gone on to his destination and all along her fear of him had been foolish nonsense.

"Which is why I lured you here. I dinnae want anyone to hear what we say to one another."

"Your wish is such a secret that only I can know it?"

"My wish is to return with you to Scotland. To meet your seanair." He stepped closer until only a few feet separated them.

His proximity made her uncomfortable, but Kenna refused to give him the satisfaction of letting him know it. She met his gaze, strong and steady, while he spoke.

He softened his voice. "My wish is to fulfill your wish to find the true heir of Granville Hall." He spread his arms. "He stands before you. I am the heir."

Even though Kenna had expected him to say those words, had even braced herself against them, hearing him say them out loud still felt like an assault. It couldn't be true. The boy-heir she'd dreamed about rescuing so often couldn't have grown up to be Angus Lennox.

"Why should I believe you? Since you overheard everything I told Liam, whatever proof you have is worthless. There's nothing you can say to convince me you're the heir."

"I don't need to say anything." Angus dug an object from his pocket. "This belonged to my father. Knowing as much as you do about the Granvilles, I'm sure you're familiar with their emblem."

He took Kenna's hand and placed a ring in her palm. The gold band had a carved design of golden vines, leaves, and flowers against an ebony background. The design was inset between raised edges.

Kenna had seen the design many times. "It's a Scottish thistle ring." According to her grandfather, the Scottish thistle was a motif often used in the carvings of Granville Hall. Because the Calhoun heritage was intertwined with that of the dukes, Seanair had incorporated it into his own designs. He'd had it engraved above the main entrance doors to the manor house and in the mantels of every fireplace.

"If you already have the ring and knew the story, then why haven't you returned to Granville?" Kenna asked. "Why live under a false name when you could have claimed your rightful place whenever you wished?"

"I've often considered it." He stepped away, leaving her to hold the ring. His demeanor had softened, as if he hoped to persuade her to believe him.

"All my life I've been told to fear my uncle's ruthlessness. I suppose I still do. If I had known I had a champion in your grandfather, that he would have supported my claim, perhaps I would have returned. But I didn't know, and so I expected to live the rest of my days in hiding. As Angus Lennox, commoner, instead of Tavish William, Duke of Granville."

"Seanair never mentioned a ring."

Angus laughed, a harsh, grating sound. "I know *your* wish, Kenna. You wished for Liam McIver to be the heir. But how could he be when he wasn't even born in Scotland? You need to accept the truth whether or not it's what you want."

"I do want the truth," Kenna insisted, no doubt with more force than was necessary. "Do you think I'd attempt to pass off someone false to my grandfather? Or that Liam himself would agree to such a scheme?"

"Nae," Angus said firmly. "The old steward believes so fiercely that the current duke is false, I'm sure he would not accept someone who didn't have proof of his claim. I wonder, though. Why does your grandfather care so much who holds the title? Is the supposed usurper mismanaging the estate? Is it not conceivable that Thomas is capable of making decisions that I, someone with no experience, could not?"

"You sound as if you're defending him." Kenna's voice rose in anger. "Do you not care that he threatened to kill you and your mother? That she had to leave Scotland to save your life? To protect you?"

"How do you know that's what happened? It could be Steward Calhoun frightened her into running away."

Kenna's heart pounded against her chest as indignation rose within her. "Why would Seanair do that?"

"I couldn't say, having never met the man." Angus's expression was inscrutable, giving her no clue as to why he would be skeptical of her grandfather's motives. A twinge of doubt raced up her spine, but her loyalty to Seanair quickly squashed it. He would not have spent his entire life bemoaning the current state of affairs at Granville if he'd played any part in bringing them about.

Needing to think, and with a dull ache throbbing at her temples, Kenna lowered herself to a nearby log without caring about the dirt she'd get on her dress.

If Angus was, as he claimed, the true heir, then she almost wished she had never come on this quest. Except if she hadn't, then she wouldn't have met Liam.

Wouldn't it be better, though, not to have met him than to return home with Angus? What a mess she'd made when all she'd wanted to do was fulfill her grandfather's lifelong hope.

"The ring has a strange inscription," Angus said, interrupting Kenna's thoughts. "Perhaps you can explain it."

Kenna peered at the inside of the ring and read the engraved words. Stunned by what she read, she repeated them out loud. "Cor immobile."

She could almost hear her grandfather repeat the words he'd said so often: *Cor nobile, cor immobile.* The Granville motto.

"I think it's Latin," Angus said. "I asked someone what it meant once. It's something to do with the heart or the spirit. I don't recall exactly. Do you know?"

He was lying.

Kenna knew with every breath in her body that he was very aware of the Latin phrase. But she'd play along with whatever game he wanted to play. Because if he was indeed the heir, then she needed to let her grandfather know that what was lost had been found.

No matter the consequences or how much she disliked the rightful duke.

If only she could be like the heroine of her dreams at this moment. But that was impossible because Angus was not the hero of her dreams.

Yet here they were, caught together in a story of brotherly rivalry as tragic as Jacob and Esau's. Unlike the Biblical twins, however, Thomas could never be reconciled with his drowned brother.

"It's Latin for 'immovable heart.'" She handed him the ring. "It's the second phrase of the Granville motto."

"What is the first phrase?"

"Cor nobile. Noble heart."

A slow, sly smile spread across Angus's face as he studied the engraving.

"You have a ring in your possession with the Granville emblem and half of the Granville motto," Kenna said. "But that may not be enough to prove to your uncle that you are the lost Granville heir."

"I think it is. And now that I know your grandfather will stand behind me, I'm eager to claim what is rightfully mine." He pocketed the ring. "We should leave immediately. You must be anxious to return home. To see your grandfather again."

Of course she was. Seanair was in her thoughts and prayers every minute of every day. But he was no longer the only man she held in her heart. As eager as she was to greet her grandfather, she was loath to say farewell to Liam.

The heroic quest she'd imagined since she was a wee lass had come to an end. But instead of experiencing the heady joy of victory, her heart was nigh to breaking.

Chapter Ten

Liam removed the mare's saddle and blanket, eager to rub her down then clean himself up after the long ride to and from Nashville. The meeting with the gallery owner had gone even better than he had hoped thanks to recommendation letters from former clients. The owner had agreed to host a small exhibit in the fall, which meant Liam needed to get busy. Hopefully, once Miss Molly saw Clyde's sculpture, she'd be willing to pose for one. And hopefully, she could talk her sister into posing with her.

On the ride back to Whippoorwill Glen, Liam had envisioned other sculptures he could add to the exhibit that would capture the character and spirit of Brown County. The stump outside his workshop. The Liars' Bench at the town square. A couple of the old-timers playing horseshoes. Even Calvin, shoulders bent and forehead propped on his hand, studying a chessboard.

He could see each one in his mind, as clear as if they already existed. It would take time, patience, and skill for each finished piece to match his vision. But he was confident in his abilities. Besides, he needed to stay busy in the months ahead, to keep his mind and his heart on his work instead of on the red-haired Scottish lass who'd turned his world upside down by pretending to know him.

She filled his thoughts whenever he *didn't* concentrate on possible sculptures for the fall exhibit.

He'd looked for her as he'd ridden up the lane to the house and around to the stables in hopes that she'd come out and greet him. His spirits had sunk a little when she didn't appear. Though why should she spend her morning waiting on his return? He only hoped she hadn't spent it with Travis or Angus even though that was a good possibility. She was still on a quest to find the lost Granville heir, and they were her only two candidates.

He wished he knew what he could do to help her, but he didn't have any ideas. He'd racked his brain to remember the lodgers he'd met in the past, especially the ones who'd been at Whippoorwill Glen more than once. But none of them seemed likely options.

As he brushed the mare, he mused that Calvin might be able to help. That is, if Kenna agreed. The three of them could go over the registries for the past few years together and make a list of the men who were in the right age range.

Kenna had said that the boating accident occurred a few weeks before she was born and that the lost heir was an infant at the time. Since she was twenty-three, then the lost heir also had to be at least twenty-three.

Just like him.

It seemed odd that he and the Granville heir were the same age and both artistically talented. He even had a slight Scottish connection through Pippa, his mother's companion. If he hadn't been born in New York City and his parents weren't both still living, he might be tempted to wonder if he was the heir.

He laughed away the ridiculous notion as he put away the grooming kit. But the thought returned even stronger. *What if...?*

He laughed at himself again. There was no *what if*. No wondering. No speculation. No possible way.

For him to be the lost heir, his parents wouldn't be his parents, he'd be Scottish instead of American, and his entire life would be a lie.

Other thoughts flitted through his mind—past reflections, snippets of memory—as he put the mare out to pasture. He perched on the top rail of the board fence, unable to get away from them.

Mother expecting him to behave like an Old World gentleman. Mother putting on airs as if she were royalty.

Her nonsensical aphorism: *"One doesn't need a silver spoon in one's mouth to eat like one does."*

Occasional whispers between Mother and Pippa that stopped when he entered the room.

Mother's occasional bouts of tears that could be attributed to nothing except a hidden sadness.

The reflections couldn't mean anything. But as he stared past the mare and the pasture and the woods to the blue sky's far horizon and played with the ring that hung around his neck, they seemed to mean everything.

"What're you doin' out here?" a voice boomed behind him, interrupting his thoughts.

Liam half turned as Mr. Green, the gardener and handyman, neared the fence and propped his arm on the top rail.

"Thinking."

"You mind tellin' me what you did to upset that redheaded gal who's stayin' with us?"

Liam startled, the question hitting his heart with the force of a sledgehammer. "You mean Kenna? What happened? What's wrong?"

He jumped off the fence and started toward the house, but Mr. Green grabbed him by the arm.

"Just hold on there a minute. No need for you to go runnin' up there like a headless chicken." When he was satisfied that Liam wouldn't take off, Mr. Green let go of him. "That gal is in her room, packin' to leave us, and it sure looked to me like she'd been crying when I took her trunk to her room. So I'm a-going to ask you one more time. What did you do?"

"I wasn't even here," Liam protested. "Her grandfather has been ill. Did she get a telegram? A letter? Perhaps a telephone message?"

The Harrisons didn't have telephones installed at Whippoorwill Glen, but the hotel in Gnaw Bone had one. Kenna's grandfather might have assumed that was where she was staying, since a letter telling him otherwise couldn't have reached him yet.

"No, no, no." Mr. Green shook his head. "No message that I know of." He stared at Liam for a long moment then shooed him away. "I reckon it's best you go see her. Off with you now."

Liam didn't wait for the burly man to change his mind. He rubbed his arm as he raced around to the back of the house. Mrs. Green's kitchen was off-limits to the lodgers—except for Kenna apparently—but Liam decided to risk her wrath and take the consequences.

He flung open the door and stopped in his tracks.

Kenna sat at the kitchen table with a plate of cookies and a glass of milk in front of her. She'd been staring out the window but shifted her gaze to him standing on the threshold.

He glanced around, but Mrs. Green was nowhere to be seen. "Are you alone?"

"Mrs. Green is in the parlor. She said something about the grandfather clock and its weight. I didn't understand it." Kenna gestured to the chair across from her. "Would you like a cookie? There's more than enough for the two of us."

"I'm not sure I should. Mrs. Green doesn't like—"

"It's fine." Kenna averted her gaze, and a small smile touched her lips. "I saw you coming this way. She knows you're here."

"I see," he said, although he wasn't sure he did. First Mr. Green manhandled him, and now Mrs. Green allowed him in the kitchen. Something strange had happened while he was in Nashville. But nothing would keep him from accepting Kenna's invitation.

"I'm glad you're back," she said as he joined her. "My quest has come to an end."

"You found the lost heir?" Disappointment knotted his stomach though he couldn't understand why. Disappointment about what? No matter what outlandish thoughts he'd struggled with before Mr. Green accosted him, he couldn't be someone he wasn't.

Kenna was packing to leave for Scotland, and he had to let her go.

"Anyone I know?"

She nodded, as if hesitant to answer him, then released a deep breath. "It's Angus Lennox. He's the grandson of the sixth duke and would have been the seventh duke if his uncle hadn't usurped the title. But now Angus can be the seventh duke. Or perhaps the eighth." Her brow furrowed. "I dinnae ken which it will be given the circumstances. Only that Thomas and his son, who by the way is also named Thomas, will have to leave Granville."

Liam didn't care if the lost heir was the first duke or the tenth. But Angus Lennox? How was that even possible?

"The clue that brought you here was what that woman, Pen, wrote in her letter," Liam said. "She said that 'T' was coming to Gnaw Bone in the spring as he'd done before. Angus has never been here until this year."

"He says he has." Kenna spoke as if she didn't care about what seemed, at least to Liam, a clear contradiction. In her mind, the matter appeared to be settled. But Liam couldn't accept that.

"Besides," Kendra added, "he has proof."

"What kind of proof?"

"He showed me a ring that belonged to his father. It shows the Granville emblem, a Scottish thistle."

"The ring could be a fake."

"I don't think so." The sadness in her eyes as she gazed at him pressed against his heart until his chest hurt. "The Granville motto is 'Cor nobile, cor immobile.' Angus's ring is engraved with the second phrase of that motto."

Stunned by what she said, Liam thought for a moment that his heart had stopped beating. "Say that again. Cor…"

"Cor nobile, cor immobile. It's Latin for 'noble heart, immovable heart.'"

"Does Angus's ring look like this?" Liam pulled the chain over his head then handed it and his ring to Kenna.

Her eyes widened as she examined the ring and read the inscription. "Where did you get this?"

"My mother gave it to me on my twenty-first birthday. She said I should always keep it." Liam's voice caught, and the back of his eyes burned. "That someday she'd tell me why."

"I don't understand." Kenna appeared as stunned as he felt. "How could she have the ring? Unless your mother isn't really your mother but her companion. Pen, the one who wrote the letters."

"How stupid I've been." An onslaught of conflicting emotions overpowered him, one after the other like crashing tidal waves. "Pen could be short for Penelope."

"Aye, I suppose it could be."

"Pippa's name was Penelope."

"What are you saying?"

Liam gripped the table with one hand to steady himself. He needed something tangible, something real to hold on to, or he feared his body would fly away into millions of pieces. "My mother is my mother. In my heart, I know she is."

"Then Pen lied to Seanair about your mother's death. Why would she do that?"

Liam snorted, a half laugh, half sob. "Mother loves mystery novels. She must have believed that if your grandfather was told she had died that the news would get back to Thomas. That it would be harder for him to find me, since he wouldn't be looking for her."

In his confused emotional state, he didn't know if that scenario made sense or not. Only his mother would be able to tell them and to answer all his other questions.

Suddenly an old memory surfaced. He'd been eleven or twelve when Mother sent him to her room to fetch something. Her gloves, perhaps, or a wrap. He couldn't remember for sure. But he remembered the framed miniature of a young man he saw on her vanity. A portrait he'd never seen before but that he now realized must have been of his father. His true father, the man who would have been the seventh duke if not for his untimely death.

With a surety he couldn't explain, Liam knew it was true. His thoughts descended into a fierce spiral as he connected the dots from the portrait to Angus.

Tavish Granville, the elder twin. Thomas, the younger one.

Kenna's words echoing in his head: *"Thomas and his son will have to leave Granville."*

Unlike Liam, who favored his mother, Thomas's son favored his father...and his uncle.

That was why Angus looked so familiar to him that night they met. Liam had seen a likeness of him before. In a framed miniature. In his father's portrait.

"Where is Angus?" Liam snatched up the chain and the ring. "Or should I call him Thomas? Like his father."

"He rode into town to make travel arrangements." Kenna stood and reached across the table to clasp his hand in both of hers. "He'll be back later today. We can talk to him then. Together."

"No." Liam pressed his lips together and shook his head. "This matter is between my cousin and me. I'll find him."

Before Kenna could say anything else, Liam raced for the garage. This time, he'd drive Calvin's Studebaker instead of riding the mare. He hoped Calvin wouldn't mind. And if he did, he hoped he'd forgive him once Liam explained the unbelievable story.

CHAPTER ELEVEN

Liam had taken what the Harrisons called "the long way" when he left Whippoorwill Glen because he intended to drive to Nashville. But now that he was at the crossroads, he had second thoughts. Had Angus gone to the Nashville train station, where he could purchase the tickets that would take him and Kenna to New York? Or had he taken "the short way" from the artist colony and driven to the telegraph office in nearby Gnaw Bone?

Liam needed to make a decision. Should he turn west toward Nashville? Or turn east toward Gnaw Bone? If Liam were in Angus's position, he'd send a telegram. Travel inquiries could be made via telegram in much less time than it would take to ride a horse to and from Nashville.

He turned east, mentally kicking himself for letting his anger cloud his common sense. If he'd taken the short way into Gnaw Bone, he'd already be at the telegraph office.

During the drive, Liam reflected on his conversation with Kenna and what had compelled him to rush off the way he did. Especially since the wiser option would have been to stay, as she had asked him to do, and talk about their options. They could have made a plan, made decisions, together. Instead, he'd taken off like that headless chicken that Mr. Green had mentioned.

But Liam's emotions were a powder keg due to everything he'd learned in such a short time. His birth father, a man he'd never known, had died, either because of an accident or sabotage. His mother had fled the country and been frightened enough of her brother-in-law's ambitions to fake her own death. Liam himself had been robbed of a heritage that was rightfully his.

Added to that, Angus had deceived Kenna. Did he really plan for the two of them to return to Scotland? Or did he only want to get Kenna away from Gnaw Bone? She was a threat to him and his father. Did they consider her enough of a threat to take her life?

The twin sorrows of grief and fear had churned into a maelstrom of anger that Liam had allowed to overcome his good sense. If he had any sense left, he would forget about confronting Angus and return to Whippoorwill Glen.

But instead of making the U-turn, he continued driving east, his mind going round and round as quickly as the wheels on the Studebaker. But unlike the vehicle, his thoughts were taking him nowhere.

How would Angus react when he learned his plans had been thwarted? He'd be angry. Perhaps angrier still to learn that Liam was his cousin, the so-called lost heir. Or did Angus know Liam's identity all along? All these questions needed answers that Liam intended to get. From Angus, from his mother, even from his traitorous uncle if need be.

He parked the Studebaker in front of the telegraph office and headed inside. If Angus had been here, he was already gone. Strange that they hadn't met along the road. Maybe he was still in Gnaw Bone or maybe he'd gone to Nashville after all.

The clerk stood from his desk and approached the counter with a friendly smile. "May I help you, sir?"

"I'm looking for somebody. A friend who may have been in here earlier. His name is Angus Lennox."

"Mr. Lennox was here, but he left several minutes ago."

"Did he send a telegram to the train station?"

"It is against regulations for me to divulge the contents of a telegram either sent or received by a customer." The clerk recited the words as if he'd said them a thousand times. Maybe he had.

"It's only that I need to make the same reservations."

"Do you wish to send a telegram, sir?"

Frustrated that his ploy didn't work, Liam shook his head and left. After all, he didn't need to know what arrangements Angus had made. Kenna would never travel with him now that she knew he was Thomas's son.

As Liam started to climb into the Studebaker, he had a thought. He returned to the telegraph office.

The clerk looked up as he entered, and frowned. "I still can't tell you anything, sir. All messages are confidential."

"I would like to send a message, please."

"Changed your mind, eh?" The clerk placed a message pad and a pencil on the counter. "You can write N.S. on the top line."

"N.S.?" Liam asked as he drew the pad closer and picked up the pencil.

"It's a common abbreviation for the Nashville station."

"This telegram is meant for my mother. She lives in Cincinnati."

"Then write the name and town on the top line," the clerk said impatiently. "Will you wait for a reply?"

Liam thought for a moment then shook his head. "When it comes, will you deliver it to Whippoorwill Glen? Only to me though. No one else."

"There's a delivery fee."

"I'll pay it. Only remember. Any reply must be given only to me."

"Oh, I'll remember." The clerk returned to his paperwork while Liam composed his message.

He wasn't sure what to say to his mother. Despite the story of her death at sea, he was confident of this truth at least—Bella McIver, not Pippa, was indeed his mother. The message, of necessity, needed to be short. And despite the clerk's assurances of total confidentiality, Liam needed to be careful of what he said.

After another moment's thought, he wrote his message on the pad and handed it to the clerk, who read it aloud. "Cor no-bile, cor immo-bile." He frowned. "What is that? Greek?"

"Latin," Liam replied. "And confidential."

He stood at the counter while the clerk keyed the message. The cryptic message would let his mother know that he was aware of the entire Granville motto, not only the phrase engraved on his ring.

He'd already written to her about Kenna's visit. She certainly would recognize the Calhoun name. As soon as she read the letter, she would know it was only a matter of time before Liam learned the truth. A truth she could have told him when she gave him the ring. Why hadn't she? Another question that needed an answer.

Once the telegram was sent, he returned to the Studebaker. The windshield wiper trapped a slip of paper between it and the glass. Liam looked around to see who might have placed it there, but no one seemed to be paying him any mind.

The note, signed *A.L.*, said *Meet me here.* A crude map showed the route to the destination.

Liam studied the map, comparing it to the mental image he had of the main road, the "short way," from Gnaw Bone toward Whippoorwill Glen. The route veered from that road with a few twists and turns. Though the map wasn't made to scale, he thought he knew where it led.

The Forgotten Cabin.

At least, that was his name for it. He'd discovered the abandoned log cabin a couple of years ago when trekking through the hills. He'd come across the little-used lane and followed it past a meadow and into the woods until he reached the clearing where the cabin had been built.

Intrigued by the place and its possible history, he'd returned again and again until he'd worn a path from the clearing to the kitchen garden behind the Whippoorwill Glen house. Since he figured the true story of how the cabin came to be built then left to ruin wouldn't match the scenarios he could conjure in his imagination, he'd never asked Calvin or Miss Molly or anyone else about it.

Somehow Angus had found it too.

If Liam had been on horseback, he could have ridden straight to the spot without following Angus's convoluted route. But since he had Calvin's vehicle, he'd have to follow the roads and take the car as far down the lane as he could. Then he'd walk the rest of the way.

He shoved the note into his pocket and got into the car. A showdown was coming, and he needed his spirit to be calm, not angry.

A verse from Psalms that Pippa taught him long ago, one of many he'd hidden in his heart, returned to him now. *Rest in the Lord,*

and wait patiently for him: fret not thyself because of him who
prospereth in his way, because of the man who bringeth wicked
devices to pass.

Thomas and Angus had prospered because of their wicked
devices. Liam would not follow that same path, no matter what fame
or fortune it might bring him.

As he drove toward the cabin and the waiting confrontation, he
prayed for that rest and freedom from fretfulness.

CHAPTER TWELVE

Kenna had no choice but to let Liam race away. But that didn't mean she had to sit in the parlor and twiddle her thumbs until he came back. In the time it took him to saddle a horse, she could change into riding clothes. He'd still be ahead of her on the road to Gnaw Bone, but only by a few minutes.

She hurried to her bedroom and was pulling her riding trousers from her trunk when she heard the roar of a car engine. *He didn't! He wouldn't!* Even though she'd only been at Whippoorwill Glen less than a week, she knew Calvin's prized Studebaker was off-limits to the lodgers.

She peered out the window and saw Liam speed past the house and down the lane. If Kenna had had even the slightest inkling he'd have the nerve to drive the vehicle, she would have raced from the house with him and hopped into the passenger seat. Now she was helpless to do anything but wave—unseen behind the window—as he drove away.

And stick to her original plan.

Undeterred by the unexpected development, she hurriedly changed clothes and pulled on her tall boots. Then rushed to the stables and saddled the gentle white-stockinged mare she'd ridden the morning she spent with Travis.

Liam could be in Gnaw Bone by now, but Kenna was determined to find him and Angus. All three of their lives had been affected by the long-ago boat tragedy. All three of them needed to talk about what to do next.

Angus had lied to her, but now that she and Liam knew the truth, he no longer had the upper hand. They did.

Instead of taking the driveway from the house to the road, Kenna cut across the gardens and a field. The mare easily cleared the ditch between the field and the road then trotted at a steady pace. Along the way, Kenna kept an eye out for the Studebaker in case Liam had met Angus returning from town.

As Kenna rounded a bend, the mare suddenly reared. A huge black horse stood crossways in the road. Kenna managed to maintain her seat and regain control, turning her head this way and that to keep the Sgàilean Dubh in her sight while the mare pranced in circles.

This was not the day nor the moment for the mysterious stranger to appear out of nowhere and try to frighten her.

"Who are you?" Kenna called.

In response the Black Shadow urged his horse forward in a slow walk. Kenna held her ground while also scouting possible escape routes. She could gallop back to Whippoorwill Glen or cut cross-country. But no matter how much she pressed the mare, they could never outrun the powerful black thoroughbred.

Perhaps her best option was to face the threat. And pray that Liam or Angus came along soon. Even Travis might be of help.

The Black Shadow halted several feet away and dismounted. She supposed he did so to put her at ease. Though she imagined he could mount again just as quickly and still outrace her, the effort to appear less intimidating worked. The mare, sensing Kenna relaxing in the saddle, quieted.

"You have nothing to fear from me, Miss Kenna Calhoun," the man said, his voice deep and strongly reminiscent of home. He removed his cap and held it deferentially in front of him. "My name is Niven Reid. Your grandfather sent me."

"My grandfather?" Kenna sputtered in disbelief. "Sent you to do what? Scare me half to death?"

"You mean when I followed you from over in Nashville? That was an unfortunate lapse on my part." He chuckled self-consciously. "Thunder takes it into his head to run sometimes when I prefer him to trot. Once we caught up to you, it was too late for me to hide but not too late to find out where you planned to stay so I could make a different choice for my lodging."

He took a careful step closer. "Your grandfather said to tell you that his chridhe is with you always."

His chridhe. *His heart.*

The message meant Kenna could trust this Niven Reid. But even though she no longer felt threatened by the big man, she was caught between embarrassment that she'd ever been frightened of him, irritation with her grandfather for sending him as if she were a helpless child, and gratitude that during her travels in a foreign land someone was watching over her.

"You've been following me since I arrived in New York. Why didn't you tell me who you were then?"

"My instructions were to ensure you made the trip to Gnaw Bone without knowing of my existence. You are more astute than I expected you to be, miss. Yet I dinnae suppose you ken the ways I ensured your safety."

"The Dayton couple?" Kenna heaved an exasperated sigh. "I thought they were my friends."

"The friendship was real, miss. I only confirmed their respectability. I was speaking of your meeting with Mr. Lennox yesterday."

Kenna made no attempt to hide her astonishment. "How did you know about that?"

He smiled. "I have my methods. Neither you nor Mr. Lennox were aware of my presence, but I heard all that you said to one another at that cabin. I know you don't trust him. Neither do I."

"He's lying about being the lost heir." She took a deep breath and prayed her trust in him was not misplaced. "Liam McIver is."

By his expression, she had managed to surprise him.

"Is he now?" Niven asked. "Are you certain?"

"He has proof. A thistle ring identical to the one Angus showed me except for the engraving. Liam's engraving is 'cor nobile.'"

"A noble heart." Niven averted his gaze as if lost in thought. "The rings were wisely given. Liam's father had a noble heart. But Thomas? His is immovable once it's set. For good or ill."

Kenna wanted to ask how he knew the sixth duke and his twin sons. How he knew Seanair. But those questions could wait for another day.

"Liam knows the truth," she said. "He left in Mr. Harrison's car to find Angus."

"He did not pass this way."

Kenna narrowed her eyes in confusion. "But I told him Angus had gone to town. Liam must have thought I meant Nashville. Perhaps he went there."

"Then we should ride to Gnaw Bone and find Mr. Lennox." Niven donned his cap and gathered his reins. "Mr. McIver will return to Whippoorwill Glen. We can wait for him there."

Kenna nodded her agreement.

Despite his large build and his limp, Niven mounted the thoroughbred with an agility that Kenna wouldn't have believed possible if she hadn't seen it with her own eyes.

"Don't worry, miss," he said, circling so their horses were headed in the same direction. "The Good Lord is looking down upon us. All will be well."

"All will be well," Kenna repeated. She wanted to believe that was true as much as Niven did. But she feared what Liam and Angus would say to each other—what they might do to each other—if she wasn't there to intercede. Maybe it was best that Liam had misunderstood her and gone to Nashville.

Now she and the Sgàilean Dubh could get to Angus before he did.

CHAPTER THIRTEEN

The Studebaker made it to the edge of the woods before Liam decided to abandon it. The track between the trees was too overgrown to risk damaging the undercarriage. When Calvin found out he'd taken the vehicle without permission, he was likely to toss all of Liam's belongings into the backyard and change the locks on his door.

Goodbye, Whippoorwill Glen.

Hopefully that didn't mean goodbye to the autumn art gallery exhibit, although if he became persona non grata in Gnaw Bone, he might have to find another theme for his sculptures. All because, for one of the rare times in his life, he'd reacted with his heart instead of his head.

Maybe he still was.

Might it be more prudent to wait for Angus at the house? If Liam didn't show up at the log cabin, Angus would eventually tire of waiting for him. He'd either come to the house or, realizing his claim of being the lost heir had been disproven, quietly disappear. Not that he could hide forever. Once Liam spoke with his mother, he'd have a major decision to make about his future. One he couldn't even contemplate at the moment.

Despite his doubts that he should go to the cabin, he continued to follow the rutted lane through the woods as if something outside himself guided his feet. As he walked, he repeated the verse, Psalm

37:7, that had calmed him earlier, and focused on the instructions it offered.

Rest...wait...fret not. Rest...wait...fret not.

As he drew close to the clearing, his steps slowed, and he paid more attention to where he stepped. He couldn't say why, but it seemed important that he didn't accidentally snap any twigs or rustle any leaves. When he reached the edge, he hid behind a large oak in hopes of seeing Angus before Angus saw him.

The sun's rays poured into the clearing at an angle and chased the shadows into the surrounding trees. Little had changed since he was here two years ago, as if the cabin was forever destined to be trapped in the past. Overgrown shrubs and vines held up what remained of the picket fence. The broken limb still pressed against a corner of the roof.

The door, though...the door was different. Instead of hanging crookedly from one hinge, it was propped against the log wall next to the tiny wooden porch.

Except for the almost silent chitter of a woodland critter, all was silent. Too silent.

Had Angus already left or was he inside the cabin?

Only one way to know.

"I'm here," Liam called out as he stayed behind the tree. "Show yourself."

A movement by the old stone well caught his attention.

Angus stood and looked his way. "You could do the same," he said. "You have nothing to fear from me."

"True." Liam took a few steps into the clearing and faced his cousin. "I'm no longer a helpless infant."

"You believe you're the lost heir?" Angus chuckled as he leaned against the well. "Dinnae Kenna tell you about my ring?" He raised his right hand to display the band he wore on his forefinger.

"I have one too." Liam pulled the chain from his pocket. His ring dangled at the end. "Mine's engraved with 'cor nobile,' the phrase I assume belongs to the eldest son and the eldest son's son."

Angus's gaze narrowed, and his eyes turned cold. "So it is you. Father told me your name, the one you live by now, but I had my doubts." He eyed the chain. "No wonder I didn't find the ring when I searched your room. You wear it around your neck like a talisman even though you know nothing of what it means."

Liam pressed his lips together. That was one mystery solved. "You hoped to steal it."

"No ring, no proof. At least none that can't be explained away. You present a certificate of birth. My father, a noble duke, accuses you of forgery. Who do you suppose has the ear of the court?"

"You admit your father is a liar. As are you."

"Because of the tale I told Kenna?" Angus snorted as if the false-hood was meaningless. "I planned on telling her the truth as soon as our ship was out at sea."

Liam wasn't sure he believed that. Kenna might have been trapped on the ship with Angus until she reached Scotland, but then she would have gone home to see her grandfather. Eventually, though, she would have renewed the quest that Angus had inter-rupted. He knew it, and Angus knew it.

A shiver went up Liam's spine. The only way Angus could have stopped Kenna from her search was to stop her permanently. Thankfully, the truth had come out before she'd gone away with him.

"Your father claims a title not rightfully his," Liam said quietly but forcefully.

"What did you expect him to do?" Angus stretched his arms out in a dramatic gesture. "Bide his time waiting for your return? If Kenna hadn't searched for you, if she hadn't told you about *my* ring, you would never have known the significance of *yours*. You wouldn't even know there is such a thing as the Granville motto."

"But she did search for me. And I do know."

Angus let out a heavy sigh and raised his eyes to the heavens as if he were speaking to a dunce. "Tell me, Liam. Or would you prefer that I now call you Tavish?"

Without waiting for an answer, he continued. "What do you know about running an estate? About crop yields and sheep ailments? Have you ever lost a night's sleep standing vigil over a ewe who can't deliver her wee lamb without your help?"

The questions didn't require an answer, so Liam didn't attempt to give one. But neither could he ignore them, because Angus was right. The title might be his, but with that title came responsibility.

"You know nothing," Angus said. "Whereas I've been training to take over the lands and the livestock my entire life. Tell me, which of us should be the next Duke of Granville?"

"I wasn't given the chance to learn," Liam said simply, though even to his ears the excuse sounded weak and pathetic. He couldn't counter Angus's arguments. He wasn't sure he wanted to try.

"You should stay here, Liam. In this country." Angus paced in front of the well, stopping to punctuate his points with more dramatic gestures. "You have the talent to be one of those rare artists who actually makes a living. Only a week ago, before Kenna arrived with her mysterious quest, that's all you wanted to do. Are you willing to give up on all you've accomplished, all you have yet to accomplish, to take an estate you know nothing about from greatness to ruin?"

By this time, the anger that had driven Liam to rush into Gnaw Bone in search of Angus had completely dissipated. The scripture, his prayers, the walk through the woods—all these had calmed his spirit. But there was still so much he didn't know about the past. About his own family. He wouldn't allow Angus to back him into a corner or bully him into making a decision that could turn out to be a mistake.

Hopefully, his mother had received his telegram by now and intuited its importance. Hopefully, he'd hear from her soon. Even if the only message she sent was a motherly "everything will be fine."

Angus started up again, and Liam found a log to sit on. He wasn't sure what his cousin hoped to gain from these monologues. Angus seemed determined to prove that Liam wasn't up to the burden of being a duke—an easy task under the circumstances—but Liam was just as determined not to make any concessions.

"I know you don't want to believe me," Angus said, "but Kenna's grandfather, Steward Calhoun, was wrong. My father had no plans to harm Isabella or you. Calhoun and my grandfather were great friends all their lives, and he went mad with grief when Grandfather and my uncle died in that accident."

Angus paused a moment to gaze at Liam, as if he'd suddenly remembered that his uncle was Liam's father.

"They quarreled, my father and Calhoun, and Calhoun lost his position. For the first time in centuries, a Calhoun no longer served at Granville. So he made up this wild story for his revenge. The rumors that my father frightened away his brother's wife and son have hung over our heads all of our lives. There are some who say he actually killed them, though now that is demonstrably false as you are sitting here before me."

"The falseness of one rumor doesn't prove the falseness of another."

Angus snorted and waved his hand as if Liam's logic was nonsense. Suddenly he changed direction and strode toward Liam until he towered over him and blocked out the sun.

"After your father died, mine did what was best for the estate. It's what he always does."

Liam stood, drew himself to his full height, and glared at his cousin. "No matter who pays the price?"

Angus returned the glare then took a couple steps back. His voice softened but remained edged with anger and frustration. "That's one of the many differences between us. I understand something you cannot and never will. Granville Hall is bigger than any of us. The estate was established centuries ago, before this country was even a thought, and it will still exist long after we are no more than portraits hanging in the gallery. That is the price we pay for the privilege of aristocracy."

He paused and took a deep breath. "You may be one of us, Cousin, but you know nothing."

Liam lowered his eyes as the weighty truth of Angus's last speech bowed his shoulders. He couldn't refute his cousin's words, but he needed to find the strength to stand up beneath them. To hold on to the truth that Angus's heritage belonged to him too.

He met Angus's gaze. "I want to know that history. It's my right to know that history."

"Aye, it is. It begins with a fight." Suddenly Angus's fist connected with Liam's jaw. The force of the unexpected blow caused him to stagger back. Before he gained his balance, Angus struck again, and Liam fell to his knees. A third blow, and Liam's world went dark.

CHAPTER FOURTEEN

First stop, the telegraph office. As Kenna and Niven stepped inside, the clerk greeted them with a friendly smile.

"How may I help you?" He picked up a message pad. "Do you wish to send a telegraph?"

"Thank you, no." Kenna gave him a gracious smile. "A friend of mine came in earlier to make arrangements for our return trip to Scotland."

The words were barely out of her mouth when the clerk scowled. "You mean Mr. Lennox? He's a popular fella today."

Niven gently nudged Kenna and casually placed his arm on the counter. "Are you saying someone else came in looking for our Angus?"

"That Mr. McIver who stays out at Whippoorwill Glen. He wanted to know what telegrams Mr. Lennox had sent and what messages he got in return." The clerk sighed as if he carried the burdens of the entire world on his shoulders. "I am compelled to tell you folks what I told him. It is against regulations for me to divulge the contents of a telegram either sent or received by a customer."

At the mention of Liam's name, Kenna's heart lurched. So Liam had come to Gnaw Bone after all. Strange, then, that they hadn't met him on the road. Neither had she seen the Studebaker parked anywhere along the street here in town.

"Do you have any idea," Niven asked, "where either Mr. Lennox or Mr. McIver went after leaving here?"

"Were they together?" Kenna blurted out.

"They weren't together, no. First Mr. Lennox came and went, and it was a while later that Mr. McIver showed up. Then he left but came right back in again. He decided to send a telegram after all." The clerk held up a finger. "But don't ask me who to, because it's against regulations for me to tell you."

"You have been most helpful. Thank you," Niven said with a smile. He turned to Kenna. "They could still be in town."

"Maybe Liam decided to stop at the boardinghouse." When they had ridden past the entrance on the way into Gnaw Bone, she'd looked for the Studebaker. It wasn't parked with the other vehicles, but perhaps he'd parked it elsewhere. "He might have wanted to see Miss Molly or Miss Alice about something."

"We'll stop in and see on the way back to the Glen."

"Something did happen I found peculiar," the clerk said as Kenna and Niven headed for the door.

They turned around to hear what he had to say. "I don't suppose it's against regulations for me to tell you."

Niven exchanged a look with Kenna then returned to the counter, a big smile on his face and his demeanor as friendly and unintimidating as a man his size could be. "Please tell us," he said, demonstrating more patience than Kenna felt in that moment.

"While Mr. McIver was writing his message, I saw Mr. Lennox through the window there." The clerk gestured toward the plate glass window that looked out onto the street. "Mr. Lennox put a piece of paper on the windshield of that car Mr. McIver was driving.

It's not his, you know. It belongs to Calvin Harrison, and he's not one to lend it around. But that's not any of my business, so I didn't ask Mr. McIver why he was driving it."

Niven maintained his pleasant expression. "Did you mention this to Mr. McIver?"

"Naw. He found the paper when he went back out. Looked like a note of some kind. He studied it then stuck it in his pocket."

"I appreciate you telling us about that. Is there anything else?"

"Only that Mr. McIver got a reply to that telegram he sent."

Kenna imitated Niven's example and smiled warmly. "We're on our way to Whippoorwill Glen. I'd be happy to deliver Mr. McIver's telegram for you."

"Normally I'd allow that," the clerk responded. "But Mr. McIver made it very clear that I was to deliver the message only to him. No one else. I'm waiting for my boy to come in so he can take it. Won't be more than an hour or two."

Kenna released a silent sigh. Could this clerk be any more annoying? She was curious to know the recipient of Liam's telegram, but she would never open a private message to him.

Niven reached into his pocket, and Kenna's eyes widened. Did he mean to offer the clerk a bribe? Instead of a wallet, he pulled out a badge of some kind. "Perhaps this will allow you to entrust Mr. McIver's telegram into my care. I promise he will receive it, unopened and unread."

The clerk stared at the badge, at Niven, and at the badge again. Without saying a word, he pulled a sealed telegram from a cubbyhole and handed it over.

"Thank you. You have been most helpful." Niven took Kenna's elbow and escorted her from the office.

"What was that badge?" Kenna asked once they were out of view of the telegraph office window.

"Didn't I tell you?" Niven shot her an amused smile. "I was with the Bureau of Investigations for a time. Retired now. Before that I did a bit of spying during the Great War."

With that background, no wonder he could switch personas so easily. Kenna would have liked to know more about his experiences, but her focus now was on finding Liam.

They rode to the boardinghouse, but neither Miss Alice nor Miss Molly had seen him. From there they returned to Whippoorwill Glen and tied the horses to the hitching post near the front veranda. The Studebaker wasn't parked in the garage, and Liam wasn't at his workshop. The gig was gone, but Kenna had overheard the Harrisons say they were spending a few hours with friends at the nearby state park. That they'd taken the gig instead of the Studebaker wasn't surprising. Calvin rarely drove the car for a trip of less than ten miles.

As they walked from the workshop back to the house, Niven suddenly pulled Kenna behind a huge lilac bush and held his fingers to his lips. He motioned toward the kitchen garden, and Kenna turned her gaze that way.

Angus emerged from the woods where the path led to the abandoned log cabin. He had a smug smile on his face while he favored the knuckles of one hand as if they were injured.

"Why would he be at the cabin?" Kenna whispered the question as quietly as she could.

"Why do you suppose Angus left a note on the car windshield instead of waiting for Liam to come out of the telegraph office?"

Kenna searched her mind for a reason but couldn't come up with anything. "I wouldn't know. Do you?"

"One probable explanation is that Angus wanted to get a jump on Liam when he arrived."

Kenna's eyes widened. She stared at Angus then shifted her gaze to the path. "Then where's Liam?"

"My guess is he's still at the cabin."

The somber tone in Niven's voice caused Kenna's heart to race. "I have to go."

Niven gently gripped her arm. "We will," he said quietly. "As soon as Angus is out of sight."

They waited for him to enter the house, then Niven led Kenna around the outbuildings into the woods. Though there was no path, he seemed confident of the direction. Kenna was grateful she was wearing riding trousers and boots instead of a dress and flats as they pushed through brush and climbed over logs.

All was quiet as they paused on the edge of the clearing. Kenna looked around for Liam then noticed the cabin. "The door has been removed. Maybe Liam is inside."

"You stay here, miss. I'll take a look."

Kenna didn't like being left behind, especially as her worry for Liam increased. Was Angus capable of taking his cousin's life? Is that why he was favoring his knuckles? She scanned the clearing again, searching for Liam, searching for a sign that he'd been there, and gasped. The door to the cabin rested on top of the well.

Kenna scurried to the well and pushed against the door with more strength than she knew she had. She managed to open enough of a gap to look inside. Despite the shadows, she was certain she could see something deep inside.

"Liam," she called quietly then again louder. "Liam, are you down there?"

Suddenly Niven was beside her. He shoved the door off the well so it fell to the ground on the opposite side with a thud. Sunlight chased away the shadows, and a groan sounded from the depths.

"Liam." Kenna grabbed Niven's arm. "He's down there."

"I see him." He patted Kenna's hand. "We need a rope. Run and get one, but whatever you do, don't let Angus see you. We'll catch up with him later."

Kenna did as he asked, running along the path till she reached the kitchen garden then making her way into the stables. She grabbed two coils of rope, draped them over her shoulder, and looked around the area to see if there was anything else that might be helpful. It wouldn't be easy, even for a big man like Niven, to pull Liam out of the well. She folded a couple of blankets over her arm.

As she started to exit the stables, a figure appeared in the doorway, his face hidden in shadow by the shoulder of the horse that walked beside him. Her pulse quickened as she stepped back. "I know what you did," she said. "You won't get away with it."

"What are you talking about?" Travis moved into the light from an upper window and stared at the items she carried. "Where are you going with all that?"

Kenna almost collapsed with relief. "Have you seen Angus?"

"He took off on that huge black horse that was tied out front. Galloped away like a posse was after him. Since no one else seemed to be around, I thought I'd unsaddle the mare."

"Don't. We may need her."

"'We?'"

"If you'll help me. It's a long story, and I'll tell you all of it. But first, we need to get Liam out of a well."

Travis looked taken aback, then he gave a good-natured shrug and took the rope, which was becoming uncoiled and dragging on the floor. "Lead the way."

Chapter Fifteen

Liam groaned as Mr. Green lifted him from the bed in the spare room and set him in an old-fashioned wheelchair that Miss Alice had stored in her barn. Every muscle in his body ached, but the worst pain radiated from his broken ankle. He was glad he'd been unconscious when Angus tossed him in the well and glad he'd lost consciousness again when Kenna's Black Shadow and Travis pulled him out.

Most of all, he was glad that Kenna's lovely face was the first one he'd seen when he came to his senses. She'd bent over him, tears shimmering in her green eyes while a smile played on her lips. He could have endured double the pain as long as she stayed beside him.

Other than that, he remembered very little after Angus knocked him unconscious. The doctor had given him a tincture that put him into a deep sleep that lasted throughout the night. He supposed it did him good not to feel the pain, but he wanted his senses about him this morning.

Mr. Green put a blanket around his legs then wheeled him into the parlor. Kenna immediately rose from the sofa where she was sitting beside Niven Reid.

"You stay right there, missy," Mr. Green ordered. "I'll park him beside you."

"Please do." She regained her seat and smiled at him. "You look much better than yesterday. When you came out of that well…" She pressed her lips together and blinked away tears.

Liam returned her smile then gazed around the room as Mr. Green maneuvered the chair beside the sofa. Calvin stood by the mantel, and Travis sat in a nearby chair, his posture unnaturally stiff. Odd, since he was usually a slouch.

He sensed they waited for him to say something, and there were things he wanted to say. An apology to Calvin for taking his car without permission. Gratitude to Niven and Travis. Gratitude and even more to Kenna. But the words seemed elusive. Probably the aftereffects of the medicine he'd been given.

"Are we supposed to bow or something?" Travis asked. "I've never been in the same room with a duke before."

At first no one said anything, then Kenna emitted a stifled giggle. Niven practically choked trying to hide his chuckle then gave in to a hearty laugh. Calvin soon joined in, and Liam couldn't help but grin.

Leave it to Travis to break the uncomfortable silence.

"I'm not a duke," he said. "Please. No bowing."

Niven dried his eyes as he got his laughter under control. "You might have to get used to a bow now and again, sir. But there's plenty of time for all of that." He pulled a box out of his pocket and handed it to Liam. "I believe these belong to you."

Liam took the box and opened it. Inside were identical Scottish thistle rings. He picked up one and silently read the engraving.

Cor nobile. A noble heart.

He'd never worn the ring, because of how much time he spent working with clay. Perhaps he should get accustomed to it. But not yet.

He put it back in the box and picked up the other ring. *Cor immobile.* An immovable heart.

"How is it you have both rings?" he asked Niven.

"Mr. Lennox had them in his possession when he was arrested for assaulting you. He was persuaded to turn them over to me."

"Where is my cousin?"

"In an Indianapolis jail cell," Niven replied. "He was arrested as soon as he got off the train from Nashville. He put up a good fight, but we bested him."

Liam didn't want to know who Niven meant by "we." He was still astounded that the Black Shadow who had frightened Kenna enough that she'd accosted a stranger for assistance had turned out to be both her guardian and his rescuer. Kenna had told him the story while encouraging him to eat the eggs, sausage links, and toast with orange marmalade that Mrs. Green had prepared for his breakfast. He had told her why he'd gone to the cabin and most of what Angus had said. He couldn't bring himself to tell her that Angus tried to blame her grandfather for his disappearance.

"I have this for you too," Niven said, handing Liam a sealed telegram. "I should have left it with Kenna, but I raced off to Indy with it still in my pocket. The clerk at the telegraph office gave it to us when we were there yesterday."

Liam unsealed the telegram and read his mother's message. YOUR SAFETY IS MY ONLY THOUGHT. COME HOME. BRING KC.

A veiled but encouraging message. Exactly as he knew it would be. He folded the paper and placed it in the box with the rings.

"Thank you," Liam said to Niven. "For everything."

Niven stood. "If you'll excuse me, sir, I have an errand to attend to."

"You will be back, won't you?" Kenna asked.

"Of course, miss. I promised your grandfather to see you safely home." He darted a glance at Liam. "When you're ready to leave, of course."

"I also have business to attend to," Calvin said.

"Before you go—" Liam began, but Calvin held up a hand.

"You don't need to explain," he said.

"But your car—"

"Is in the garage. No harm done."

"I am sorry for taking it."

"All that matters now is that you regain your health. If there's anything Mrs. Harrison or I can do for you, please let us know."

After Niven and Calvin left the room, Travis moved from the chair to the sofa and leaned toward Liam. "There's something I need to tell you," he said. "It's awkward."

Liam exchanged a glance with Kenna, who shrugged, indicating she didn't know what Travis intended to say. "What is it?" Liam asked.

"I don't have any excuse. Except, I suppose, I was jealous. You and I started coming here about the same time, but now you have people interested in your work. And I don't." He pressed his lips together for a moment then sighed. "I've been sneaking into your room. Taking your mail. Even taking a bit of money now and again when I ran a little short."

He sighed again, deeper this time. "I took the sketches you made of Kenna too." Suddenly the words came out in a rush. "It was wrong of me, and I'm sorry. I hope you'll forgive me."

Liam stared at him, unsure what to say, then chuckled. "You helped save my life, Travis. Of course I forgive you. But I want those sketches."

"Absolutely," Travis rushed to assure him. "I kept everything in a box. I can put it in your room if you want."

Is he kidding? Apparently not. Struggling to hide his amusement, Liam nodded. "Why not?"

Travis clapped him on the shoulder. "I'll take care of it right now. I'll have to give you an IOU for the money. See you two later."

As soon as he was out of the room, Liam and Kenna started laughing. Liam wrapped his arms around his aching sides though his arms ached too. According to the doctor, his body was covered with scrapes and bruises. He'd been fortunate that there wasn't enough water in the well to drown him and that he hadn't hit his head on a rock.

"I'm glad Travis didn't turn out to be the lost heir," Kenna said. "I never wanted it to be anyone but you."

"My mother wants me to come home." Liam handed Kenna the folded telegram. "She wants you to come too."

Kenna's lips turned up in a mischievous smile. "There's something I need to tell you."

"Have you been breaking into my room too?" he teased.

She gave a playful shake of her head. "Mrs. Harrison intended to send a telegram to your mother. I asked her if I could instead."

He must have looked alarmed, because she immediately placed her hand on his arm. "We only told her there had been an accident. She'll be here tomorrow."

Liam relaxed and covered her hand with his. "I'm glad you'll get to meet each other."

"I'm glad of that too."

A wave of tiredness suddenly swept over him. So much had happened in such a short time, churning his emotions into whirlwinds. Yes, he'd been physically battered. But he was holding Kenna's hand in his, and his mother—who knew all the secrets that had been hidden from him—was on her way. Soon all his questions would be answered.

Until then, he would *rest, wait patiently,* and *fret not.* God had His own plan for taking care of men who prospered because of their wickedness. Would He use Liam to bring them to justice?

CHAPTER SIXTEEN

Though he was weary of sitting in the wheelchair, Liam refused to return to the bed Mrs. Green had prepared for him in one of the ground-floor rooms. The Harrisons had driven the Studebaker to Nashville to meet Liam's mother and bring her back to Whippoorwill Glen, and he wanted to be in the parlor when she arrived. He wished Kenna was with him too, but she was in the kitchen helping Mrs. Green prepare refreshments. She thought Liam should have a few minutes alone with his mother before he introduced them.

Shortly after the Studebaker parked in front of the house, Bella McIver strolled into the parlor wearing a fashionable blue dress and matching hat. Though she greeted him with a warm smile and a gentle kiss on the temple, her eyes welled with tears.

"I'm a sight, I know," he said. "But much better now that you're here."

She gripped his hand in both of hers as she perched on the edge of a nearby chair. "What happened to you? The telegram said an accident. But these bruises. These cuts."

"It's a long story, Mother." He'd asked the Harrisons not to tell her what they knew. He needed to tell her himself, in his own words and in his own way. And with Kenna beside him.

"He found you, didn't he? My poor boy. After all I tried to do to keep you safe."

"None of us could have foreseen this," he said to comfort her. "My body will heal."

"I should have come as soon as I received your letter mentioning Miss Calhoun. I thought about it. But I feared by coming, I'd accidentally give myself away and that would endanger you even more. But if I had come, perhaps this wouldn't have happened. You would not have been hurt."

"All that matters is you are here now. You can meet Kenna, and your secret doesn't need to be a secret anymore."

"I suppose it is time for you to know the truth. All the truth."

Liam rang the little silver bell that Mrs. Green had left within easy reach for him on a side table. A few moments later Kenna entered with a tray of pimento cheese sandwiches, sliced carrots, homemade cookies, and a pitcher of lemonade. She placed it on the coffee table then stood beside Liam as he made the introductions.

Kenna curtsied when Liam's mother stood to greet her and placed her fingers on Kenna's cheek. "You have your mother's eyes. But I believe you must take after your grandmother. She was a lovely woman. My own mother died when I was a young girl, and your grandmother was most kind to me."

"I wish I had known her."

A shadow crossed his mother's face.

"It was a sad day for all of us. So much loss." She smiled at Liam then took her seat. "Sit beside me, Kenna, and we will talk about the past, and we will cry. But we will also laugh, for there were many happy days before the tragedy."

The afternoon passed quickly. Liam explained about Angus and being tossed in the well. Later, Liam and Kenna sat spellbound as they listened to his mother's stories. She told the most difficult one first.

Shortly after the funerals for his father and his brother, Thomas made his intent clear. He had always believed that he could manage the estate better than his twin and deserved the title. Bella admitted that Thomas's assessment that he was the better manager may have been correct—her husband preferred more educational pursuits such as scientific advances and astronomy over getting his hands dirty in the barns.

When both the Duke and Tavish died on the same day, Thomas saw his opportunity. He had no interest in devoting more than twenty years of his life to the estate only to turn it over to his nephew.

"Thomas was a cruel man." she said. "So unlike his brother. I believed him capable of the worst deeds. I have no doubt he would have killed us if we had stayed at Granville."

Kenna's grandfather helped Liam's mother flee along with Penelope, her companion. On the voyage, the two women concocted the plan to write to Mr. Calhoun with the sad but false news of Isabella's death. They believed Thomas had a spy in the Calhoun household and hoped the falsehood would find its way to him. If he searched for his nephew, he'd search for a baby being raised by one woman, not by two.

The other deceptions were easy. Within a year of arriving in New York City, Liam's mother married and changed her name to Bella. Her new husband, Ross McIver, adopted her son, and his name was changed from Tavish William Granville to Liam Ross McIver. She'd even managed to obtain a birth certificate stating Liam was born in New York.

Until Liam was sixteen, they never stayed more than two to three years at any one address. Gradually they made their way westward, moving from New York to Virginia to Pennsylvania until finally settling in southern Ohio.

"Why didn't you tell me all this when you gave me the thistle ring?" Liam asked.

"You were born to that life. But you haven't lived it." His mother took a sip of her lemonade as if she needed a moment to gather her thoughts. "Your father—I mean Ross—and Pippa and I talked about what was best to do. For months it seems we talked of nothing else."

She set her glass on the tray and folded her hands. "We were all so proud of you. The man you'd become. All that you were accomplishing and dreaming of accomplishing. We still are. It might not have been right of us, but we decided to wait at least a few more years. It appears God had other plans."

"So He did." Liam reached for Kenna's hand.

"Now you will tell me what brought you here," his mother said to Kenna. "And everything there is to tell about your family. Your grandfather, how is he?"

Liam leaned back in the chair as Kenna and his mother chatted. He wasn't sure, but he might have even dozed for a short while. They talked until dinner, when they joined the Harrisons and the other lodgers in the dining room.

Over the next couple of days, Liam often talked to his mother and Kenna about his conflicted thoughts. He'd taken to heart what Angus had said about managing the estate and knew he wasn't capable of taking on the task. But neither could he allow Thomas to retain a title he'd stolen.

Angus had also said that Granville would "still exist long after we are no more than portraits hanging in the gallery. That is the price we pay for the privilege of aristocracy."

But part of that price, Liam believed, was respecting the traditions that stretched into the past, including the responsibility of the title.

Liam might never be the duke his father would have been or that his grandfather had been, but he would not deny that opportunity to his children and his grandchildren. He would not deprive them of their birthright.

For their sake, for his, and hopefully for Kenna's, he determined to fight his uncle for what belonged to him. He determined to win.

CHAPTER SEVENTEEN

Dressed in her traveling clothes, Kenna stood on the platform of the Nashville train station with her hand resting on Liam's shoulder. He sat in a more modern wheelchair than the wooden one Miss Alice had lent him. Kenna knew, though, that he chafed from the confinement and was counting the days until he could walk again.

Niven Reid, her personal Sgàilean Dubh, stood a discreet distance away while keeping a watchful eye on them. Passengers were already boarding the train to Cincinnati, but Liam's mother was finding it difficult to say goodbye.

"Who knows when we will see each other again?" Tears shimmered in her eyes.

"You must come visit us," Kenna urged her, even though she already knew Bella's answer. During long conversations about the future, Bella had explained that America was her home now and she was happy in her life. Besides that, she had no desire to return to the place where she'd known such crushing grief.

"Seanair would welcome you with open arms," Kenna added.

"You must kiss him for me," Bella replied. "Then, after this business with Thomas is done and there is another Tavish William who will someday be Duke of Granville, you must return to visit me. Promise me you will."

Kenna's cheeks warmed as she exchanged a glance with Liam. His warm smile and the love in his eyes told her all she needed to know—their hearts had been knitted together, quickly and securely, in the few days since she climbed from a wagon and took his arm. Whatever the future held for them, both the joys and the heartaches, they would face together.

And once again, hopefully in the not-too-distant future, the Granville and Calhoun families would be joined together again in a new and abiding way.

"We promise." Liam pulled a box from beneath the robe that covered his legs and handed it to his mother. "Open it."

She removed the lid to reveal the two thistle rings that rested inside. She gasped and stared at Liam. "You cannot give me these. The rings of Granville must stay with you."

"Kenna and I want you to have them," he said. "Angus said my ring was proof of who I am. Now they are proof that you will always be a Granville too."

The whistle blew the last warning for the passengers to board. Bella startled at the sound then closed the box and tucked it in her bag.

"I will keep them for your son," she said. "Now I must go."

She kissed Liam on the forehead and gave him an awkward hug then wrapped Kenna in a warm embrace. "Take care of one another," she whispered. "Cor nobile, cor immobile."

"We will," Kenna promised as tears stung her eyes.

With a last wave to them, Bella boarded the train that would take her home.

Now it was their turn to travel north to Indianapolis then eastward to the New York Harbor.

Kenna had fulfilled her quest. She had rescued the lost heir from danger, and he was the hero of her dreams. It was as if the best of her youthful imaginings had come true.

CHAPTER EIGHTEEN

September 1934

The grandeur of Granville Hall was greater than anything Kenna could have imagined. She stood in the center near a marble table holding a huge urn of chrysanthemums from the estate's greenhouse and tried to see everything at once. The portraits of Liam's ancestors. The tapestries. The heavy wooden furniture. The medieval swords displayed above the mantel of a fireplace large enough for her to stand in.

"Is it not magnificent, mo chridhe?" Seanair whispered, bending close to her.

Her return home, with Liam by her side, had done more to improve Seanair's health than any medicine.

"I can't believe this will be our home." She directed her gaze toward her new husband, who stared at a portrait of two young boys, twins, playing with a dog. It was impossible to know who was Tavish and who was Thomas. From the expression on Liam's face, though, Kenna guessed that his heart told him which twin was his father.

A moment later, a servant ushered them into the library, where they joined Thomas and a team of lawyers for both sides around a long table. During the past few months, Liam's true identity had been confirmed with the legal documents provided by his mother.

Both her marriage license and his birth certificate had been confirmed as authentic.

To avoid a long legal battle he knew he would lose, especially once Angus was found guilty of the attempted murder of the rightful heir, Thomas had relinquished the title to Liam. Finally, all the details had been decided and written in legalese.

Kenna grasped Seanair's hand as the final documents were signed and Liam Ross McIver was formally and officially declared to be Tavish William, the Eighth Duke of Granville.

The lost heir had returned home.

RINGS OF DECEIT

by

DANA LYNN

So do not fear, for I am with you;
do not be dismayed, for I am your God.
I will strengthen you and help you;
I will uphold you with my righteous right hand.

—Isaiah 41:10 (NIV)

◌ CHAPTER ONE ◌

Gnaw Bone, Indiana
Present Day

"Call me as soon as you leave the lawyer's office," Eve's mom demanded.

Eve Granville bit back the sigh threatening to break free. Her mother had called her three times in the past twelve hours with the same command. "I know, Mom. Listen, I'm getting ready to leave for the lawyer's office now. I don't want to be late, okay? I'll call you later."

Her mother disconnected while Eve was still speaking.

Eve grimaced. It had always been like this. Her mom would say what she wanted then leave the conversation. No goodbyes or I love yous. She'd hang up without warning. Eve glanced around the hotel room, checking to be sure she had everything she needed for the reading of the will. Her stomach muscles tightened. She dreaded the meeting. Her mind couldn't quite grasp the concept that Nana was gone. Fiona Granville had been a constant in her life. She'd seen her grandmother less than two months ago, back at the end of May. Nana had appeared tired, but her mind had been as quick and clever as ever, and her joy in life had refreshed some of Eve's weariness.

She'd returned to her demanding career as a pediatrician in Pittsburgh, promising Nana she'd return to spend some quality time with her for the holidays.

If only she'd known that would be the last time she saw her grandmother, she would have taken a leave of absence earlier and spent the time with her. Now, she'd never get the chance.

She heaved a sigh. Instead of spending the holidays with her beloved nana, she'd be alone in her apartment. Which was her fault as well. If she hadn't broken her engagement, she and Vincent would be married and celebrating their first anniversary.

Not that she regretted her decision. She hadn't been in love with Vincent. Sure, he was a great guy and a talented doctor. He was the ideal husband, her mother had reminded her when Eve shared her misgivings. Instead of counseling Eve to listen to her instincts, her mother had done her best to persuade her to go through with the wedding.

It would have been a farce. She couldn't do it. She returned Vincent's ring, ended the relationship, and did her best to ignore her mother's snide comments.

Enough. Wiping away the moisture clouding her vision, Eve glanced in the mirror. Her mother would have approved of her fashionable black slim skirt, matching fitted blazer, and modest navy blouse. It was sleeveless, so she'd ditch the blazer when she was out in the blistering mid-July heat.

She left her hair down, which her mother would have criticized had she been there. Mom was all about appearances. Well, this one time, Eve wore her hair the way Nana had liked it. Nana claimed it made her look like the young, vibrant woman God had called her to be rather than the unapproachable professional her mother insisted she act like. Eve tucked a strand of her long red hair behind her ears. Her hazel eyes were bloodshot from weeping, and the pale skin she'd inherited from her Scottish grandparents appeared colorless.

She had a few minutes. She opened her makeup bag, pulled out her blush, and dusted some color onto her cheeks. Then she slicked a thin layer of coral gloss on her lips.

She didn't bother with eye makeup. If she cried again, it would streak down her face. That was also why she'd opted to wear her glasses rather than her contact lenses. Another choice Mom wouldn't approve of.

She couldn't stall any longer. After slipping her phone and hotel key card into a pocket of her tote bag, Eve pushed her feet into simple black pumps with two-inch heels, knowing her feet would be screaming by lunchtime. She left the room and wandered through the air-conditioned halls and lobby of the hotel and out into the bright morning sun.

Gnaw Bone, Indiana, wasn't truly a town. Barely a blip on the map with a population hovering around 200 people, it was an unincorporated township located in Brown County. The lawyer handling Nana's will was based in Nashville, Indiana, a mere five-minute drive from Nana's house. She'd elected to stay at a chain hotel less than two miles from Samson and Son's Law Office. She could have walked, and if she had been in comfortable clothes, she would have. But since she wore these awful heels, she got in her bright blue Honda CRV and left the parking lot.

Three minutes later, she reached her destination. There were a few cars there but none that she recognized. If she didn't hurry, she'd be late. Not happening. Eve was hardwired for punctuality. When Eve was growing up, her mother always showed up to events chronically late—or what she called "fashionably" late. Eve didn't care what she called it. It mortified her every time her mother forced others to wait for her, and by extension, her family. Her father had been indulgent, though she knew it bothered him as well.

He'd been gone seventeen years. Her heart ached every time his memory popped into her head.

Drawing in a deep breath, Eve stepped from the vehicle. After locking the doors, she dropped her keys into her overlarge purse then pulled out her phone to silence it, grimacing when she saw another text from her mother. She would deal with that later.

"Eve? Eve Granville?" a voice called.

Pivoting, Eve narrowed her gaze at the man approaching her. Her eyes widened as recognition dawned. She'd know those dark eyes and wild brown curls anywhere.

"Carter?"

He nodded, and she frowned. The Carter she'd known had possessed a wide, contagious smile with a dimple in his right cheek. The man staring down at her was more reserved. Wary. That startled her. They'd been best friends as kids until the day her widowed mother had decided to leave Nana's house, the only home Eve knew, and move them to an apartment two states away in Pittsburgh. At first, the switch had stifled Eve. She clung to her friendship with Carter for a year through letters and phone calls, but when he left for college, those slowed to a trickle until the day she left him a message and he never called her back. He never knew how terrible life got for her.

And here he was, seventeen years later, a grown man of thirty-three.

"I'm sorry about your grandmother. My entire family was out of state at a family reunion when she died. We didn't even hear about it until we returned home two days after the funeral."

She'd wondered why none of the Grant family had attended.

"Thanks. It was a shock. I saw her in May. I didn't know she was sick."

They began walking toward the building. He opened the door for her, gesturing for her to enter. He followed close behind.

"She was eighty-six, right?" His voice was barely a whisper.

"Eighty-five." She spoke in hushed tones too. Then she felt foolish. They weren't sharing any secrets. "Her birthday's in October."

Tears stung her eyes. She blinked rapidly to hold them off. The last thing she wanted was to enter the lawyer's office with tears streaming down her cheeks. She cleared her throat. Jerking her shoulders back, she straightened her jacket.

"Shall we?"

He nodded. Briefly, he touched her elbow. Then he stopped to let her walk past.

She took three steps into the room and halted, her jaw dropping. "Nadia?"

The tall blond seated in front of the lawyer's desk stood, smoothed her pale yellow pantsuit, and sauntered over. She held out her arms and hugged Eve, the bracelets on her wrist jangling. A cloud of floral perfume surrounded them.

Eve returned her hug, holding her breath against the intense fragrance. When Nadia backed away, Eve let her go. She couldn't stop the grin from spreading across her face. She hadn't seen her half sister in five years, not since Nadia and Mom had a massive blowout of an argument. Eve had always adored her sister. Nadia was eight years older, but growing up, she had tolerated her little sister tagging along wherever she went. Nadia was six when her widowed mother met and married Richard Granville, and Eve was born two years later. Eve's father had treated his stepdaughter as his own.

"It's good to see you! I didn't know you were coming," Eve said.

Nadia shrugged one shoulder. "You know me. I have trouble keeping in touch."

That was a major understatement. She'd stopped responding to Eve's texts a couple of years ago.

Nadia's phone vibrated. She glanced at the screen and grimaced. Eve caught a glimpse of a picture of Nadia with a young man who wore a black beanie. Nadia put the phone away and rolled her eyes at Eve. "My ex-boyfriend keeps bugging me."

The door behind the desk opened, and a short, grandfatherly man in a dark suit with a red tie entered the room. "Please, make yourselves comfortable."

Eve glanced around, startled. "Is it only the three of us?"

Somehow, she'd expected more. Nana's funeral had been well-attended. The line for visitation had extended down the hall and out the front door. The day of the funeral, fifty cars had processed from the funeral home to the cemetery. It seemed everyone in Brown County knew Fiona Granville. She'd been a member of four county-wide committees, including the local historical preservation committee and the church hospitality board.

Mr. Samson smiled over his glasses. "Yes, Miss Granville. Mrs. Granville awarded her contributions to the church and other local groups before she died."

"She knew she was dying?"

Why hadn't she said anything?

"She knew it would happen eventually. She was getting up in years. She didn't want to leave anything to chance."

Eve heard what he didn't say. Not like what had happened with her grandfather or her dad. Both men had died before their time.

An hour later, it was done. Eve sat in her chair, shocked. After a few moments she gathered herself, thanked Mr. Samson, and left the office. Carter walked her out to her car.

"Eve, are you all right?"

Pushing her hair back, she leaned against the car and stared up at him. "Did I imagine that, Carter? Everything? She left me everything?"

He tilted his head, his lips quirked in a half smile. "Not everything. Nadia inherited some money."

"And so did you," she reminded him.

"Not much. Do you mind?" Concern rang in his voice.

"That you inherited? No!" she declared, amazed he could think it. "According to her will, you were indispensable to her this past year. I could never begrudge you the money. If anything, you should have gotten more."

"I don't need anything." He glanced away. "What are you going to do with the house?"

She dropped her head in her hands. She could feel a tension headache coming on. "I haven't the slightest clue. I grew up in that house. I have so many memories there."

"But?"

She gave a humorless laugh and met his gaze. "But I have a career in Pittsburgh. I can't see keeping the house and renting the apartment both."

He frowned. Was he disappointed? Or was that disapproval? She shifted her stance. She was exhausted. Suddenly, it was too much. The weight of her job, her grandmother's death, and this looming decision. The tears she'd been refusing to shed all morning burst through in a torrent of deep, painful sobs.

Immediately, Carter was there, wrapping her in his arms. He didn't speak. Just held her while she let all the grief and uncertainty pour out, drenching his shirt under her cheek. Finally, the tears stopped rolling down her face. She pulled away from him, embarrassed. His arms dropped, and he stepped back.

"Sorry about that. I guess it all got to me. That, and I'm just so tired I can hardly think."

"Can I make a suggestion?"

She forced herself to meet his gaze, her face hot. "Of course."

"You need a break. Why not take some leave? You can come stay in the house for a few weeks. Give yourself time to deal with your grandmother's death and decide about all her things before you put the house on the market."

She considered his words. "I haven't had a vacation in three years," she mused. "I could take time off. Family leave. That's what I'll do."

He smiled, the first genuine smile she'd seen from him today. "Great. How can I help?"

"Can you keep an eye on the house while I'm gone? It'll take me a week or so, I imagine. Ten days at most."

"No problem. Let's exchange numbers. You go home and do what you have to. I'll be here when you return."

She nodded and waited for him to unlock his phone. He took a picture of her then plugged in the number she rattled off. She repeated the process then sent him a quick test message. When his phone hooted like an owl, he gave her a thumbs-up. She hopped into the car and took off.

She should call her mom, but she resisted, knowing she needed a few minutes alone to regroup. She had sobbed like a teenager all over his shoulder! Good grief. She hadn't cried like that since her father died. It had seemed unreal, seeing Carter again. She would do as he suggested. However, she needed to exercise caution. No matter how much time off she took, she had a career and a life somewhere else, so she couldn't afford to forget how he'd ghosted her.

Her phone rang. Her mom. Of course.

"Hey Mom."

"So?"

She really didn't want to do this. "Look, I'll be home this evening. We'll talk about it then."

Her mom protested. Eve did something she'd never done in her life. She ignored her mother's complaints and hung up. She'd pay for it later, but she needed a few more hours of peace even though she knew it wouldn't last. Mom would be livid when she learned her daughter was "risking" her career by taking leave instead of selling the house and furnishings outright. Eve pressed her lips together. She knew the truth. Mom needed money to pay off debts she'd accrued through the years.

Debts she had tried to hide from her younger daughter.

When her mother called back thirty seconds later, Eve let the call go to voice mail.

It was time to take charge of her life.

Ten days later, Carter checked his phone for the fourth time in ten minutes. Eve had texted at six o'clock that morning to tell him she was on her way and would arrive around two in the afternoon. It was twelve forty-five now. He wasn't sure how he felt about having her in his life again.

Seventeen years was a long time. At one point, he'd thought they had become more than friends. Then her father died, and their relationship disintegrated. And while he'd admit that it was his fault they lost touch, he'd moved on.

He strolled along the rows of headstones in the cemetery. Eve would want to visit when she arrived. She'd ordered flowers. He could have gone at the same time she did, but he wanted to make this visit alone. He moved with the confidence of someone who'd made this journey often, as indeed he had. Carter had been a weekly visitor at the cemetery for the past four years, regardless of the weather.

He paused before a gravestone. All the markers in this new portion of the cemetery were flat stones flush with the ground so the riding lawnmower wouldn't bump into them and damage anything. Squatting down, he brushed away the freshly cut grass.

Michaela Ann Grant
Beloved wife and daughter
Born September 3, 1992
Went to Jesus November 7, 2019

What would their life have been like if Michaela had lived? If cancer hadn't ripped the floor out from beneath them? He'd fallen so hard for her. Their life had been rich. They'd shared everything and planned to have a large family one day. Then, within the span of eight months, all those dreams were dust.

Never again would he open himself up to that kind of agony. Watching her waste away, knowing there was nothing he could do except sit with her and hold her hand, had nearly killed him. He couldn't go through that a second time.

His phone rang, jarring him from the melancholy wrapping around him like a thick fog. He unlocked the phone and answered it while walking back to his car.

"Buddy," his friend Doug said, "you need to get to the flea market."

"The flea market? Why? We were just there Saturday."

"Trust me. You're gonna want to see this. I'll meet you there."

Carter sighed. Doug had a tendency to be mysterious. "Fine. I'll be there in ten."

After shoving his phone into his pocket, he got in the car and started it, cranking the air conditioner on high to combat the sweltering heat. It was the last Monday in July, and the temperature had hovered in the nineties all week. Hopefully, whatever Doug wanted to show him wouldn't require him to walk the entire length of the flea market. After spending an hour this morning working on the lawn at the Granville place, then another fifteen minutes at the cemetery, he was ready to get someplace cooler.

Doug approached his car and stood beside it, bouncing on the balls of his feet, while Carter shut it down and locked it.

"You're like a kid at Christmas," Carter joked. "What has you so amped?"

"I can't tell you. I want to see your reaction. I think it's something you might want to acquire for the museum."

Now he was really intrigued. Carter had been a museum curator for a decade. He'd often traveled hundreds of miles to investigate a possible piece to add to the museum's collection. Doug had never, in his memory, sought him out this way. And to say he needed to check at the flea market? Carter discreetly looked at his phone again. If he wanted the time to shower before he met Eve, he needed to leave right now. But Doug was so excited, Carter couldn't disappoint him.

Fifteen minutes later, Carter held the object of his friend's zeal in his hand. Realizing his mouth was hanging open, he shut it.

"Well? Is it genuine?" Doug whispered.

Pulse hammering in his chest, Carter examined the antique thistle ring sitting in his palm. The etchings were exquisite. Marvelous craftmanship.

"It's genuine," he said slowly. Then he turned away from the seller and glanced up at his friend. He kept his voice low. "It's also stolen."

Doug's jaw dropped. He held up both hands. "Wait... Wait a minute. Stolen? Dude, are you sure?"

Nodding, Carter showed him the inscription. "See this? 'Cor immobile'? It's part of a set. The other ring reads 'cor nobile.'"

"What does it mean?" Doug squinted at the inscription.

"A noble heart is an immovable heart," Carter translated.

"Wow. Sounds majestic," Doug said.

"Exactly." He turned back to the seller. "Do you have a second ring like this?"

The man shook his head. "Nope. That's the only one. You want it?"

"Yeah." He pulled out his wallet and paid for the ring. The asking price was a pittance of its true worth. He also grabbed one of the business cards next to the cash box. Once he talked with Eve, he'd know what to do. Although he was sure the ring had been stolen, he had to verify it before calling the police. He'd save the card for them. If he was correct, they would be paying the vendor a visit. He jerked his head, signaling to Doug it was time to leave.

"Why did you buy it if it's stolen?" Doug thrust his hands into his pockets as they made their way to the parking lot.

"Because I know the owner. If my memory is correct and this is her ring, she'll want to check and see if the second one is still in its place. Then we'll call the cops."

"When did you last see these rings?"

"At least seventeen years ago. I'm pretty sure I'm right, but I'll know once I see Eve."

He checked his phone again. Almost time. He'd stop and pick up a pizza and some soda, then head over to Eve's. He hopped in his car and stowed the ring in the glove compartment. He'd feel better when it was back where it belonged.

By the time he arrived at the Granville house, his stomach was growling. Eve's car was in the driveway. He parked beside it and jogged around to the passenger side. After retrieving the ring from the glove compartment, he shoved it into his pocket then gathered the pizza and the ice-cold six-pack of Pepsi and made for the front door. Eve was waiting in the doorway by the time he reached it.

"I was hoping you'd bring food," she said with smile.

"I'm starving," he said, returning her smile. "But I need to show you something first."

She quirked an eyebrow at him and led him to the kitchen.

He placed the pizza and drinks on the table and then took the ring from his pocket. The moment her gaze landed on it, she blanched. Her hands flew up and covered her mouth, but he still heard her gasp.

"Where did you find that?"

"At the Olde Tyme Flea Market." He hesitated. "I'm a museum curator. Part of my job is to locate antiques and objects of local historic relevance. When my friend Doug saw this ring, he had no idea what he'd found. He just knew it looked old and antinquish. He called me to come look at it, and I recognized it the moment I saw it. I asked the vendor if he had a second ring, but he didn't."

She spun and dashed down the hall. He followed her into the office. She lifted a picture from the wall, revealing a sleek black safe. It looked different than he recalled, shiny and stylish. Deftly, she punched in the passcode. He heard a faint click, and the door swung open easily.

"The papers are all messed up."

Her voice quavered. She grabbed the box near the back of the safe and brought it out. Her hands trembled as she opened it.

Sure enough, all that was left of the rings was their indentation in the felt lining of the box.

CHAPTER TWO

Eve couldn't wrap her mind around it. Her grandmother's rings had been stolen.

"I can't believe this," she whispered, staring at the empty box. "They were here."

"When?" Carter's voice startled her out of her frozen shock. "Eve? When did you last see them?"

He squatted down in front of her. She didn't have to think about it. The last visit was still fresh in her brain. "I saw Nana near the end of May. Around six weeks ago. She showed them to me that weekend. We were talking about the history of her...of our family. Do you know it?"

He frowned. "I'm familiar with some of it. I know your family is descended from nobility."

She couldn't stay in this room. She strode back to the kitchen and grabbed a can of Pepsi to keep her hands busy. Then she faced him and continued the story.

"That's right. Scottish nobility. The Dukedom of Granville. My great-grandfather, Tavish William Granville III, was the legitimate Seventh Duke of Granville. His grandfather, who was the duke at the time, died in a boating accident along with the duke's son, who was Tavish's father. His mother, my great-great-grandmother, Isabella Granville, escaped with him to America to protect him from his uncle. Tavish III was just an infant at the time, and his mother was afraid his uncle would kill him to usurp the title. Years later, when Tavish returned to Scotland to take his rightful place, she remained here in America. Tavish married my great-grandmother, Kenna Calhoun, and had twin boys. Kevin was his heir and my great-uncle, and Rory was my grandfather. Rory traveled to America to meet his grandmother, Bella, and ended up settling in Gnaw Bone."

"I vaguely remember this story. When did he arrive in Gnaw Bone? Mid-fifties?"

She took a sip of her Pepsi. "Yes, '56 or '57. Somewhere around that time."

"Is this the house your great-great grandmother lived in?"

She shook her head. "I'm coming to that." She paused, trying to keep her thoughts straight. "Rory stayed with his grandmother for a few months. He intended to return to Scotland. His plans changed, though, when he met my grandmother. I hear it was love at first sight. He wouldn't marry her, of course, until he had a house for her. He built this one. He called it their little wedding cottage."

Carter snorted, nearly choking on his Pepsi. She grinned. There was nothing little about the house Rory Granville had built for Fiona Bruce. It had five bedrooms and three and a half baths. Plus a huge kitchen, a dining room, a front family room with a picture window, a second family room, a den that also served as an office, and a finished basement.

"I know. Remember how we used to study in the fallout shelter in the basement?" She smiled at the memory.

"Yeah, that was fun. I remember setting up a desk down there. We had one side, and your grandma had shelves built on the other side to keep all the fruits and veggies she canned."

It was a good memory. She had to clear her throat before she could move on.

"Well, they got married and settled here. My dad was born a year later."

She leaned against the sink and stared out the window. The flowers in her nana's prized garden were in full bloom, creating a riot of colors. There were black-eyed Susans, butterfly weed—an awful name for such gorgeous flowers—and Virginia bluebells, along with several other species she didn't recognize.

"Eve? How are you? Are you okay?"

She gave herself a mental shake. "Sorry, lost in thought. Anyway, on her deathbed, my great-great-grandmother Bella gave Rory the thistle rings. They were part of the collection of jewels from the Granville dukedom. Tavish III left them with her when he returned to Scotland. Bella told my grandfather they were to be passed on to each new generation as a reminder of our heritage."

"So, they're what, hundreds of years old?"

She nodded. "At least. Oh, Nana would be heartbroken!"

Carter moved to her side and placed a warm hand on her shoulder. "Eve, we have to call the police. The second ring is out there somewhere."

He was right. They were wasting time talking. Shoving herself away from the counter, she went to retrieve her phone near the microwave where it was charging. She'd missed another call from her mother. She groaned.

"What's wrong?" Carter strode to her side, concern etched on his handsome face.

"Nothing." She started to turn away, but then the frustration proved too much. "Okay, it's my mom."

Deciding to get it over with, she dialed her voice mail then put the phone on speaker. She already knew what her mom was going to say.

"Eve Granville, are you ignoring me? I need you to call me back. I don't know why you're being so selfish. That house should have been left to me. I was married to her son, after all. Eve, listen, I have a friend, he's lawyer. He can help you put the place on the market fast. I'm contacting him. It's ridiculous that you were left the whole estate. What do you know about dealing with—"

Eve hit delete. When she faced Carter again, his mouth was tight, and his brown eyes were narrow slits. She'd never seen him so furious.

"She wants to take your inheritance? What kind of mother is she?"

His automatic support gave her spirits a boost.

"She's in debt. I don't know how deep. She's never told me, but I happened to overhear a conversation a few years back. We were meeting for lunch, and she was talking on the phone when I arrived. She was stressed about several letters she'd received from creditors."

"Why would she think you'd give her the money from selling the house?"

"Because I've done everything she's wanted up until now. I didn't want to take my current job. I wanted to have a small practice in a small town, but she insisted I was wasting my education and opportunities. I caved, and now I'm stuck in a job that's sucking the life out of me."

"Then change it."

in *Gnaw Bone, Indiana*

"How?" She leaned against the countertop. "I've worked hard to get where I am at the hospital. It's taken me years. And I was recently invited to join a practice connected to the hospital. If I leave now, I'll have wasted a lot of time."

The curl of his lip was there and gone so quick, she could have imagined it. The closeness of a moment ago, however, was gone.

"Right," he said, backing away. "Sorry. I don't know what I was thinking."

"Carter." She reached out an imploring hand.

"We should call the police." His words dropped like ice crystals in the quiet kitchen.

Eve stared at him for a moment, aching to return to their former camaraderie. After a few seconds, she sighed and looked up the police department on her phone. "I'm not bothering with 911, since this isn't an emergency. The rings could have been stolen weeks ago."

"I agree."

She waited a second. When it became clear he had nothing more to say, she pressed her lips together to hold in a sigh and dialed the number. She startled when a person answered. She'd expected a robotic menu.

"Officer Schiller here. How may I help you?"

For a second, her mind went blank. When he repeated his greeting, annoyance in his tone, she hurried to respond. "Hi. My name is Eve Granville. My house was robbed."

She cringed at the words "my house." In her heart, this was her grandmother's house. And although a part of her would always treasure the years she'd spent here, she couldn't let that trap her. She had to move on, which meant this was not her house. Not for long.

"Are you safe?" he barked out. "Is the thief still on the premises?"

"No. Whoever did it is long gone. They took my grandmother's rings and left." She gave him the address.

The sharpness left his voice. "I'll be there soon, ma'am."

"What's wrong?" Carter asked her when she ended the call. "You seem a bit, um, unsettled."

She turned away from him and grabbed the Pepsi at her side. The can was slick with condensation, and the cold drink felt good as it slid down her throat. A jolt of caffeine couldn't hurt right about now. "I'm not used to having a real person answer the phone. I was all prepared for an automatic answering service or an operator."

He stepped to the table and picked up his own beverage. "That's a small township for you. We have an officer on duty. He's in charge of the phones too. It's not often there's an actual call he has to go on." He pointed to the pizza. "We should probably eat now. It might be a while before we get another chance."

She sat and put a slice of pizza on her plate. After eating three bites, she pushed it away. "I can't eat. My nerves are too tight."

Carter paused, a slice oozing with cheese two inches from his mouth. She chuckled. "You can eat, silly. I'll finish mine later."

Eve picked up the box and slid it into the nearly empty refrigerator. She'd meant to go grocery shopping this afternoon. That would need to be delayed a bit.

Carter polished off his slice and took the dishes to the sink. He rinsed them and then popped them into the dishwasher.

"Thanks," she murmured as the doorbell rang.

"I'll wait in the office." Carter slipped past her and disappeared through the office door.

Eve drew in a deep breath and went to let Officer Schiller in. There was a second officer standing at his shoulder. Eve gestured for them to enter and ushered them down the hall and into the office. Their feet sank into the plush carpet, cutting off the loud clopping their hard-soled shoes had made on the polished hardwood in the hall and entry-way. Carter glanced up from the book he was flipping through, unease slithering across his face and disappearing just as quickly.

He stood and nodded to Officer Schiller. "Phillip."

Any hope he had of keeping his personal life quiet died the moment his brother-in-law entered the room, followed by Phillip's partner, Officer Theresa Kent, who preferred the nickname Teri. "Hey, Teri."

Phillip paused midstep. Carter understood. There were no hard feelings between them, but their meeting was always a reminder to the young officer that his older sister was gone and not coming back. Phillip's gaze cut to Eve then back again. "Carter. Hey. I didn't expect to see you here."

The slight emphasis on the last word irritated him, as if his brother-in-law felt Carter's presence was some sort of betrayal of Michaela's memory. Carter had adored his wife. But she'd been gone for four years. Since her death, he'd never even considered dating again. The judgment emanating from the man before him seared through him, leaving a bitter taste on his tongue.

"Eve and I are old friends." He clamped his mouth shut before he said anything more. As much as he respected Phillip, he owed him nothing.

Eve's hazel eyes narrowed. He waved his hand, trying to signal to her that he'd explain later.

Eve switched her gaze to the police officers. "My grandmother's rings?"

Phillip's cheeks reddened.

Teri frowned at him and took over. "Yes. When did you notice the rings were missing?"

"I inherited this property after my grandmother, Fiona Granville, passed several weeks ago. I had no idea they were gone until Carter brought it to my attention this afternoon."

Once again, he was the focal point. Stiffening his shoulders, he succinctly explained how he came to have one of the thistle rings in his possession. The officers, their professional demeanor back in place, asked the routine questions. Carter handed Phillip the card he'd taken from the vendor at the flea market. Teri began taking pictures of the ring.

"Where were the rings kept?" Teri lowered her phone and spoke to Eve.

"Over here." She led them to the safe then stood aside so they could complete their investigation. She looked so alone, her arms folded across her stomach, her jaw tense. He had the impression she was fighting against either a torrent of tears or a scream of rage. Carefully, he crossed the room to stand beside her, making sure there was a safe space between them. He didn't want to stand close enough to give the wrong impression, but neither would he leave her to face this new situation on her own.

He could be her friend without becoming too emotionally involved, couldn't he? After all, he'd been in love with his wife, and he already knew the agony of losing her. He'd not be weak enough to get mixed up in a relationship again.

Not even with Eve, his first love, although she'd never known it.

"Why would someone do this?" Eve murmured, still staring at the officers.

"I wish I knew." Phillip slipped his phone back into his pocket and pushed himself to his feet. He and Teri joined them near the wall.

"Well?" Eve demanded, her gaze ping-ponging between them.

Phillip scratched his head. It was his tell for when he was puzzled. "Well, ma'am, there's not much we can say. I noticed there were a substantial number of documents in the safe. Was anything else missing?"

She shrugged. "Not that I could tell, but I don't know everything Nana kept in there."

"You say you saw the rings in May?"

"Yes. I hadn't looked in the safe again until this afternoon. I would never have thought to look at the flea market though."

"Yeah. I'm glad Doug called me about it." Carter shook his head, still awed. "Has anyone else been in the safe that you know of? Anyone else know the passcode?"

She tugged on a hank of hair and curled it around her finger. A clear sign she was distraught. The familiar gesture was at odds with the sophisticated woman she'd become.

"I don't know. I doubt Nana shared it with anyone else. However..." Her glance flashed to the safe. "This is a new safe. The last time I was here, it had just been installed, but the passcode remained the same."

Phillip and Teri both straightened. Their eyes grew sharp, focused. Phillip stepped up to the safe and wrote down the brand and serial number. "The person who installed it would know where it was and the passcode. Any idea what company she went through to get this safe?"

Eve shook her head. "I'm sorry, but no."

"What about any cameras on the premises?" Teri asked.

"Cameras? I've never seen any. I lived here until I was fifteen. There were none then, and Nana has never mentioned any that she had installed after I left."

Disappointment shivered across Phillip's face. "We'll try to find out who installed the safe. And we need to check into the vendor at the flea market. Those two are high on the list of leads."

Or suspects. He didn't say it out loud, however.

"I'm sorry we can't tell you more," Teri said. "In a case like this, it's possible the second ring might never show up. Especially since we don't have a real time for the disappearance."

"Does that mean this isn't a priority?"

He could almost visualize steam seeping from Eve's ears. Her temper had always amazed him. She started on a slow simmer and worked her way up. But she never screamed or yelled. The madder she became, the more she withdrew into herself, until the simmer turned into icy, frigid calm. So cold, sometimes he almost believed he'd get frostbite from standing too close to her.

Phillip must have caught the edge of anger dripping from her words. He held out both hands in a defensive, calming motion. "No, ma'am. I don't mean that at all. We'll search. As I said, we'll start with the contractor who put in the new safe. If you find any receipts, or anything else you think may be helpful, let us know. We'll do everything we can. The truth is, any evidence or clues may be long gone by now. In your own words, the thief may have had up to six weeks to cover his or her tracks."

She deflated like a balloon stuck by a straight pin. He could only imagine what was going on in her mind. The Eve he knew wasn't materialistic. The monetary value of the jewels would be irrelevant to her. No. The importance, he was certain, lay in the fact that the two rings had been part of the heritage her grandmother had entrusted her with.

And she'd lost one before she'd even fully taken ownership of the house.

The officers promised to contact her if there was anything else they needed. Or if they uncovered information regarding the thistle ring. Carter didn't say it out loud, but that was unlikely.

At the door, Phillip turned to him. "You should stop by tonight, Carter. Jen would love to see you."

Carter and Phillip had been friends since middle school. And when they left for college and he started dating Michaela and Phillip was dating Jennifer, the foursome had done everything together. Now it was just too painful to be with them.

Carter shrugged. "Maybe some other time."

His brother-in-law's lips tightened, but he merely jerked his head in a nod and followed Teri out the front door. Carter stood at Eve's shoulders, watching the officers get into their cruiser and drive away. Finally, she shut the door and spun to face him.

She pierced him with her hazel eyes. "I hope you didn't decline his offer because of me. I don't want to take you away from your friends."

She had to know sometime, and it might as well come from him. "You're not. Besides, Phillip isn't just my friend. He's my brother-in-law."

Her brows shot up. "You're married?"

He steeled himself for the sense of loss that always accompanied the words. "I'm not. Not anymore. My wife died of cancer four years ago."

The sting he'd expected didn't come. Instead of the staggering agony and loneliness he always felt when he spoke of Michaela, there was a dull ache. He still missed her, but he could breathe through it. Was he beginning to heal at last?

～ CHAPTER THREE ～

Eve blanched. Carter's shocking statement hovered between them. Her mind swirled with questions. She shushed them. Now was not the time. His face was closed, telling her he had no intention of discussing anything personal.

She could respect that. Too many years had passed between them. It wouldn't do any good to remain in Gnaw Bone anyway. As she'd already told him, her place was in Pittsburgh, focusing on furthering her career. A career that didn't bring her much joy, true, but it was still hers, something not even the pressure of her mother's constant attempts to control her life could rob from her.

Thoughts of robbing brought her mind back to the situation at hand.

"I need to find the missing ring," she blurted.

Carter frowned. "The police are on it. They'll keep searching. It's their job."

She waved her hand like she was swatting at a fly. "Yeah, I heard that. I also heard that they don't have much hope of finding it."

She pivoted on her heel and began to pace the length of the hallway. "Carter, someone came into this house and stole the heritage handed down from generations of the Granville family. We didn't publicize that the rings were here. As far as I know, no one outside of the family was ever told."

"Well," he interrupted, "you told me."

She hit him with her best glare. "You know what I mean. And for all intents and purposes, you were family."

Were. Until her mother moved her from the life she'd always known into a life of chaos and uncertainty.

He flinched. So he felt it too, the injury their abrupt departure had caused. It wasn't just her life that had been ruptured by her mother's actions.

She strode into the kitchen, snatched up her half-full Pepsi, and drank several long swallows, feeling the burn as the carbonation hit her throat.

"You don't have to do this alone, you know." Carter lounged in the doorway, his right shoulder against the frame.

Did she know that? It had been so long since she'd had someone she could turn to. Not since her father had passed away. Her mother had never been interested in what she needed, and Nadia disappeared soon after that. Nana would have helped, but she was so far away, and Eve hadn't been willing to be a burden to the one person who loved her unconditionally.

Even Carter had let her down when he left for college and ghosted her.

But she couldn't make this about her. The heritage her grandparents had taken such pride in needed to be her priority. Something Carter had told her clicked.

"You said you're a curator?"

"Yes. I work with several museums in Brown County."

She tapped her chin. "If you're a curator, you have contacts with others who are familiar with antiques and historical objects. Not to mention, you've actually seen the real ring. Which means you'd recognize it, like you did the one at the flea market."

"True." He folded his arms across his chest. "I said I would help you, and I will. I'm assuming you want me to use my contacts to gather some information?"

She started pacing again. "That's it exactly. Between you and your contacts, if someone decides to sell the other ring, it's possible that one of you will see or hear something."

"It's a long shot."

She stopped pacing and met his gaze. "I know that. But I'm kind of low on options. With the exception of you, I don't know anyone in this area anymore."

It made her sad. Seventeen years ago, she knew everyone. Now she was reduced to a lawyer and Carter. Not much. Her heart ached for the connection they had once shared.

She backed up, putting more space between them, and shut that train of thought down. Carter was off-limits. Not only was he firmly rooted in the small community of Gnaw Bone and the surrounding area, but it was obvious his deceased wife was still a very real presence in his life.

"Okay," he said, stretching the word out. "Fine. I'll help you. And let's say you find the ring. What then?"

She huffed. Why was everyone so keen on pinning her down, knowing her plans? First, she had her mother calling every other hour, getting more strident with every call, her demands escalating. Now Carter.

"I haven't decided," she hedged. "I've taken a month off work. That's all the hospital would give me."

"And?"

"And what?" Why wouldn't he drop it?

"You said you had a new job. So, what will you do with this place?"

"I haven't decided yet." She stalked into the living room and halted before the cushioned bench nestled in a small alcove under the large picture window. She had spent hours sitting on that bench, dreaming as she stared out the window or reading whatever novel had captured her attention at the moment. She turned around and saw the handmade rocking chair across the room. Nana would sit there, her knitting needles flashing as she worked. Nana's craftsmanship had been superb. She'd had a consistent business and would sell her afghans, scarves, and cardigans at a small eclectic shop on the border of Gnaw Bone and Nashville, the next town over.

Blinking back tears, she averted her gaze.

"There are so many memories here."

She hadn't meant to say that out loud.

He sighed in her ear. Eve startled. She hadn't heard him approach. She opened her mouth to complain, but her stomach grumbled, interrupting her. Heat flooded her face.

"Look, Eve, why don't you go ahead and change into comfortable clothes. I'll heat up the pizza, and we'll plan while we eat. I'm still hungry. That one piece of pizza is all I've eaten today."

Change her clothes? Frowning, she glanced down at her slim light blue skirt and sleeveless blouse. She'd decided against nylons in light of the July heat. Her sandals were stylish, although, she admitted, not the most comfortable.

He must have caught her confusion. "You can't be serious. Eve, those shoes look like torture. It's July. You're on vacation. Going through a house is sweaty business, regardless of the central air, and it can be dirty work."

For a moment, her pride raged with her common sense. Finally, she dipped her chin, acknowledging his plan. Then she ran up the stairs, the idea of ditching her expensive, well-made clothes for comfort suddenly appealing.

Besides, it wasn't like changing her clothes would change who she was.

Carter watched Eve disappear at the top of the steps. His initial thought was that she'd dressed in her normal professional attire because she had business to attend to that morning before coming to the house and he'd arrived before she'd had an opportunity to change. Her reaction had him rejecting that theory.

"I hope that's not her idea of casual now," he muttered, striding to the large, airy kitchen. He grabbed a couple of plates from the cupboard and loaded several slices of the pizza. He added two glasses filled with ice on the table for their sodas. She had her drink with her, but he dumped the rest of his into a glass. The ice crackled, and a white frosty fog escaped from the top. By the time he had the pizza warmed up and had it placed in the middle of the table, she was padding into the room.

He looked at her new outfit and gave her a thumbs-up. She rolled her eyes, but he caught the pink tinge in her cheeks. She'd gone with shorts and a green and white T-shirt with pink flowers, and she'd twisted her red hair into a messy bun. He'd always loved the color. It reminded him of autumn.

His eyes dropped to her feet, and he grinned. Gone were the fussy sandals. In their place she wore comfortable shoes that matched the color of her T-shirt.

"Much better."

She sank into her chair and immediately poured her Pepsi over the ice. "I hate to admit it, but I feel better."

Unwilling to say anything that might get her defenses up, he ignored the statement. "Should we say grace?"

After a quick prayer, they ate for a few minutes in silence. Finally, she wiped her lips with a napkin and pushed her plate away. He took a long swig of his drink then set his glass aside and grabbed the notepad and pen he'd found while she was changing.

"I jotted down a list of people I can contact. Most of them, I can send an email. A couple I only have phone numbers for."

He shoved the pad toward her. She tugged on the necklace around her neck while she read the list. His breath caught.

Did she realize that was the necklace he'd given her right before she moved away and broke his heart? Of course, now he knew it hadn't been her fault. They'd exchanged letters for a year, but then he'd gotten involved with college, met Michaela, and one day he got a letter and never got around to answering it.

He couldn't regret it though. Michaela and he shared a beautiful love until the day she died.

But he did pity Eve. All she had was her mother.

"Well." Eve glanced at the clock. "You know the other ring was nearly an exact copy of this one, with the exception of the inscription."

She placed the ring on the table between them. He took out his phone, snapped a quick picture, and then began composing emails. He sent the image in a text to the other two numbers.

One text bounced back. He did a quick search and found the dealer had retired. He wouldn't worry about him. Once the emails were sent, he rose to his feet.

"I'll let you know if anything comes of these." He wouldn't be holding his breath.

She frowned. "Oh. Fine. I guess you have things to do."

He paused. Did she want him to stay?

Warning bells went off in his mind. He couldn't stay. She was only a temporary fixture in his life.

"I need to get home. And you," he said as he put his dishes in the sink, "are probably looking forward to going through your grandmother's things."

She sank into herself, and the corners of her mouth drooped. "I can't do that. Not yet. Maybe tomorrow."

He understood. That would make her nana's death final.

Feeling mean for leaving, he still forced himself to walk out the door and drive home. He hit State Road 46 and followed it a little over half a mile. Most people drove through Gnaw Bone without even realizing it. The entire town was only about a mile long. It didn't even have a post office or a single stop light. When he was a kid he couldn't imagine a better place to live.

He parked in his driveway, entered his empty house, and walked from room to room. It felt empty after spending hours with Eve. Maybe it was time he invested in a dog. He'd always loved animals. Granted, his job sometimes required travel, but he could stay in hotels that allowed animals. Or leave the dog with his mom. She'd enjoy that. His mom had never met a dog she didn't fall in love with at first sight. They would have had several growing up if his dad hadn't put his foot down and limited it to two dogs and one cat.

After a while he decided to work in his garden to occupy himself so he wouldn't pick up the phone to dial Eve and check on her. She was a grown woman with a high-pressure career. She could handle a night alone in the house she grew up in. Besides, his phone was nearly dead. He took it into his bedroom and plugged it into the charger. He'd check on it later.

It was nearly ten o'clock before he thought to check his email. He'd had several responses. None of the dealers had seen such a ring, but they would let him know immediately if they saw it or heard of it. One email suggested he contact a dealer named Basil Curry.

Of course! He'd forgotten Basil, but the man was an acquaintance. They hadn't spoken in years. He thanked the sender for the advice and then fired off an email to Basil. Then he placed the phone back on the charger and got ready for bed.

There was nothing else he could do until tomorrow. He vacillated between hope and dread of hearing that someone had found the ring. He wanted Eve to have the rings together again. He couldn't regret helping her. It was the right thing to do.

He didn't like spending too much time with her though. Despite his decision to keep his distance, he worried she might find her way into his heart again. He'd gone down that road before. Emotional attachments were risky and messy. He'd had more than his share of that kind of pain.

But she had no one else.

Before falling asleep, he sent up a prayer for wisdom.

And for the strength to resist the temptation that was Eve Granville.

CHAPTER FOUR

Eve woke up to her phone blaring like a fire alarm next to the bed. Groaning, she rolled over and slapped her hand on the device, dragging it closer to the edge of the nightstand. She sat up and slid her finger across the screen, turning off the alarm.

She needed to find a new sound to wake her up.

Then she looked at the time and dropped back down on the pillow. Why did she still have the alarm set for six? She was on leave. Flipping over in the bed, she closed her eyes, determined to get another hour of sleep.

Unfortunately, she'd always struggled returning to sleep once she woke up. Now was no different. After fifteen minutes of willing herself to sleep again, she surrendered to the inevitable and threw the blankets off. She shivered as the central air blew an arctic blast through the house. She padded to the main controls in the hall and adjusted the temperature to a reasonable seventy-four degrees.

She might as well get ready. She pulled out a sundress then paused. Who knew how dusty she'd get today, going through Nana's things? She decided on a pair of shorts and a lightweight T-shirt then headed into the bathroom.

Twenty minutes later, she was showered, dressed, and seated in the window seat with her Bible. The weight of everything that had happened in the past month pressed down on her. She could barely straighten her shoulders, the burden was so heavy. She had no one to turn to, really. Her mother had her own agenda, and Eve couldn't trust her. She wanted to trust Carter, the way she used to, but the divide caused by those seventeen years apart seemed insurmountable. He was helping her, true, but it wasn't hard to sense the emotional barrier he'd placed between them. It wasn't fair. He was the one who'd abandoned her when he left for college, but he acted like it was her fault. She was a kid when her mother dragged her away from Gnaw Bone.

She couldn't even tell him about how terrifying those years were for her. If it hadn't been for her grandmother, her escape to college wouldn't have been possible.

She smoothed her hand over the leather cover of her Bible. She hadn't been as faithful as she should have been this past year. She'd been busy, but that was a poor excuse. The truth was she'd started to lose hope. She hadn't lost her faith, but it had taken a beating.

She opened the Bible randomly and found herself in the book of the prophet Isaiah. She started reading. When the tears gathered in her throat and clouded her vision, she paused and swallowed. When she could see again, she slowly read Isaiah 41:10 aloud. "'So do not fear, for I am with you; do not be dismayed, for I am your God. I will strengthen you and help you; I will uphold you with my righteous right hand.'"

In her grief, she'd forgotten. God was bigger than all of her problems. He knew what would happen. He knew what she needed.

"I'm sorry, Lord. I didn't trust You. I'll do better. Help me overcome my fear and lack of trust."

She spent a few more minutes in prayer then began planning her day. At eight, she decided she'd waited long enough and tried to call

Carter. His phone went to voice mail. Impatient, she snapped out a message for him to call her. After disconnecting the call, she paced the room. Had he made any headway?

There was a chance she'd never see the second ring again. She fought the shame that tried to take root. She hadn't been here to stop the theft. That wasn't her fault. She'd come as soon as she could. Besides, the theft might have happened before Nana died. If it had been the man who replaced the safe, Nana must have let him in the house herself!

Eve needed to occupy her thoughts. She walked to the kitchen and began sifting through Nana's cookbooks. Baking always made her feel better. She didn't see anything that looked good in the first book. Then she spied Nana's recipe box. Ah, that was promising. Nana had hundreds of handwritten recipes, many passed down from her mother or grandmother.

She skipped the main course recipes. She wanted to make something sweet. She flipped through the cookies and candies. When she got to the cakes, she paused. Orange Marmalade Cake. Grandfather's mother had given the recipe to Nana on their wedding day. It sounded like a great summertime recipe. But did she have all the ingredients? She riffled through Nana's spices. Cinnamon, nutmeg, and clove. Check. What about marmalade? She went to the refrigerator and pushed aside the jelly jars that Nana had stocked. No orange marmalade. She chewed on her lower lip while she considered her options.

She could try and find a different recipe. Except she could almost taste this one. She could try swapping the marmalade out. Nope. She needed to go to a grocery store. She grabbed her phone and searched for grocery stores in the map app. There was one less than three miles away. It opened at nine.

She dropped her phone and keys into her purse and left. If she hurried, she could bake the cake and still have time to work in the house this morning.

She zoomed into the store and asked the first employee she saw where the marmalade was. When he pointed her in the right direction, she gave a brisk thanks and strode in the indicated direction like a hunting dog on the scent.

She snatched the last jar sitting on the shelf and beelined to the checkout. After leaving the store, she dug in her purse for her key.

"Eve? Eve Granville?"

Lifting her head, she was pinned in place by a familiar pair of brown eyes surrounded by a halo of mahogany curls. Olivia Grant was the female version of her older brother.

"Livvy?"

The younger woman ambushed her, wrapping her in a hug so tight, Eve squeaked in laughing protest.

"I can't believe you're back!"

Eve braced herself to talk about her grandmother. "I'm only here for a few weeks. I have to take care of Nana's estate."

Sympathy darted across her former friend's face. "I'm sorry about your grandmother. We all loved her. I couldn't make it to the funeral."

"I know. Your brother explained." Reminded of her mission, she quickly made her excuses. "I have things I have to do today with the estate. Can we get together later?"

They exchanged contact information, promising to make plans later in the week. Eve popped into her car and returned to her new house. Once there, she shed her shoes inside the front door and padded to the kitchen.

She gathered all the ingredients together, and soon spices and flour dust were flying in the air. When she mixed the batter, she paused. Going on instinct, she added a little extra marmalade. She preferred her cake moist. She poured the batter in a prepped Bundt pan and put it in the oven. Soon the scents of warm cinnamon and orange permeated the air. She sniffed appreciatively.

Once the cake finished baking, she gently removed it from the pan and let it rest on a cooling rack.

It was almost ten thirty. She tried Carter's number again. When the call went to voice mail, she didn't leave a message, not wanting to appear anxious. Although he'd see that she called. Again.

She couldn't force him to answer his phone. All she could do was wait.

Carter heard the phone ringing as he reentered the house, his arms full of tomatoes, green peppers, and zucchini from his garden. Well, whoever was calling him would have to wait. He cleaned the vegetables and put them on the counter to dry then went to check his voice mail. Eve's voice whipped down the line. Despite the seriousness of the situation, he couldn't hold back his grin. She hadn't completely changed in the years they'd been apart. Her temper and impatience were still a part of her personality. Maybe those character traits weren't strengths to some. Carter had always found her sharp nature exciting. It matched her hair.

He'd shower and shave then return her call.

Twenty-five minutes later, he wandered back downstairs and found his sister waiting for him, her nails tapping out a staccato beat on his kitchen counter. "When were you going to tell me Eve is in town?"

He blinked at her. "Hello to you too, Sis. Um, I hadn't thought about it. She's dealing with things." He didn't want to discuss Eve's business with others, not even his sister. "I'm giving her a hand. In a few weeks she'll be gone, and life will go on."

Olivia frowned. "That's cold, Carter. She was my friend. And yours. I'd think you'd be more enthusiastic."

He ran his fingers through his hair, yanking as they snagged on a stray curl. He needed a haircut. "I am glad to see her, don't get me wrong. But we're not close anymore."

Olivia's face grew sad. "Aw, Carter. Who else does she have?"

He refused to get into an argument with his sister. "Look, Olivia, I appreciate what you're saying. Just so you know, I am going to help Eve today. I really need to get ready."

Scowling, she hopped off the counter she'd been using for a chair and sauntered out the door. He hadn't heard the last of it, but he couldn't worry about what Olivia thought. It was already eleven o'clock. Eve was probably fuming because he hadn't returned her calls yet.

He picked up the phone to call her. To his surprise, he saw he had an email from Basil. He recalled the quiet dealer with his dry wit. Basil had introduced himself long ago with the comment that, yes, he did indeed have a "spicy" name. So did all his siblings. His parents were avid gardeners. He'd resisted giving his daughter such a name. Chuckling, Carter opened his email. Two sentences in, he nearly dropped the phone.

He read the entire email through a second time.

He picked up the phone and dialed Basil's number. No answer. Frustration bit at him. They were so close. He dashed off a reply to Basil telling him he was on his way. Then he punched in Eve's number. She picked up the phone so swiftly, he suspected she'd been waiting for his call.

"Don't go anywhere," he greeted her. "I may have a lead on the ring. I'll be at your house in five minutes."

He hung up before she'd finished gasping.

Racing to his car, adrenaline propelled his legs to move faster than they'd moved since he'd left the university and the track team behind. He jumped behind the wheel and backed out of his driveway. For the first time in years, he thanked God for the blessing of living in a small town with no traffic lights.

Eve met him at the door in shorts and bare feet. Behind her, he caught a whiff of a sweet smell intermingled with cinnamon. The appealing aroma distracted him from his quest.

"Are you baking? It smells good."

She waved his question away. "Yes. We'll have it with lunch. Later. Tell me about the ring."

"I'll tell you on the way there." He spun back toward the car then thought of something and whirled around. "Bring the other ring. You might need it."

He didn't say for what, but he figured Basil might want to see it to be sure he wasn't being tricked out of a profit. Not that Basil was mercenary. He wasn't. But he was a stickler for keeping things fair and up-front.

Carter respected that.

Eve dashed inside the house. He didn't have to wait long. She joined him in the car within two minutes. She must have run to get the ring so fast. He knew finding the second thistle ring was a priority for her.

"Where are we going?" Eve drew her seat belt across her torso and buckled it securely. "I take it one of your contacts paid off."

He dipped his chin once. "Yes. A dealer I've met a couple of times through the years, Basil Curry, emailed me this morning."

Her eyebrows climbed her forehead when he said the dealer's name, but she didn't make any comment. Her focus remained on the missing ring. "What did the email say? Has he seen it?"

He tossed her a grin. "More than that. He called to tell me the ring is in his shop."

Her mouth fell open, and her eyes widened. "I can't believe it! The police were so sure we'd never find it."

He placed a cautionary hand on her arm. "Eve, this may be a wild-goose chase. Remember, he may know antiques, but Basil has never set eyes on the real thing. It may just be another old ring."

Some of the sparkle left her eyes, and guilt curled in his gut. He hated being the one to kill her enthusiasm. But she had to be realistic.

He opened his mouth to apologize, but she never gave him the chance. Holding up a hand to stall his words, she lifted her chin. Her lips pressed together in a firm line for a moment then eased up. He'd seen her do that in the past when she needed to stop herself from saying something rude or angry.

"I know it might be a waste of time. But I won't give up hope. Not yet."

"I haven't given up hope," he protested, turning his gaze back to the road. "I just don't want you to be disappointed."

"Thanks. But I can take care of myself."

He didn't respond, knowing they were on edge and anything he said might result in an argument.

When they arrived at Curry's Antique Boutique, there were no parking spaces on the street in front of the building. Carter drove to the corner and turned right then made a second right turn into the parking lot. He left his side of the car and walked around to get Eve's door for her. She smiled her thanks.

They had to go up two steps to enter the shop.

"This must be icy in the winter." Eve frowned at the narrow steps. "They need a railing here."

"It could be a problem," he agreed, holding the door open for her. They stood in the dimly lit shop, blinking to allow their eyes to adjust. Eve moved her sunglasses to sit on top of her head. She wasn't wearing her prescription glasses today, which meant she probably had contacts in. Carter found he missed the glasses. They had character.

"Welcome!" A young woman approached them, her face fixed in a professional smile. "If there's anything I can help you with, please, let me know."

Her gaze turned quizzical as she looked at Eve.

"Something wrong?" Eve asked.

The woman blinked then smiled again. "No. You just looked familiar, is all."

Carter glanced at her name tag. JILL CURRY. "Are you related to Basil?"

Her lips parted into a natural smile, flashing perfect teeth. "Yes, he's my dad. Do you know him?"

"We're acquaintances. He asked me to stop in and see him this morning. He had a ring to show me."

Her forehead creased. "He never mentioned it to me. He's not here right now."

"When do you expect him?"

She shrugged, her gaze shifting. "I can't say. He's normally here before me. I just got here a few minutes ago, and he wasn't here yet."

Carter didn't like the sound of that. He took out his phone and saw that he hadn't received a reply from Basil. "We'll just look around while we wait for him."

"No." Eve waved her hand impatiently. "I don't want to wait around." She turned to Jill. "Your father wanted us to see an antique ring. It's a thistle ring. It might have looked like this."

She reached into her purse and brought out a small jar. She unscrewed the lid, dumped it upside down, and the ring Doug had discovered tumbled into her open palm. Jill covered her gasp with her hand and leaned in.

"Yes! It looks just like that." She scurried deeper into the shop on her three-inch heels at an impressive speed.

"I'd fall on my face in those heels," Eve whispered, something like envy in her tone.

Jill led them to a long rectangular glass case filled with rings, bracelets, earrings, and necklaces. A few were cheap baubles, but the vast majority of the jewels were tagged with exorbitant prices. In the center, the thistle ring stood out like a rose amongst the weeds.

He felt Eve stiffen next to him. Carter frowned. "Something's wrong."

Eve shot him a wide-eyed glance at his soft comment but showed no other reaction.

He pointed at the ring. "Can we see it, please? Out of the case?"

Jill paused before agreeing. Eve held out her hand, and Jill placed the ring in the center of her palm.

Eve considered the ring from every angle. Instead of satisfaction, he watched confusion dawn on her face. She held both rings in front of her, one in each hand. "This one feels lighter."

Carter heard the doubt in her tone. He in turn lifted his hands, asking silently for a chance to examine them. Eve tipped her hands and let the rings fall into his. The ease with which she trusted his judgment over her own about the legitimacy of the second ring struck him. He bent to inspect them.

"I see what you mean. The second ring is lighter. And look at this." He pointed to the inscription. "The second *M* used the wrong font. This is not one of the Granville heirloom rings."

"What are you saying?" Jill asked.

He looked between them then his eyes settled on Eve. "This ring is a fake."

✑ CHAPTER FIVE ✑

"We should call the police." Carter set the fake ring on the glass case.

Eve picked up the other ring and returned it to the safety of her purse. "But it's not the stolen ring."

"Yeah, but obviously it's connected to the theft. Someone went through a lot of trouble to put a fake ring here. Which means they have the real one. I mean, why else bother?"

Eve's deep disappointment was evident. He wanted nothing more than to gather her in his arms and comfort her. In fact, the desire was so strong, he crossed his arms across his chest to keep himself from yielding to the temptation.

"I see your point," she conceded.

Jill's face had lost all color. "St-stolen?"

Carter let Eve deal with the flustered Jill. She was a natural. Watching her comfort the young woman, showing such calm sympathy, he could easily envision her in a white doctor's coat, treating children and working with worried parents. She truly had a gift.

It was a shame she was so burned out. He believed it was more an issue of being too close to her mother's dominating personality and accepting the wrong position rather than being in the field of pediatric medicine. Not that it had anything to do with him.

Except the Eve he'd once known, the vibrant and courageous young woman she'd been, was still there. He'd caught glimpses of her in the short time she'd been back. It seemed wrong to let that spirit drown in the pressures of a job she didn't want when he knew she'd be able to find work more suited to her somewhere else.

He shook off his thoughts and returned to the task he'd taken on. He dialed the police station and explained the situation when Teri answered the call. "Phillip and I will be over there right away," she told him.

Hopefully, Basil would arrive before they did.

When Teri and Phillip came through the door ten minutes later, Basil still hadn't arrived. Phillip insisted on seeing both rings together and feeling the weight of them.

"You're right. I can feel a difference. Are you sure that's not normal?"

"Officer Schiller, I've seen these rings all my life. And held them many times. I've never noticed a weight difference. Except for three letters in the inscription, they are supposed to be identical." Eve leaned over and tapped the inscription on the ring he held. "The ring you have is not the ring we're searching for."

Teri peered over Phillip's shoulder to see the rings better. "I've got to admit, until you pointed out the differences, I would have sworn it was the original ring. How did you know to search for it here?"

"I emailed all my business contacts and sent them a picture of Eve's ring. I struck out with most of them. But then Basil emailed me this morning and said he thought he had the ring I wanted. When we got here, however, Basil wasn't here. He hasn't been here at all this morning, according to his daughter."

Carter tilted his head in Jill's direction.

"She showed us the ring." Eve picked up the narrative. "We knew almost at once that it wasn't genuine. But it's a very good counterfeit."

Phillip's eyes shrank to narrow slits. "And where is Mr. Curry now?"

He looked at Jill. They followed his gaze.

"Do you know where we can find him…" Teri glanced down at her name tag. "Jill?"

Jill's eyes grew large. "I don't know. My dad is never late. He never called to say he wouldn't be here. He's not answering his phone. I'm starting to worry."

She dropped her head in her hands.

Phillip kept his expression and his tone all business. "Let me see the email from Basil, Carter."

Carter slipped his phone from his pocket and opened up his email. He handed it to Phillip, using his finger to indicate the email trail they were discussing. They all waited while Phillip read the messages.

Finally, Phillip held the phone out to Carter, who took the device and returned it to his pocket.

"We're going to keep this ring. Lock it up in evidence. Right now, Basil Curry is a person of interest."

"No!" Jill stormed back to the group, her face a mask of fury. "My dad would never steal anything. Never. He doesn't have a dishonest bone in his body."

"I agree with Jill." Carter met Phillip's sardonic look with a level stare.

"We're not saying your father is a thief," Teri told Jill. "We just want to speak with him. He's the last person who might have any knowledge about where the false ring came from. Maybe he'll be able to help us locate the real one."

"Right." Phillip straightened. "We'll need a recent photo of your father."

"Of course." Jill swiped away a tear and scrolled through the pictures on her phone. "Will this one do? It was taken a couple of months ago."

Phillip glanced at it. "Yes, that'll work. Look, I want to be thorough. Walk me through your dad's normal morning routine."

Eve remained next to Carter as Jill and the officers moved off into the next room.

"I'm worried about Jill's father," Eve murmured. She didn't turn to him as she spoke. "I hate to think something might have happened to him."

Carter reached out and gave her hand a quick squeeze. "I know. I'm concerned too. But we need to let the police do their job."

A few minutes later, they heard Jill exclaim. Carter and Eve exchanged startled glances then followed the voices to the back office. A broken mug lay in a puddle of liquid. Papers were strewn on the floor, and the desk chair was on its side.

Phillip narrowed his eyes. "I'd say there was a struggle. Your dad may have been abducted."

Jill put her hand over her mouth, and tears filled her eyes.

"Miss Granville." Teri approached them, urgency in her stride. "Have you figured out who your grandmother hired to put in the new safe? It wasn't anyone in Gnaw Bone, so it was probably someone in Nashville."

Eve shook her head. Her hair brushed Carter's cheek, and he smelled gardenias. "No, I haven't. I'll look through her desk today when I get back to the house. My grandmother was highly organized. If she hired someone, there'll be a record of it in her desk somewhere."

"Call us immediately if you find anything."

Phillip tilted his head at Eve. "These rings are valuable, right?"

She nodded. "They are. They're heirlooms from a Scottish dukedom. Whoever has it could make a tidy profit off of it."

"He'd get a lot more money if he had both of them." Teri stepped over to Eve. "Does anyone else know that you have the other ring in the set?"

Eve's stomach plummeted. "You mean someone might try to steal this one again?"

She whirled to face Carter. "We emailed a photo of it to all the collectors in your contact list."

He looked stricken. "Yeah, we did. Doug also knows. He was the one who found the first one."

She groaned. "I never told Mom that the rings were stolen. She'll assume I have them. You know her. She'll tell everyone who's interested that she should have gotten more. I don't know if she'll think of the rings. She's never been interested in my dad's family history. But she knows they exist."

"Too many leaks." Officer Schiller stalked over to where she stood with Carter. For the first time since she'd met him, he eyed her with concern rather than suspicion. "Eve, I know these rings are important to you. I think you should let us take yours back to the department and put it in our safe there until the investigation is complete. You already know someone can get into your grandmother's new safe. We'll talk to the vendor at the flea market ASAP. See what he knows. But I doubt he's the thief. If he was, he'd want to sell it for more than he charged Carter."

Every instinct screamed to say no, to keep the ring close. It was, after all, her history.

Her mind, though, recognized the sense of his plan. The original thief—she refused to believe it was Jill's father—had breached the safe once, as Officer Schiller had said. In theory, it could happen again.

Her fingers shook as she passed the ring to him. It was more than a ring. It was a connection to Nana and her dad. "Please keep it safe. My nana trusted me with it."

His hand closed around it. "I promise you, Eve, Teri and I will keep it safe. We will do what we can to reunite it with the other thistle ring too."

There was nothing more they could do here. She glanced at Carter. He understood her silent message.

Eve's stomach was grumbling by the time she and Carter buckled themselves into the car to return to her house. Which was ironic, because her stomach also felt like she'd swallowed a bucket of rocks. How she'd be able to eat feeling this way was a mystery.

Carter didn't try to talk on the short ride. He reached over and squeezed her hand again. To her surprise, he left their hands connected. It wasn't as much a romantic gesture as a supportive one. It felt like when they were fifteen again. Carter had always *got* her. He had some inner radar that told him when she needed him.

No one in Pittsburgh had ever been there for her like he had been. Not even Vincent.

She glanced out the window. They were nearly back to her house.

To Nana's house, she corrected herself. She couldn't let herself think of Gnaw Bone as home. Her home was in Pittsburgh. Regardless of the fact that she had felt more at home in the past two days in her nana's empty house and in the small-town setting than she had in seventeen years in Pittsburgh. Theft or no theft, Gnaw Bone was in her blood.

CHAPTER SIX

Carter pulled into her driveway and shut off the engine.

"Stay for lunch?" Eve shifted in her seat to face him.

He tilted his head, considering her. "Are you sure you want the company? You've had a bit of a rough morning."

She nodded. "That's why I need the company." She flushed. She wasn't used to showing her vulnerability to anyone. But she was too raw to hide how she felt. "I don't know how to handle going through her desk alone. I have to find the contractor hired to do the safe."

"Then yes, I'll stay."

That was it. She marveled at how easily he arranged his plans because she needed him. Her mother would have scoffed and reminded her that she was thirty-two and could handle this herself. Despite the fact that Mom often demanded help with *her* problems, she never offered her daughter the same consideration.

Maybe that was why Nadia had taken herself out of the family circle. It wasn't much of a family.

Entering the house, she sniffed. Some of the tension rolled off her shoulders. She'd forgotten about the cake. The smells of early morning baking mingled with the warmth of the sun shining through the windows.

Home. She was home. The rocks in her stomach dissolved. The scripture she'd read—*was it only this morning?*—breathed through her mind and settled in her soul.

"What are you thinking?"

She smiled, closed her eyes, and recited the first half of the verse. "So do not fear, for I am with you; do not be dismayed, for I am your God."

"Isaiah?"

She pivoted on her heel. Carter stood at the door watching her, his face conflicted. "It was the verse I was reading this morning. I was having a pity party, and God reminded me that He's stronger than my problems."

The corner of Carter's mouth tipped up in a half smile, melting away some of the protective ice she'd built around her heart through the past seventeen years. "He is. I've been reminded lately that my own faith has gotten stale since Michaela died. I haven't trusted Him the way I should."

He looked away, the tips of his ears glowing.

She stepped toward the kitchen to spare him more embarrassment. "Come on. Let's eat lunch first. Then we can take our cake into the office."

She paused in the middle of the kitchen. With one hand pointing to the Keurig machine and the other to the refrigerator, she said, "This is the real dilemma. Coffee or Pepsi?"

He snickered. "It's eighty degrees outside. I'll get the glasses and the ice."

She grinned, feeling lighter than she had since she arrived, despite the missing ring. The rings were important, yes, but they were only things. She had to remember that.

"I bought a rotisserie chicken yesterday on my way here. I can cut some up, and we can have chicken salad sandwiches with a spinach leaf salad?"

"Sounds good."

A few minutes later, they sat down to eat. They didn't speak as they ate. Strangely, the quiet wasn't uncomfortable, not like a silent meal with her mother. Even with Vincent, she'd always felt compelled to fill the silence. What did that say about her relationships?

She didn't want to go there. While Carter cleared the table and stacked the dishes in the dishwasher, Eve placed two small plates on the counter and got out a large knife. It slid through the cake like warm butter. She refreshed their glasses with a couple of new ice cubes and opened another can of Pepsi to top off their drinks.

"I don't have a tray to carry these."

"It's all right." Carter picked up his glass and one of the plates. "We have two hands."

She smiled and chuckled under her breath, picking up her own dessert. Her smile wilted at the door to the office. She sucked in a deep, fortifying breath, straightened her shoulders, and entered the room. Carter's presence braced her. She sat in the large swivel desk chair. For the next few minutes, the only sound in the room was silver forks hitting the plates as they enjoyed the rich sweetness of the cake. When her piece was gone, she set her empty plate on the desk and leaned back in the chair. She swiveled it from side to side.

Carter groaned. "I knew you'd play when you sat in that chair."

She made a face at him, but she had to laugh. She couldn't resist spinning in swivel chairs. Ever. They were too much fun.

"All right. That's enough silliness. Left or right?" she demanded.

Carter tilted his head to one side. "Um, right?"

"Right it is." She forced herself to open the lower drawer on the right side of the desk. It was deep, and Nana had used it as a filing cabinet. "Wow. There are a lot of files in here."

So many, it was a bit overwhelming.

Carter came around to her side of the desk and whistled when he saw the packed drawer. "Is the other side the same?"

She hooked the handle of the left drawer and tugged it open. While it was equally as deep, inside were mostly office supplies, such as a stapler, a three-hole punch, rubber bands, pens, and paper clips.

"Oh!" She pulled out a plastic container filled with cookies. "Sorghum cookies. I haven't had these in ages!"

She lifted the lid, and the sweet syrupy scent wafted from the container. Carter grinned. "I love those cookies. I'll bet she bought those at the Gnaw Bone Country Store and Bakery."

"She always had these in her desk when I came in here." Eve used her foot to swivel the chair from side to side. "I remember coming in to do my homework while Nana did her work or balanced her checkbook."

"Sounds like a good memory."

Sighing, she put the cookies back and closed the drawer. "I'm still full from lunch. So those will have to wait for another day."

"What's that?" Carter reached past her and pinched a newspaper clipping with his forefinger and thumb. She looked at the picture. Heat flowed up her neck and into her face. She cupped her cheeks with her palms, warming her hands. If she had to guess, her face and hair probably matched.

"I didn't think she'd hang on to that."

Carter read the engagement announcement. "Wait. You were married?"

She winced. He sounded shocked.

"No. I broke the engagement off several months before the wedding."

"What was wrong with him?" He dropped the clipping above the open drawer, letting it float back to the bottom. Then he scowled. "Did he cheat on you?"

For a moment, the anger in his words stunned her. Then she realized he was waiting for her to answer. "No. Nothing like that. I realized I liked him a lot, but I didn't love him." She rubbed her face with her hands. It seemed so ridiculous now. "I didn't expect him to ask me to marry him. I'm not sure why I said yes. When I wanted to change my mind early on, my mom convinced me it would be stupid. After all, he was a doctor with great connections. I went along with it until one day I thought, I want more out of marriage than a business arrangement. That was when I realized that most of my decisions seemed to be based more on trying to please my mother, who is never satisfied, than on whether or not they would make me happy."

His hand landed on her shoulder. She appreciated the support, but now that she'd gotten that off her chest, it mortified her that she'd shared so much with him.

She sat up straight, dislodging his hand in the process. "Time to tackle the files."

He didn't protest the change of subject. He moved away from her chair and returned to the front of the desk. He stopped suddenly.

"Hey, Eve. I wonder. Could the invoice be among the papers in the safe?"

She tugged on her hair, thinking. "I don't think so. But, considering that the ring was in there, it couldn't hurt to check."

Spinning away from the desk, she stood and strode to the safe then punched in the code. "Nana was a smart woman, but she should have picked a better passcode."

"Why? What did she use?" Carter joined her at the safe.

"She used 3760. For 1937 and 1960. The year my grandfather was born and the year my dad was born."

She gathered the mess of papers from the safe and brought them to the desk. "You know, if something was taken from these documents, I wouldn't even know it."

The next five minutes were silent except for the sound of papers rustling. Eve found a large document envelope at the bottom of the pile. The top was folded down and secured with a binder clip. After releasing the clip, she unrolled the top and tipped the envelope over, dumping the contents on the desk.

A clump of smaller envelopes, held together with a rubber band, lay before her. She undid the rubber band then sorted the letters, oldest to newest.

"Carter," she breathed, "look at these envelopes. At the stamps."

He peered at them. "They're all from Scotland."

She tapped the last one. "This one is only a few months old."

She opened it and read it, eyes widening. "It's from my great-uncle Kevin. He invited Nana and me to join him and his family at Granville Court."

"I wonder if she answered."

Shaken, Eve stared at him. "This was just before she died. Carter, I wonder if they are even aware of her passing?"

Burning with curiosity, she went through the rest of the letters. One, in particular, affected her. She read it, blinking as the page blurred in front of her. Finally, she handed it to Carter to read. Then she dropped her head back against the seat, drained.

Carter accepted the letter, concerned at the sudden shift in Eve. Five minutes ago, she'd been lit from within, sparkling with the wonder of discovery. This letter had changed that. Glancing down, he began to read.

> *Dear Fiona,*
>
> *We are grieved beyond measure to hear Richard has passed. Our children have long hoped to meet their American cousin and learn of his life in the States. I am especially grieved to know I will never see the son of my brother. I have felt Rory's absence from my life every day since he left us for America.*
>
> *Fiona, I would like to meet his daughter someday. She is the last remaining link to my brother. The older I become, the more I treasure our family and its rich history. I would love to share this love with her. My wife and I would also enjoy meeting you.*
>
> *Again, we send our condolences, along with our love and our hopes that we will one day meet.*
>
> *Sincerely,*
>
> *Kevin Granville*

"Eve? Are you all right?"

She opened her eyes and blinked up at him. "Yes. It's just so sad, Carter. They never met. When did my grandfather last see his twin brother? Did he ever go to Scotland? I know they never came here. And my father. Carter, they've been writing for years."

She scrambled to sit up then picked up another letter. "This one was written a month after my grandfather's death."

She opened it and read. "Yep. I can't doubt that their grief is real. Look—" She pointed at a spot on the pristine parchment. "Maybe I'm being fanciful, but I'll bet Great-Uncle Kevin was crying, and that mark was from a tear falling on the paper. Why didn't someone make the plans and travel? They missed the opportunity to meet family."

Carter held up his hands, halting her rant. "Now, I don't know what they were thinking. I can't remember your grandmother ever traveling though."

That caught her attention. "Not by plane." She tapped her chin. "She'd use a train. Or she'd drive. Never by plane."

"Maybe she had a fear of flying."

"Maybe."

"Anyway. The invoice isn't in the safe. Let's tackle the desk files."

She made a face but didn't argue. Instead, she picked up the pile of letters and returned them to the safe, carrying them like they were fragile crystal. Then she strode back and grabbed a clump of files, lifting them out of the desk with an exaggerated groan as if they weighed fifty pounds.

He rolled his eyes.

She winked and thumped them down on the desk. "Let's do this."

They spent the next thirty-five minutes going through the files. Some they didn't even bother to open because the titles made the contents obvious.

"Wouldn't it be ironic," he said, placing the file marked *Bake Sale Plans* on the growing stack of unopened files, "if your grandmother had a complicated system for how she filed things? Like, what if she had a secret code, and 'Bake Sale Plans' means something entirely different than what we think it means?"

She snickered. "Nana was smart, but she wasn't exactly into codes and spy stuff. But, if we don't find anything the first time through, I'll rethink that as we go through these files. I doubt we'll find it here though."

She set another file labeled *Save The Trees!* on the discarded pile.

Five minutes later, he found it. "Here it is." He held the stapled pages out to her.

Eve dropped what she was perusing and snatched the papers from him. They shook with the force of her trembling.

"It's an invoice to a hardware store. They removed the old safe and put in the new one. This is so anticlimactic," she said.

He was already picking up the phone and dialing the police station. Phillip answered. "Hey, Phillip. It's Carter. We have the information on who put in the new safe."

"I'll bet Nana had him program the passcode," Eve murmured.

He raised his eyebrows and repeated that information to Phillip. Then he put the call on speaker. It was, after all, Eve's business more than his.

"Which means the man had everything he needed to break in and steal the rings, even if Fiona had them at the time of installation."

"But there was no forced entry. My grandmother wouldn't have given him the key to the house."

"Eve, did your grandmother hide a key in case she got locked out?"

"She did. She kept one under the welcome mat at the front door."

Phillip's voice was matter-of-fact but Carter imagined him rolling his eyes. "Which would have been one of the first places he'd have looked to find the key. If he knew the value of those rings, which I looked up, by the way, he would have been highly motivated to find the key."

"What's the value?" Eve asked.

He named an outlandish sum that had both of them gasping.

"If he has only one ring, the value decreases significantly, though it's still a lot of money."

Eve brushed her hair off her face. "What do I do now?"

"Now? You wait. Teri and I will have a conversation with the contractor. Don't leave town. We'll be in touch."

He hung up.

"He has such a lovely bedside manner," Eve complained.

He grinned at her snarky comment. "True. But he's a good cop."

Eve stood and stretched. He watched her saunter to the window. "I feel a little lost without something to do."

He knew how that felt. "You need to get out of the house. Come on."

Startled, she jerked around. "Out? Where are we going?"

He grabbed her hand and gave it a gentle tug until she moved to stand beside him. Strange, how natural her hand felt, tucked in his. "It's time you got reacquainted with Gnaw Bone, Indiana."

CHAPTER SEVEN

Eve wasn't sure it was smart to refamiliarize herself with the town she grew up in, but she couldn't help herself. She'd only been away from Pittsburgh for a couple of days, but the idea of returning to the rushed life she'd escaped left a bitter taste in her mouth. She'd liked waking to the sound of frogs and crickets rather than traffic and tenants upstairs arguing. In a weird way, she even liked knowing that she had to wait for the grocery store to open. She'd gone shopping at three in the morning before, and aside from it being a novelty, she hadn't enjoyed it.

She started to slide on her sandals.

"Nope."

She looked up to find Carter shaking his head at her. "No sandals. You're going to be doing a lot of walking, so I would suggest comfortable shoes."

Excitement sparked in her. This was going to be an adventure. She ran upstairs and riffled through her suitcase for a pair of ankle socks. Then she shoved her feet into her running shoes. She started to bounce out the door but halted as she caught sight of her reflection. No. She was going to enjoy this adventure without sweaty hair flopping in her face. She grabbed her favorite lime-green scrunchy and twisted her abundant hair into a bun on top of her head. Then she went into the bathroom and removed her contacts. Glasses would be a better bet if it was dusty.

There. She was ready. She grinned. Mom would have a fit. She looked like a teenager. No makeup. No contacts. Hair in a haphazard do. Yep. She was ready to go.

She skipped down the stairs and halted in front of Carter. Then, feeling impish, she whirled with her arms out. "How about this?"

She stopped. He was grinning. Not the half smile she'd grown used to, but the grin she remembered from her youth. Her pulse kicked up.

"Nice."

Nice? That's it? But she was too excited to let irritation weigh her down.

"Do you know how Gnaw Bone got its name?" Carter held the front door open for her. She locked it behind her and pocketed the key.

"Well, the story I heard was it was originally named Narbonne by French settlers, and that gradually devolved to Gnaw Bone."

He grinned. "Oh, you've heard the nice story."

"The nice story? I take it there's a not-so-nice one?"

He shrugged, digging his fingers in his hair to locate the sunglasses sitting on top of his head. She held back a grin. His hair was worse than hers when it came to getting things snarled in it.

"Well, the story my parents always told Livvy and me was that there was a man in town who knew everything about this place. Whenever someone needed to find a place or a person, they were told to ask the man sitting in front of his store 'gnawing on a bone.'"

She laughed. "That can't be real."

"There are at least five different stories I've heard through the years."

"Are there still only two hundred people in Gnaw Bone?"

"About that."

She'd never forget the next few hours, no matter how many years she lived. He took her to the Gnaw Bone Country Store and Bakery, which resembled a large log cabin. They visited the trading post and the antique mall. He also drove her past a motorcycle dealer, which made her smile. Finally, he parked the car and they got out and hiked along Gnaw Bone Creek.

It was all so different from where she lived, but she felt her memories stirring. There were several abandoned buildings. One of them was a rickety one-room schoolhouse. They crossed a creaky wooden bridge. She wasn't quite sure it was stable, but they made it safely. After an hour, they circled back and stood on the bank.

Two canoes paddled by, and they waved at the people sitting inside wearing bright orange and green life vests.

"I remember coming here with you and Livvy." She watched the fish swimming under the water. "We'd hike or ride our bikes."

"Yeah. That was great." He stretched his arms over his head. "Or we'd canoe. One summer we tried to build our own raft."

That startled a laugh out of her. "I'd forgotten that. Epic fail. My mother was so mad when I walked in the house covered with mud."

"Don't forget the leeches."

She shuddered. "Thanks for reminding me."

For dinner, they went to a small restaurant that specialized in barbeque. After the waitress took their orders, Eve settled back on the seat and glanced around. "I've never been here before."

Carter sipped his water. Condensation dripped from his glass onto the table. "Dad and I come here sometimes for some father-son bonding time."

Leaning forward, he clasped his hands on the wooden surface. "I've been thinking. Instead of writing a letter, you should call your great-uncle."

She choked on her water and spluttered for the next minute. Finally, when she could talk again, she wheezed, "Say that again? I'm not sure I heard you right."

"Call your uncle. He deserves to know about your grandma now. A letter across the ocean can take a while. What if it gets lost on the way?"

"So I should call the house of a duke and ask to chat with him?"

He snorted. "No. I think you should call your uncle, announce your connection, and leave a message. Then it will be up to him to call you back. But at least you'll have let him know about your grandmother."

Part of her mind said it made sense. The other part said it was a ridiculous, foolish idea. But the longer it simmered in her head, the more the idea took root. Carter was right. Her uncle deserved to know. Especially since her grandmother had received an invitation to visit. Obviously, the man wanted to meet his brother's family.

"You know what? I think I will call him." She looked up the time on her phone. "It's almost 11 p.m. in the UK right now. That's hard to wrap my head around. I'll do it tomorrow. If I call at eight in the morning, it'll be one in the afternoon there."

It was after six when Carter parked in her driveway.

Her mother was already there.

Carter had planned to hightail it home the second he dropped Eve off at the door. He didn't intend to step foot out of the car himself. He'd had a very long, tiring day. And while he had enjoyed almost every moment of it, he wanted nothing more than to go home, take a shower, and go to bed early. Tomorrow promised to be another long day.

The moment he saw Cheryl Granville, however, his plans changed drastically. There was no way he was going to let Eve deal with her mother on her own, not after the past few days. She had been through the wringer, and then some. Cheryl had never been a restful person. Just being in her presence caused tension. Especially in her daughter. Eve had nearly married a man she didn't love to win her mother's approval.

He wasn't leaving until he absolutely had to.

He ignored the little voice in his head questioning why his protective instincts were stirred up if he and Eve were only friends. He only knew he couldn't abandon Eve. One glance at her stricken face told him all he needed to know. Cheryl's appearance was not only unexpected. It was also unwelcome.

"Do you want me to tell her to leave?"

She sent him an incredulous look. "Why? She's my mother, and this is my house."

She put her hand on the door handle then glanced over her shoulder at him. "But could you stay for a while?"

She flushed. No doubt she was embarrassed she felt the need to ask. He nodded, grateful she'd invited him to remain.

She visibly braced herself then climbed out of the car, appearing far more confident than she had a few seconds earlier. She strode up to the front door, almost marching. There was purpose in every step.

Admiration welled inside him. He knew how unsure she felt, but she faced it head-on.

Cheryl met them at the door. Her blond hair was artfully styled, and her makeup was still fresh. She eyed Eve's clothes with distaste. "Really, Eve, you've been out looking like that?"

Eve halted before her. "Mother. What are you doing here?" She waved her arm at Carter. "You remember my friend, Carter Grant, don't you?"

Nice. She'd completely ignored her mother's veiled insults.

Cheryl's nostrils flared even while she pasted a smile on her face. "Carter. How lovely to see you again. Eve, I've come to stay for a few days."

Eve unlocked the door and stood back, gesturing for her mother and Carter to enter the house.

He ducked his head to bring his mouth close to her ear. "Will you let her stay?"

She rolled her eyes. "She's my mom. I can't just kick her out."

He didn't necessarily agree with that, but he wasn't going to push.

She sighed. "I've changed my mind. You should go home. I'll be fine. She stresses me out, but that's all."

He didn't want to go, but he couldn't stay when she'd told him to leave. "I'll go, but I'm only a phone call away. I can be here in under ten. No matter what time it is."

"I know. And I appreciate it. But I'll be fine."

He got in his car and drove away, against the instinct to remain. Once at the house, he sent her a text.

I'm home. Do you want me to come back??

LOL. No. I'm fine. See you tomorrow?

Tomorrow was Wednesday. Normally, he'd be at work, but after she'd asked him for help yesterday, he'd made arrangements to take the rest of the week off as vacation time. He'd earned it. He hadn't taken any time off since Michaela died.

Yes. What time do you want me to show up?

As early as you can.

He grinned. I'll be there by 9.

He was exhausted. After he plugged his phone in to charge, he got cleaned up and prepared for bed. During his prayer time, he had trouble keeping himself focused.

"Lord, I apologize for my lack of attention tonight. So much has happened. I need Your strength and wisdom if I'm going to be any help to Eve."

He thought about Basil as he slipped under the top sheet. Where was he? Had he shown up today after they left? He needed to call the antique shop tomorrow morning.

After tossing and turning for an hour and praying for Basil's safety, he fell asleep. His dreams were restless. When his alarm went off, he groaned and hit snooze three times before finally throwing back the covers and rising for the day. It was already seven forty-five.

He hoped Eve had rested better than he had.

∽ CHAPTER EIGHT ∾

Eve dragged herself out of bed Wednesday morning. Her body ached as if she'd spent the night wrestling someone twice her size. Her eyes were dry and gritty like they had sand in them. There was no way she could wear her contact lenses today. That would be one more thing her mom would complain about.

But at the moment, Eve couldn't care less what her mom thought of her appearance. She was tired, and she was cranky. Maybe that was why she felt grief carving a hole in the center of her chest. She missed her grandmother and her father so much she could barely get a full breath. In a weird way, she also missed the relationship she could have had with her Scottish relatives. Her father's relatives.

She had no idea why that relationship had never happened. With modern technology and cell phones and the internet, there was no excuse.

A tension headache simmered behind her eyes. She staggered to the bathroom, grabbed the over-the-counter pain reliever, and swallowed one tablet. She didn't take medicine often, but she knew if she didn't stave off this headache before it took root, she'd be useless the rest of the day. She needed to be able to function.

Her shower was longer than usual. At least it revived her a little. What she really needed was a steaming cup of coffee.

She dressed quickly in a comfortable sundress, one she'd picked up at a consignment shop on a whim, and quietly went to the kitchen. Hopefully, she'd have her first dose of caffeine before her mom decided to join her.

Barely lifting her feet off the floor, she shuffled to the Keurig and hit the power switch. Hooking her finger around the handle of one of the mugs hanging on the rack on the wall, she removed it and placed it under the spout. After selecting her favorite morning blend, she inserted it, closed the lid, and hit ten ounces.

Hot water spurted from the spout with what, to her overly sensitive ears, seemed like the sound of a jackhammer. She tensed and waited for her mom to burst into the room.

She relaxed when the coffee stopped pouring and her mom still hadn't made an appearance. She added some french vanilla creamer and brought the mug to the table.

The mug was halfway to her lips when Mom entered the room. "I have an appointment this morning, Eve. Don't expect me for lunch. I might do some shopping this afternoon."

Without asking how her daughter was, her mom breezed out. Five seconds later, the front door slammed shut.

Rather than feeling relieved, suspicion bloomed in Eve's heart. Her mom hadn't kept any contacts here in Gnaw Bone. After they left, she'd acted as if the town no longer existed. Who could she possibly need to see this early in the morning?

Well, there was one good thing about her mother being absent. She wouldn't be there when Eve called her great-uncle in Scotland. She still wasn't sure calling him was the best idea. In fact, if it hadn't been over two weeks since her grandmother died, she wouldn't have given in to Carter's recommendation. At this point, however, too much time had been wasted.

Eve walked to the front door and checked the driveway to make sure her mother's car was gone. It could be awkward if she walked in while Eve was on the phone. If there was one thing she was certain of, it was that her mother would not approve of her contacting the Granvilles at all. Just to be safe, she twisted the bolt on the door, locking her mother out.

Then she had second thoughts. What if Carter arrived while she was on the phone? She sent him a quick text, letting him know what she was doing and that the door was locked. Almost immediately, her phone buzzed. Carter texted that he would wait until she told him it was all clear to come over.

It was up to her now.

Finding the number wasn't difficult. Her great-uncle had written it on each letter he had sent over the years. The first time she tried to dial it, she got so nervous she hung up. She paced up and down the office, wiping her hands on her sundress, trying to calm herself. She wasn't doing anything wrong. This was family. Even if they'd never met her, she had an invitation from the duke himself. How much better could it get than that?

Steeling herself, she drew in a deep breath and tried again. This time, the phone rang. When it was picked up, the woman answering the phone had to repeat herself twice before Eve could understand her through the gorgeous, thick accent.

"Oh, yes! Granville. Um, I'm calling from the United States. My name is Eve Granville. My grandfather was Rory Granville and—"

The woman on the other end interrupted her, her words so fast they tripped over one another. Eve couldn't understand ninety percent of what she said until the woman asked her to wait.

She bit her nail while she waited, all the while hoping she'd heard correctly.

She waited and waited as the minutes ticked by. She hadn't been disconnected. Should she stay on the line? Hang up?

"Eve? Eve Granville?" A deep masculine voice, slightly shaky with age, interrupted her musings.

"Y-yes."

A jubilant laugh echoed in her ear. "Eve! I'm your great-uncle Kevin."

She blinked in disbelief. She'd done it. It was a difficult conversation due to their communication issues. They both had to repeat themselves often. When she told her uncle about her grandmother's death, he sounded as though he wept. Tears slid down her own cheeks. They talked about her grandfather and her father too.

"Eve, I can't fly to the States. My wife is too frail for me to leave her. You are welcome to visit us."

She sniffed and swallowed a sob. "I would love to visit, but I can't right now. I need to figure out what I'm doing with Nana's estate and my job. But soon."

"Good. Your cousins will be so excited to meet you. And I'd love to show you your land."

She scrunched her forehead. She must have misheard him. He would enjoy showing her the family lands. She had no land in Scotland.

They disconnected after fifteen minutes. But those fifteen minutes had changed her life. She had family who wanted to meet her. Steel entered her soul. Her mom would whine, but Eve would meet her Scottish relatives.

What had happened to set her mother against her meeting her father's family?

Shaking her head, she unlocked the front door and sent Carter a text.

ALL CLEAR. COME ON IN.

After unlocking the front door, she returned to the kitchen and reheated her coffee while she waited for him to arrive. He strolled into the house fifteen minutes later.

"So why the lockdown?"

She described her mom's hasty exit that morning. "I can't figure it out, but my gut says she's up to something."

He helped himself to some coffee. "It sounds like it. I called Jill Curry before I came here. Her dad is still missing. She's pretty shaken up."

She slumped against the kitchen counter. "That poor girl. What a horrible situation."

"I don't know what else we can do. The police are checking on the contractor and searching for Basil. I've heard back from all my email inquiries, and Basil was the only one who'd seen the ring."

"And I talked to my great-uncle." Grinning, she replayed the conversation for him.

"Will you go meet them?"

She nodded. "Absolutely. I don't know when, but I will."

He hesitated. "I don't want to bring up a sore subject, but what about your job? Will you be able to take leave again so soon?"

"I'm having second thoughts about keeping my current job."

Carter froze. Had he heard her correctly? "What are you saying? I thought that was your dream job. You said you'd worked so long to achieve it."

She turned her head and fused her gaze with his. He felt that look all the way down to his soul. "I have worked hard. Since I've been here, though, I've been able to distance myself from my life in Pittsburgh. So much of my effort has been for the wrong reasons. I didn't want to join a large-city practice. My dream has always been a small-town practice where I can know my patients by name. My mom was the one who wanted the prestige of that position. Just like she tried to handpick my husband for the same reason. I've spent so long chasing a career to win her approval."

She walked away from him and stood in the door leading to the back deck. He set his mug down and approached her. "What are you planning, if you don't want to take the position?"

She shrugged. "I haven't completely made up my mind. One thing I do know. When I decide, it will be based on what I want, and not on what someone else wants for me. And I won't live a lie anymore."

Something else was going on here. "What do you mean? Eve, what happened to you after you and your mom moved?"

She sighed. "My mom was a wreck. She promised we'd be wealthy and be deliriously happy. But the truth is, she'd developed a bad habit of overspending. Her credit cards were maxed out. We spent a lot of time in homeless shelters. When we would find an apartment that we could afford, Mom would disappear for days at a time."

He shuddered. She'd been alone, and then he abandoned her. "How did you afford college?"

She bent her head. "I wrote to my grandmother and asked her to help me. She wrote back and funded a 'scholarship' for me. No one could spend it on anything other than my education. It was the only way of being sure."

He heard the words she didn't say. It was the only way of being sure her mother didn't steal it.

His hands clenched at his sides. Blood pulsed in his ears. Squeezing his eyes shut, he prayed for God to take away his rage. Anger wouldn't help Eve. She needed his support, not his vengeance.

Her hand eased its way into his, and he calmed at her touch.

"It's okay, Carter. I'm fine. Actually, the person I feel sorry for is my mom. Something must have happened. I don't know what. But she's lost her way."

Her merciful reaction overwhelmed him. Shame burned up the rest of the anger stalking in his chest. She was the injured one, and she reacted with mercy. It was an example he should follow. It was difficult though.

A loud, jarring ringtone shattered the silence. She jumped, brushing against his arms. He hugged her briefly, then released her. She went to her phone and answered it. A second later, she whirled to face him.

"It's my grandmother's lawyer. He says I need to come to his office. It's an emergency."

"I'll drive you."

The drive to the lawyer's office was quick. "It seems surreal, doesn't it? This is where we met again, two weeks ago."

Her eyes flared open. "Was it only two weeks ago? It feels like it's been months."

He grabbed the door and opened it for her. In his mind, he could see her as she'd been that day two weeks ago. Unapproachable, in her professional clothes and aloof manner. Only the red-rimmed hazel eyes had indicated how hurt she was inside.

He'd been so close to walking away without speaking to her.

Only now could he admit he was glad he hadn't followed that impulse.

They walked to the same office where the will had been read. Mr. Sampson greeted them and surveyed Carter briefly.

"Eve, what I have to tell you is sensitive. If you don't want anyone else to hear it…"

She smiled at the man. "I want Carter here. It will save me the trouble of repeating what is said here to him later."

Mr. Sampson made no further attempts to change her mind. "Then I will proceed. This morning, I had a visit from your mother."

Eve's face paled. The lawyer continued. "Your mother is trying to contest the will. She wants the house and the contents. She said that you would not argue this and would agree that she should have inherited."

Eve stared at him, nonplussed. "I knew she wanted the money, but I never dreamed she would do something like this. She's actually taking legal action against me?"

He nodded. "I told her she'd have to find another lawyer. I represent you, as you are the legal heir to your grandmother's estate."

"After the reading, she told me she had a new lawyer who was looking into it for her."

"*Humph.* Well, I suppose this new lawyer found there wasn't anything he could do." Mr. Sampson opened the top drawer. "I had hoped to never have to reveal this. But your grandmother left this in my care a long time ago."

He pulled out a file folder. "Years ago, right after your father died, your mother went to your grandmother and begged for her help in paying off some of her debts. Your grandmother helped her with a generous gift, but she took the precaution to photocopy the check before she gave it to her."

Eve reached out and grabbed Carter's hand. She held on hard. He winced but didn't complain. She needed his support. He could bear the discomfort for a few minutes.

"What did my mother do?" she rasped.

"Your mother took the check and changed the amount. I have your grandmother's photocopy of the check she'd written for one thousand dollars and the bank statement showing a check your mother cashed for ten thousand. Your grandmother let her have the money. But she gave her an ultimatum. If she didn't change her spending habits and get a job, she wouldn't get a penny more out of the Granville estate. Your mother left the next day and took you and Nadia with her."

Fifteen minutes later, Eve staggered to her feet and stumbled to the door. Carter held her arm to steady her. They didn't speak as they walked out into the sun to the car. Carter waited until they were both seated and the air conditioner was running before he did what he'd been aching to do for the past half hour.

Turning to Eve, he gently tugged her toward him. She fell against his shoulder a second before the first sob ripped from her. His arms closed around her. As he did two weeks earlier, he held her while she broke down.

CHAPTER NINE

She rarely cried. Now she'd soaked his shoulder twice in two weeks. It was becoming a bad habit. Shifting, she put space between them. She bent her head in order to avoid his eyes.

When his warm hand touched her jaw, she flinched. Then she leaned against his hand. He gently nudged her head up. Compassion swam in his gaze. If she had any tears left, she would have wept a second time.

"I got your shirt wet again."

He grinned at her inane remark. "I don't care. You can do that anytime."

His grin faded. She knew he was thinking about her mom.

"She wanted me to sell the antiques to help her pay off her debts. I refused. I told her I needed to go through everything and make a decision then. She couldn't wait. Why would she try to steal from me?"

He searched for an answer. "I think she must have some kind of compulsion, like a sickness. I'm sorry she keeps hurting you this way."

She went still, her already pale face appearing bloodless. "Carter. What if it was my mom who stole the rings?"

His mouth dropped open. "Your mother?"

She nodded. "If she's willing to contest the will to take the inheritance away from her own daughter, what would stop her from stealing the rings?"

"Did she know where they were kept?"

"I don't know. Nana never showed them to me in front of her." Her head began to ache again. "It wouldn't have been hard to figure out where they were stored. I can't stand this. Do I have to tell the cops my own mother should be a suspect?"

He pressed his lips together and turned to gaze out the window. A second later, he put the car in drive and headed back toward the house. She didn't know what she'd do. She blocked the question from her mind. She'd decide later. Hopefully, she'd have a chance to talk with her mom and get some answers.

A thought popped into her head. Jill had said Eve looked familiar. All the Granville women resembled each other, even though she had red hair. Would her mom lie to her?

That was the thing she didn't know. She'd never believed her mom to be dishonest before, only ambitious. Now she had to admit she didn't know her mother at all.

They pulled into the driveway, and she heaved a sigh of relief. Her mother hadn't returned. That was a blessing. She wouldn't have to deal with her yet.

"Let's go in and have lunch," she said. "I guess I'll spend this afternoon going through Nana's things. That should keep me out of trouble until the police get in contact with me."

He raised his eyebrows. "So you're not going to tell them about your mom?"

"Actually, I'm hoping they find the ring in the contractor's possession and it won't be an issue."

At the house, she meandered through the kitchen, opening and shutting the cupboards. She toyed with several ideas for lunch but discarded them all. For the first time in her memory, baking held no interest for her. Her equilibrium shattered, she didn't know what to do with herself.

Carter popped his head into the kitchen and watched her for a moment. "Why don't I go get something? That way, there are no dirty dishes and you can stop stressing about what to fix."

She paused. The idea had merit. "Are you sure?"

He shrugged one shoulder. "Yeah, why not? You've had a nasty shock. Go lie down. Or read a book. I'll be back soon."

He disappeared. She wandered into the front room and sat on the window seat. Her heart grew heavy in her chest. Bowing her head, she offered her pain to God. "I can't solve this problem, Lord. Only You know the best ending."

She stared out the window at the variety of blooms gracing the front lawn. Gradually, the colors merged, and the shapes of the flowers became fuzzy and indistinct. Her head drooped as sleep overtook her.

Carter reentered the house, carrying a bag of Chinese food. He'd had to travel a bit for it, but he recalled how much Eve enjoyed cashew chicken and eggrolls. He strolled into the kitchen. She was nowhere to be seen. He hoped that meant she'd taken his advice and was relaxing.

He opened the boxes and set the plates and chopsticks on the table. Then he went in search of Eve. She didn't respond when he called her name. Finally, he looked in the front room. The vision of her snuggled asleep on the window seat tugged at his heart. She was so weary. He was tempted to let her sleep, but he knew she needed to eat as well.

He walked to her and gently shook her shoulder. "Eve. Eve, honey. Wake up."

Her breathing hitched, and her eyelids fluttered open. "Oops. Sorry."

"No need to apologize. Come on, sleepyhead. I brought Chinese."

Those smoky hazel eyes widened, pleasure sparkling in their depths. "Oh, yum! I'm awake."

He could gladly spoil her on a daily basis.

The thought sent a warning spiraling through him. He froze midstep following her to the kitchen. What about the pain he'd suffered with Michaela's death? He'd promised himself he'd never leave himself vulnerable to that kind of pain again. His mind whirled with the impact of that choice. In effect, he was saying that his love with Michaela hadn't been worth the devastation of her loss.

It had been, though. The joy of love had been worth the pain. He'd never wished they hadn't met and fallen in love. But for the past four years he'd been stifling his emotions. Was a life without full participation really living at all? He'd buried his heart with his wife.

Eve, by the force of her personality, had dug his heart back up. He wasn't in love with her, not yet. It was too soon. But he knew, if she stayed in Gnaw Bone and gave them a chance, he would be. Their bond of friendship grew stronger each day.

If he didn't want this relationship to blossom, he needed to nip it in the bud.

The thought of letting her leave, of cutting her off, made his heart ache. He rubbed his chest. He couldn't do it. He couldn't return to hibernation. He wanted to be alive and feel all that God sent his way, the good and the bad.

What if she left? It would break his heart again. It would also mean he'd lived while she was here.

His choice made, he rejoined her in the kitchen. They'd finished eating and were cleaning up when the doorbell rang. Eve dried her hands on the dish towel and frowned.

"It's not my mom," she said. "She'd waltz in like she owned the place."

The shadow of her mother's duplicity stalked them to the door. Eve swung it open.

Phillip and Teri entered the house. Carter ground his teeth. He'd hoped, for Eve's sake, that any more confrontations would wait until the morning.

"Phillip. Teri. You have news?" Eve greeted the officers, the epitome of a gracious hostess. At her sides, her hands clenched into fists then relaxed. It was the only sign she was disturbed.

"Eve," Teri began, "we found the man who installed the safe. He has an alibi for the time when the ring was likely stolen. He was in a motorcycle accident the day after he installed the safe. His leg was broken in three places. He's been recovering and in rehabilitation therapy for the past two months. There's no way he could have stolen the rings."

Eve's face softened. "That poor man! Will he recover? What about his job?"

Carter shook his head. She was amazing. With all she was going through, her heart still had room for concern for others.

Phillip waved his hand. "You don't need to worry about him. He has good insurance, and his company will hold his job. He's a stellar worker. They don't want to lose him."

Phillip exchanged a glance with Teri, and Carter stiffened. They had something else on their minds. Phillip shifted. "The thing is, the night he was here, he overheard an argument between Fiona and another woman."

"An argument? What about?" Eve's glance bounced between the two officers like a ping-pong ball. "Did he see the woman?

"He didn't see her. They were at the front door. Apparently, the other woman tried to enter, but Fiona wouldn't allow her to come inside the house. He didn't understand Fiona's side of the argument. Her voice was too soft. The other woman was practically yelling. She wanted Fiona to give her money. She kept saying she was cheated when Richard died."

Eve's jaw tightened. "Richard was my dad."

Phillip nodded. "Eve, we need to talk with your mom. I need her contact information."

"I'll give it to you." Eve buried her face in her hands for a moment. "I think you should know that my mom arrived last night. She left early this morning, and my grandmother's lawyer called me. My mom is contesting the will. The one that left me this house. My lawyer refused to represent her because it would be a conflict of interest."

"I'm sorry, Eve." Phillip seemed to mean it. "We have to investigate your mom. She's a suspect now."

"I understand. I don't want to believe my mom could do such a thing. But I never thought she'd try to contest my inheritance either."

"Have you seen her today?"

She shook her head. "She left this morning and hasn't called or contacted me since. I have no idea if she'll be back tonight or not."

"Call us if she returns."

She nodded reluctantly. Carter waited until the door closed behind the officers before speaking. "You didn't tell them about the check."

"That was years ago. My grandmother didn't report it, so I'm not sure it's relevant."

He walked over to her, lifted her chin, and gave her a brief kiss on the forehead. "I know this is hard. But you're not alone."

Her eyes grew bright. "I feel like I am. I don't want to stay here tonight, not if she might be here, but I also don't want to leave the house empty."

He couldn't stay, as much as he wished he could. It wouldn't be right. "Hold on."

He pulled his phone out and sent Olivia a quick text. When she replied, he grinned.

"Problem solved."

Eve raised her eyebrows at him. "Oh? How did you solve my problem?"

He showed her Olivia's text. "My sister's husband is on a weeklong Boy Scout hike with their son. She's been complaining about being on her own. She'd be thrilled to join you for a slumber party tonight."

Eve laughed. "I haven't had a sleepover since we moved away. What a great idea!"

He read the relief behind her laugh. He shared it. He could leave, knowing someone would be here with her.

Eve had forgotten how energetic Livvy was. And how talkative. From the moment she arrived on Eve's doorstep, she chatted constantly. Eve found her responses pared down to single words. Then Livvy was off again.

She didn't mind. Livvy had the most positive outlook she'd ever seen. She bubbled with good cheer, and it rubbed off on Eve. By the time the clock struck eleven, Eve's stomach muscles ached from laughing. Several times she wiped tears from her cheeks.

"Why weren't we better friends when I lived here?" she demanded, munching on tortilla chips and guacamole.

Livvy gave her a mocking look. "Because you and Carter thought I was obnoxious."

She considered that. "Yeah, you were. Three years seemed like a huge difference."

"Those three years don't matter now. Not when we're all adults." Livvy sighed and leaned back against the couch. They were both sitting on the floor around the coffee table. "I'm glad you're here. Carter seems more like his old self. I haven't seen him so, I don't know, so animated since Michaela died."

Eve didn't respond. She was glad her presence helped Carter. She wasn't sure how she felt about the growing connection between them. For so long, her mother had orchestrated her life. She'd let that happen. Now she had a chance to make life decisions for herself. Getting involved in a romantic relationship, even with her former best friend, the one person she'd trusted over everyone else, might not be the way she wanted to go. Plus, she didn't know if Carter's feelings for her were real or if he was just on the rebound from mourning his late wife. True, Michaela had been gone for years. There was no set length of time appropriate to grieve. It would absolutely destroy her if she fell in love with Carter and he didn't feel the same way.

"Do you think you'll stay here?" Livvy asked, completely unaware of the struggle going on in Eve's head.

Eve shrugged. "I haven't decided what I'm going to do yet. I still have a couple of weeks. I need to go through my grandmother's things. I've been so distracted by the rings I haven't done much of anything yet."

Livvy bit into another chip and chewed thoughtfully. She swallowed and took a long sip of iced tea. "What about the treasure?"

Eve's hand halted over the bowl of guacamole. "Treasure?"

"Don't you remember? You and Carter heard someone talking about some mysterious treasure that your grandfather had hidden. I remember listening to you guys planning a treasure hunt."

Stunned, Eve dropped the chip in her hand to the plate in front of her. She ran to the kitchen to grab her phone and dial Carter's number. The moment it started ringing, she grimaced. One minute she was unsure of letting their relationship grow, and the next she was calling him in the middle of the night. She glanced at the clock. Eleven fifteen. Good grief. He was probably asleep. She lifted the phone away from her ear, planning on hitting end, when he picked up.

"Eve! What's wrong?" he yelled, concern ringing in his voice.

She laughed self-consciously. "Sorry. Nothing's wrong. I was talking with your sister and forgot that some people sleep at night."

His warm laugh sent a flush to her cheeks. Livvy snickered beside her. Eve pivoted so her red face wasn't on view for her friend to gawk at. "I wasn't asleep. Not yet. What's on your mind?"

"Livvy reminded me of a story. Do you recall when we heard that my grandfather had a treasure?"

"I haven't thought about that for years. Yes, I do. We were going to find it. If I recall, you moved before we could set our plan into action."

"Do you think I should mention it to the police tomorrow?"

He yawned. A pang of guilt swamped her. "You could tell them. My guess is they'll dismiss it. After all, as far as we know, no one else ever mentioned it. But every angle should be considered."

"I'll tell them. You go back to sleep." She disconnected and made a show of returning the phone to the charger in order to give her hot cheeks time to cool before she faced Livvy again.

It didn't help. Livvy smirked the moment their eyes met, and Eve's face flamed again.

The front door opened. Eve heard the click of high heels in the hallway a few seconds before her mom waltzed in and stood inside the doorway, taking in the scene as if she hadn't tried to betray her daughter that morning. Her lip curled as her narrowed gaze skimmed over Livvy standing by the kitchen table in her pajamas. When her mother's gaze met Eve's, the lack of remorse on her mother's face sent a rush of anger flowing through Eve's body like lava from a volcano. Eve pressed her lips together to keep the bitter words on her tongue from spewing out.

"I didn't know we were having guests."

It was the "we" that did it.

"*We* are not. *I* am. This is *my* house, remember?"

Her mother's eyes narrowed. "*Hmm*. Maybe."

"You mean because you plan to contest the will to take the inheritance left to me by my grandmother?" Eve threw caution to the wind.

Mom's blue eyes widened. Under her makeup, her face paled.

"You didn't think I'd find out? Mom, how could you? To try and take your own daughter's inheritance? What kind of mother are you?"

Mom's chin lifted. "I'm not trying to steal from you. I'm trying to get what should be mine."

Eve snorted. "The way you stole from Nana all those years ago?"

"What—"

She didn't let her finish. "I know what you did. Your actions ripped me from this house, where I was loved, and ruined my childhood." When her mother backed up, she pressed her advantage, stepping closer. "We had a good life here. I had friends. I had my grandmother. We left, and I spent the next few years wondering if we'd even have a safe place to sleep at night. Or if you'd come home. If Nana hadn't helped me, I wouldn't have been able to go to college. And still, you tried to control my whole life. Who I married. Where I worked. I should have known you'd try something when you badgered me to sell Nana's stuff to pay off your debts. And now the thistle rings Grandfather passed on have been stolen. I got one of them back, but the other one's still missing. Well, you should know that the police think you're a prime suspect for the theft. I couldn't even defend you."

"I never stole anything!" Mom gasped, her eyes wild. "I didn't know they were missing."

"I don't know if I can believe you. When the police said you were a suspect, I wasn't surprised. Isn't that sad?"

Eve had never understood how loud silence could be until that moment. Mom's face had aged in the past minutes.

"I didn't do it."

"I don't believe you." Eve crossed her arms over her chest. "Did you ever really love me, Mom?"

Shock blazed across her mother's face. "Of course! How could you ask that?"

Eve shrugged. "Well, you never acted like a mother."

Her mother cast one last wild look around, and then she spun and staggered from the room. Eve listened to her running down the hall. Then the front door slammed shut. What had she done? Never in her life had she spoken that way to her mother—or to anyone else, for that matter. She hadn't known she was capable of such vitriol.

Livvy came up to her and gave her a hug. Eve was too stunned at the scene she'd just created to cry.

"What kind of daughter am I? I can't believe I said all that to my mother."

"You needed to let her know how she's hurt you. I hope she'll take a look at her life and repent."

Repent. Eve bowed her head. She'd promised to trust God. She'd failed again.

"God will forgive you, Eve." It wasn't until she heard Livvy's words that she realized she'd spoken aloud. "Jesus made sure of that. If we're truly sorry."

Eve sighed. "I am. But I think the police won't be happy with me when I tell them what I did."

CHAPTER TEN

"You should call your girlfriend."

Carter lifted his head and scowled up at his sister, squinting to see her face with the sun peeping out around her head like a halo. He slapped his hands together to dust them off, sitting back on his heels next to his garden. He'd been working for the better part of an hour. It was a good time to take a break.

"I don't have a girlfriend." He stood and reached for the basket he'd filled and offered it to Livvy. "Want a tomato?"

"Love one." She grabbed a Roma tomato and took a bite then swiped her chin to remove the dribbling juice. "I like teasing you. Seriously, though. She's pretty freaked out right now. Her mom showed up last night, and Eve told her off. It was intense."

He blinked, stunned. "Eve went against her mother?"

"Dude, she completely went off on her."

He groaned. "I'll bet she's feeling bad about it now."

Secretly, he was glad she'd had the nerve to wrest control of her life away from Cheryl, but she was still Eve's mother. Something like that would bother Eve.

"Yes. Which is why you need to call her. Now."

He stood up. "Thanks for letting me know. I'm going to clean up and head over there."

"Oh, nice. She can cry on your shoulder."

She'd already done that, twice, but he'd never tell his sister that. He jogged up the stairs and cleaned up quickly, not even taking the time to let the water warm up. Eve needed him more than he needed hot water.

In under ten minutes, he was back downstairs and out the door. Olivia sat in her car, texting on her phone. "I'll see you later, Liv!"

She waved without looking up. "Don't mess up."

He scoffed. In his heart, he worried he'd do just that. Before he had his thoughts together, he was standing outside Eve's door. She didn't meet him at the door this time. He rang the doorbell then shoved his hands in his pockets while he waited for her to open the door. The morning air was hazy. It was going to be another hot one.

The door opened. Livvy was right. Eve had been crying. "Liv said you had a hard night."

"I thought she'd tell you." She met him on the porch, closing and locking the door behind her. "Just my mom. As usual."

She clearly didn't want to discuss her mother's latest drama. He let the subject drop. Right now, he was more curious about where she was going. Her purse was slung over her shoulder.

"Anyway, I'm glad you dropped by."

He tilted his head. "So am I. But why are you glad?"

"I was on the phone with Teri when you arrived. She and Phillip want us to meet them at the hospital in Nashville. I have no idea where it is."

There were several hospitals in Brown County. "I can take you. Which one?"

She rattled off the name. "The reason she called is they found Basil Curry."

His stomach muscles tightened. "Is he okay?"

"He opened the shop early to get the ring for us and was attacked by a couple, a woman and a man. He was abducted and beaten up, but nothing too serious. He somehow escaped but fell on his way home and got a concussion. They sedated him and want to keep him for observation."

Poor Basil. He was a kind man, one who would go out of his way to help a neighbor. He certainly didn't deserve to be mistreated. He frowned. "I don't like your mother much, but I really can't see her getting violent and attacking or kidnapping someone."

Relief fluttered over her pretty features. "I don't think she would either." A shade of doubt entered her gaze, dimming it. "Yet, at the same time, I never expected her to go to the lengths she has to get my inheritance. The funny thing is, I don't care about the money. If that's all she wanted, I'd help her out. But she always wants more than I can give."

"We'll have a chance to talk with the police. I do agree they shouldn't stop looking for a suspect. I don't see your mom going to the trouble of creating a fake ring."

He pulled into a parking space at the hospital and shut off the engine. Eve met him at the back of the car, ready to march in and confront this new situation. He could practically see the determination vibrating off her skin.

On the way into the hospital, he reached over and touched her hand. She flipped hers over and entwined their fingers.

His heart skipped a beat. She didn't mean anything by it, he knew that. She was accepting the support he offered.

Suddenly, though, support wasn't enough. He wanted her to see him as something more than a former friend she'd met again.

He wanted the chance to move on. Together.

Impatience raced through her blood. Only Carter's hand wrapped around hers kept her from losing her calm. Their footsteps echoed on the tile floor in the lobby. Phillip and Teri stood as they entered.

Basil was awake when they came in, but he was groggy.

"You only have a few minutes," the nurse told them. "The painkiller will knock him out."

Phillip nodded and opened the door for her to exit. He returned to the bed. Basil blinked up at them, his eyes bleary. He was half asleep already. "Basil, do you recognize this?"

Phillip showed him the fake ring then the real one.

Basil frowned in concentration. "Not the same one. They took it."

Eve ground her teeth when his lids slipped completely shut. What a waste of time.

"Well, he says this isn't the ring he had," Teri mused. "Which means the other ring is out there. I think we need to watch for someone trying to sell it."

All she wanted was her life to go back to being boring. She wanted to have the peace to make the decisions she needed to make and not worry about thieves.

Eve was done being a victim. She needed to stand on her own two feet for once and make her choices based on what was best for her. If she returned to Pittsburgh, it needed to be because that was the job she wanted to do. Along the same lines, if she decided to make her home in Gnaw Bone, it needed to be her choice, and not because of Carter. As wonderful as he was, she didn't want to base her life on someone else's wishes ever again.

She needed to know that she was in charge of her future.

Something had changed while they were inside the hospital. Eve kept a full foot between them on the way back to the car. When they arrived at the house, she shifted to look at him, her manner remote.

"I have to go through Nana's stuff. I've put if off long enough. I'll talk to you later." She turned to exit the car.

"I can help," he offered, desperation clawing inside him. Why was she pushing him away?

"No thanks. I'll talk to you later."

She was out of the car and striding up to the front door fast, as if someone were chasing her.

He had no option except to return home.

For the next two days, whenever he called, she was unavailable. He couldn't figure out what he'd done, but he wouldn't stop trying until he did.

Saturday afternoon, he got a call from a jeweler just outside of Nashville. This particular jeweler specialized in antique gems.

"Ryan. What can I do for you?" He liked Ryan. They'd worked together at several estate sales.

"Carter. I had a woman come into my shop yesterday. She sold my partner a ring. When I got back to the shop and looked at it, I realized it was the same ring you've been searching for."

Carter sat up. "Did your partner get the woman on video?"

"Unfortunately, not. There was aah, let's say there was a glitch in the system during the time of the transaction. Very convenient. My partner is highly agitated at the thought that he aided and abetted a criminal."

"Is it real? The ring? This woman tried to give someone else a counterfeit."

"Oh, it's real. I weighed it, checked out the insignia, and compared it to the documents I found on the Granville Dukedom thistle rings. It checks all the boxes."

Carter absorbed the information and thanked Ryan. He immediately called Phillip.

"I know where the ring is." He told Phillip the news. Within two hours, Phillip, Teri, and Carter were standing in the police department conference room, waiting for Eve. Carter had both rings sitting on the table in front of him. He'd confirmed they were the original rings.

Eve strode into the room, her face pale. Her eyes fell on the rings and widened. Gasping, she scooped them into her hands, tears streaming down her face. "I can't believe it's been found."

He knew she'd felt she failed her grandmother. Locating the ring removed that burden.

"Eve," Teri said, her voice serious, "the jeweler's partner described the woman. She fits the description we have of your mother."

Some of the sparkle left her eyes. "I understand."

"We also talked with the vendor at the flea market. He has a solid alibi for the time when the rings were initially missing. He was out of state for a month helping his son."

Why wouldn't she look at him? When she left the conference room, he followed her outside. "Eve, wait."

She halted.

"Can we talk for a moment?"

Her shoulders tensed. Slowly, she pivoted to face him. "What do you want to discuss?"

"Why are you upset with me? Did I do something wrong?"

She sighed. "No. Look, Carter, I have some big decisions to make about my job, what to do with the house. I need to make them without feeling like someone is pressuring me. Not my mom. And not you."

He stumbled back a step. "Whoa. What pressure? I'm your friend. I haven't put any pressure on you."

Had he?

"Maybe not. But I need to make my decisions myself, based on what I want and not dependent on someone else." She hesitated. "And another thing. I don't want to get emotionally tangled up with someone who is essentially on the rebound. And I don't want to be in a position where my feelings are stronger than someone else's. I can't make a choice based on whether you'll be there or not. I've decided to save myself some heartache."

She spun and walked away.

Anger swooped in. How dare she make such assumptions. On the rebound? He was thirty-three years old. Not a teenager.

It didn't matter. She'd made herself clear. She didn't trust him. Not enough to give them a chance.

CHAPTER ELEVEN

Why had she said those things to Carter? Eve regretted them the moment she'd arrived home two days ago. He had again become her best friend, and she'd shoved him away in a moment of fear. She needed to find a way to make things right.

Needing to clear her head, she went for a walk. On her way back, she passed a car sitting along the road. A man was in the front seat, reading a newspaper. He looked out of place, wearing a hat in July. She frowned. He looked familiar.

Increasing her pace, she returned home. She should call Carter and apologize. And tell him she'd made her decision.

The doorbell broke into her self-recriminations. Groaning, she walked to the door and flung it open. She stared at the woman on her porch. Although their coloring was different, they bore a strong resemblance to each other.

"Nadia!" She gaped at her half sister.

"Hi. Aren't you going to invite me to come in?" Nadia gave her a tight smile.

"Oh!" Eve's face heated. "Sorry. I didn't expect you to show up here on my doorstep."

Nadia laughed. Eve frowned at the sharp, sarcastic sound. "Nadia?"

"Eve. Are you going to greet me the same way every time you see me? Of course you didn't expect to see me. I didn't tell you I was coming." Nadia stepped over the threshold and scanned the hall, her mouth twisting. "This place hasn't changed much since the last time I saw it."

Eve closed the door behind them and followed her sister's meandering steps. Something was off, but she couldn't quite put her finger on what it was. Nadia seemed angry. Not like the loving half sister she'd met at the reading of the will.

Her sister's phone made an owl hooting sound. She glanced at it and scowled.

"Is that ex-boyfriend still bugging you?" Eve asked.

Nadia snorted. "Nah. He's ancient history. I have a new boyfriend now. This is some place. I guess you'll be selling it soon, huh?"

"What? Oh no." She tried to keep up with her sister's rapidly changing topics. "No, I've decided to keep the house. I'm moving to Gnaw Bone."

Her sister swung back to glare at her. The open hostility in Nadia's expression shocked her.

"What do you need with a house like this? And what about your career? You've worked hard for it, or so I assume."

Eve rolled her eyes at the familiar argument. "Not you too. Mom hounds me about my career enough. Which reminds me... Have you seen her? She came by a few days ago, but now she's disappeared. I have no idea where she's vanished to."

Nadia gave a delicate shrug. "I talked with her the other day. She called and said the thistle rings had been stolen."

"You know about that?" Eve led the way into the kitchen. Nadia followed her.

"Yeah. She said you found one of them."

Eve's stomach knotted. Something was wrong.

Her phone rang, interrupting her thoughts.

"Hold on for a sec." She unlocked the screen and answered the call. "Hello?"

"Eve. Are you at home?"

She relaxed at the familiar voice. "Hey Teri. Yes, I'm home. What's up? Did you and Phillip plan on coming over?"

"We might later. Listen, I thought you'd want to know we found your mother."

Eve straightened, her fingers tightening on the phone. "Really? Where? Is she okay?"

"Yeah. Apparently, whatever you said to her the last time you saw her sank in. She checked herself into an addiction therapy center. We went down there, and she talked to us."

Eve hesitated. For some reason, she was reluctant to talk about their mom in front of Nadia. But the need for the truth trumped her reluctance. "Was it gambling?"

"No. Your mother has depression. She dealt with it by compulsive spending. She has four credit cards, all maxed out. Which sent her into deeper depression. It's a vicious cycle. She wanted us to tell you that's why she pushed you to accept that job and to attempt to marry well. She wanted you to help her get out of debt. She never thought about what she was doing to you."

Eve silently considered this new development.

"Eve?"

"I'm thinking. I guess I understand. It might be a while before I can trust her after this."

"I totally get that. No judgment here. But there's something else you should know."

Eve braced herself. "I'm listening."

"Phillip and I went to the hospital and talked to Basil again. We showed him a picture of Cheryl. He said she isn't the woman who attacked him. The woman he saw had the same coloring. Blond hair, blue eyes. She resembled her but was much younger."

A chill traveled down her spine. The woman who'd taken the rings was standing behind her. The man in the car. That was the man she'd seen on Nadia's phone when they'd met at the reading of the will.

Nadia had stolen the rings and attacked Basil. Eve didn't dare look at her. She recalled her sister's bitter laugh. Would Nadia hurt her? She couldn't take the chance.

Think! She had to let Teri know that she was in trouble.

"I'd love to see you and Phillip today. Carter's coming over later too. But I can't talk long now. My half sister is visiting. I don't want to be rude."

Teri paused on the other end. Eve practically heard the wheels turning in her head. Her voice was softer when she spoke. Probably to keep her questions from being heard by Nadia. "Does your sister have blond hair and blue eyes?"

Eve forced a small laugh out. "Absolutely!"

"Eve, you're in danger."

"Oh yes, I know." Nadia moved in closer to her. The hair on the back of Eve's neck rose, and she shivered. She had to hang up before her sister suspected something. "I'll see you when you get here. Bye."

She ended the call and returned her phone to her pocket. "Sorry about that. I didn't mean to be rude. I have some friends stopping by in a bit."

"You've never been a good liar, little sister." Nadia stepped closer. Eve compelled her feet to remain planted.

"Why would I lie?"

"I heard her talk about Mom. Who were you really talking to?"

Eve shook her head, unable to think of a countering argument fast enough. She wished Carter were here. He had become a steady source of strength since she'd arrived. But instead of thanking God for sending her someone like Carter, she'd foolishly sent him away and closed her heart to what was growing between them. She was on her own until the cops arrived.

"You were talking to the police, weren't you? I don't plan on being here when they arrive. I need the other one."

Eve gritted her teeth and smiled. Nadia didn't know she had both rings again. "Nadia, I don't understand you. The other what?"

Nadia thrust her face an inch away from Eve's. "I didn't go through the trouble of stealing those rings to lose this opportunity."

Eve's eyes popped open wide, and she stepped back. Her sister planned to sell the second ring to the same dealer. She knew they were worth more if she sold the pair. "Why? The rings mean nothing to you!"

Nadia closed the gap between them again. "I lived in this house with you as Richard's daughter until our mother messed up. I called that woman Nana just like you did. But she left me pittance compared to you."

Nadia looked around. "You got all this. I hoped when you sold it I could convince you for a loan. But I couldn't count on that. I'd heard about the rings a few times. I'd even seen the old woman showing them to you when she thought you were alone. After the reading of the will, when you returned to Pittsburgh, I snuck in. I'd made a copy of the key under the porch mat long ago, just in case. It was easy to guess the code for the safe. I put the rings in my purse, but the zipper was broken. One must have fallen out, because I couldn't find it later. I got nervous and sold the one I had to a pawn shop."

Eve licked her dry lips. So that was how it ended up at the flea market. "But the other ring—"

Nadia sneered. "I kept my eye out for it. I saw it on the antique shop website. When I saw the price on it, I knew I'd been cheated. My boyfriend is a skilled counterfeiter. He made me a copy. We planned to swap it for the real one. I hoped to sell it for its real value before anyone realized the one at the shop was a fake."

She'd never seen the avarice in Nadia's character. Maybe because Nadia had left while she was still innocent of such things. Suddenly, she wondered how far her sister would be willing to go to keep the truth under wraps. The sister she'd loved hadn't existed. The woman in front of her wouldn't hesitate to hurt her to get what she wanted.

Eve shoved Nadia away and dashed from the room. Nadia yelled and came after her.

Eve hit the front door and pulled it open. She launched herself out of the house and bolted down the driveway, Nadia at her heels.

It had been two long days.

If he didn't want to lose Eve, Carter knew he'd have to find a way to fight for her and their friendship. A friendship that had the potential to be so much more. He hopped in his car and headed her way without making a conscious decision. He would prove to her that she wasn't a rebound to him. He needed to show her that he meant to be a part of her life, in whatever capacity she'd allow. It might take a long time, but Eve was worth it.

He approached her house and saw Eve running toward him. Her sister ran up behind her and leapt, tackling her from behind. He slammed on the brakes and put the car in park. After jumping from the still-running vehicle, he dashed to the two women rolling on the ground.

"Nadia! What are you doing?" He reached down to separate them.

Nadia kicked at his legs. He released her and assisted Eve to her feet. Nadia tossed him a wild look then took off running in the opposite direction, her escape hampered by the spike heels she was wearing.

"She's the thief! Carter, she stole the rings and attacked Basil!"

Carter moved to go after her. A police cruiser pulled up. Phillip jumped out, and Carter shouted at him to go after Nadia. Within moments, she was in handcuffs. Eve told Phillip that Nadia's boyfriend had been around her house. Phillip took the information and got back into his car to search for the man.

Carter returned his attention to Eve.

She hurled herself into his arms. He forgot about Nadia and held on to Eve. She was shaking so hard, it was a miracle she remained on her feet. He tightened his hold, his throat constricting. He'd been so unsure of his welcome.

"Eve, what happened?"

She pulled away but kept her hand on his chest. His arms looped loosely around her waist. She was still trembling. If she started to fall, he'd catch her. He'd always catch her.

"Nadia showed up at my house. While she was there, I got a call from Teri. They showed Basil a picture of my mom, and he didn't recognize her but told them about someone that fit Nadia's description. Nadia heard part of the conversation." She told him everything that had occurred since her stepsister showed up on her doorstep.

He whistled. "I'm glad your mom is getting the help she needs."

"Me too."

His phone rang. It was Phillip. Nadia's boyfriend was in custody.

He hung up and looked at Eve. There was so much he needed to tell her, but suddenly, all the words he'd planned flew out the window. He needed to go with his gut.

"Eve, I'm sorry if you felt I was getting in your way. I never wanted to make you feel pressured. I—"

Her fingers against his lips halted his words.

"I'm the one who's sorry. You didn't pressure. You supported. Always. I got scared and reacted. It's one of my biggest faults. I realized I was starting to depend on you, Carter, and I needed to make choices for me."

He kissed her fingers then took her hand in his, frowning. He didn't want to get this wrong. He'd do anything for her. Even if it hurt him. "What scared you? What did I do?"

She leaned her head against his shoulder. He breathed in the scent that was hers. Gardenia and cinnamon. "You didn't do anything. I got worried that I would lose myself in what was growing between us and then you'd leave. Carter, my family was always leaving. My dad died, my mom forced me away from the home I loved then left me, literally, all the time. My sister left."

"I left too." How could he ever forgive himself?

"You were in college. I wasn't there. It was a normal part of life."

He tangled his fingers in her bright curls. "How do I prove to you that I'm here to stay?"

She backed away. For a moment, fear pressed his throat closed. Then she smiled, and the sun came out again. "You don't have to. Carter, I think God brought me here for a reason. We don't need to hurry. We've reclaimed our friendship. If God wills it, in time it will grow to be more. I'm open to that possibility now."

He leaned in and gently brushed his lips against hers. "I will always be here for you. You are not a replacement for Michaela. You have a special place in my heart and my life all your own."

Her hand settled over his heart, and her smoky gaze met his. She smiled, sending rays of sunshine into his soul.

∾ CHAPTER TWELVE ∾

October

Carter bent and brushed the grass and dried flowers from Michaela's headstone. He arranged a new bouquet of flowers, her favorite carnations, in the plastic floral holder anchored in the ground. She would have enjoyed the colorful blooms.

"Good morning, Michaela." He shoved his hands into his pockets and stared at the cold granite marker. "Your brother's a little irritated with me. I'm engaged to be married."

He frowned. Phillip had given him a cold congratulations when he'd told him the news. Michaela's parents, however, were delighted. Her father had brushed away his tears, hugged him, and said, "It's about time, and that's the truth. Michaela would want you to be happy. Don't worry about Phil. He's very sensitive where his sister is concerned. You know he'll mellow once he gets used to the idea."

He shook off thoughts of Phillip's reaction.

"You'd love Eve. I know I told you about my best friend growing up. Well, she's back. She inherited her grandmother's house, and we're going to live there and build a life together. The wedding will be in January. She wanted to get married on her nana's birthday, so we will."

He squatted down and touched the grave marker. "I never thought I'd be blessed to find love and happiness again. God had other plans."

He spent a few more minutes at the grave. When he heard the grass rustle, he stood and pivoted slowly. Eve approached, a second bunch of flowers cradled in her right arm. She took his breath away. The Eve he'd remembered from his youth had returned, her hair flowing over her shoulders, a gentle breeze blowing the vibrant red strands across her cheek. She brushed them aside, and the gold solitaire on her ring finger glistened in the sunlight. The tailored suits had been traded in for jeans and a lightweight jade-green sleeveless T-shirt under an open blue and green flannel shirt. Besides her ring, the only jewelry she wore were two necklaces, the one he'd given her so many years earlier and a thick chain around her neck holding the thistle rings.

He sauntered across the lawn, liberally strewn with red, orange, and yellow leaves, and greeted her with a soft kiss. She smiled under his lips.

"All done?" she asked. "I can walk a little while longer if you need more time."

He raised a hand and slowly brushed a red strand off her forehead. "No. I'm good. I see you have the flowers for our next stop."

She nodded. "Yep. I think Nana would have liked these."

He took his place at her side and entwined their fingers. They meandered through the cemetery until they arrived at the Granville plots. They stopped briefly in front of the resting place of her great-grandparents.

Eve brushed the front of the monument with her fingers, an affectionate touch, not a mindless action. Next, they stopped at a smaller headstone. It was a pale gray stone carved in a simple rect-angle a foot-and-a-half tall.

Richard Granville 1960-2005

Wow. Carter had never realized how young her father was when he died. He couldn't imagine being fifteen and having to adjust to life without his dad. Eve hadn't had a choice. Plus, she had to deal with moving to another state and starting from scratch.

And then her best friend had abandoned her.

No. He wouldn't relive that. They had moved on. He wouldn't dwell on past mistakes. Not when they had a future together. He intended to be truly present to her and any children God blessed them with for however long they had together.

He noted Cheryl's name on the headstone. Would she be laid to rest beside her husband someday? She'd made progress in the past few months. She and Eve still didn't have an easy relationship, but they were working on it. He'd been skeptical at first. Cheryl had years of bad hab-its to break. But she was trying to turn her life around. When she announced two months ago that she'd surrendered her life to God, he let all the rancor go. After all, some of Christ's apostles had led unsa-vory lives before they'd met Him. Who was he to deny grace to Cheryl?

After a few minutes, Eve shifted to stand in front of the massive tombstone marking the graves of Rory and Fiona Granville. It was an enormous heart with a majestic angel leaning against the left side, almost as if it were embracing the marbled marker. In addition to their names and the dates of their births and deaths, the date of their wedding had been carved. Below the wedding date, the image of the two thistle rings had been painstakingly cut into the stone, the words *Cor nobile, cor immobile* etched in delicate lines.

"Arabella font," Carter murmured.

"Excuse me?"

"The words are written in Arabella font. It was created in 1936." He shrugged and smiled. "One of the advantages of being a museum curator. You learn all sorts of interesting facts."

"That so?" She leaned in closer, lines furrowed across her forehead. "Carter? Doesn't that stone look odd? Almost like it's been cut out."

He squatted to see it better. "Hmm. I think it has been. Let me see if I can move it. Or would you mind?"

It might seem rather disrespectful to try and remove a piece from her grandparents' headstone.

"I think you should. My gut tells me this is important." Her words were confident, but he detected a tremor running through her voice. Her face, however, was firm and resolute. He knew that expression. Her mind was made up.

He carefully jiggled the stone. It moved under his fingers but didn't come all the way out. There was no way he'd be able to pull it the rest of the way with his bare hands. His fingers were too big to fit into the crevices and maneuver the piece. Glancing upward, he took in Eve's avid gaze. She met his eyes and nodded. He grabbed his pocketknife from his jeans and worked it open. After sliding the blade into the left side of the rock, he jimmied it until it crept forward half an inch. He switched to the other side and repeated the movements. It took one more attempt on either side before he could grasp the stone with his fingers. With one pull, remarkably easy now that the stone had been edged forward, it cleared the remainder of the way and came free.

"Whoa." It was a clean hole, obviously cut deliberately into the stone.

Eve dropped to her knees and peered into the empty slot left behind. "Hey, Carter! There's something in here!"

"Careful!"

She rolled her eyes. "Of course."

She grabbed her phone and used the flashlight app to see inside the small space. Then she reached into the hole and pulled out a slim cylinder. After opening it, she tipped it over. A brown envelope, rolled up and protected inside layers of plastic wrap, slid into her trembling hand.

"Carter, could this be the rumored treasure?"

He tilted his head and considered the item in her palm. "I don't know. Seems pretty small for a treasure. I guess there's only one way you'll know for sure though."

Grinning, she gently stripped the plastic away from the brown envelope. "This is like Christmas."

He laughed.

"Can I borrow that?" She pointed to the pocketknife.

"Sure." He flipped it over and held it out, handle first.

She used the knife to open the envelope then gave it back to him. She removed the documents inside and gasped. "Carter. This is a deed to land in *Scotland*!"

"Scotland?"

She nodded and picked up the smaller, folded paper sitting on top of the deed. "Oh!"

"What? What's wrong?"

She sniffed. When she spoke, her voice came out choked. "It's a letter from my grandfather."

Eve drew in a deep breath, attempting to calm herself. Seeing her grandfather's letter to her father brought the confusion of loss and love to her heart.

"It was written a week before my grandfather died."

"Can you read it?"

There was no pressure in his voice. Dear Carter. If she had said, no, put everything back, he would have done so. For the first time in so long, she knew without a doubt that someone besides her nana loved her unconditionally and only wanted what was best for her and would never try to use her for their own means.

His presence in her life was nothing short of a blessing. A gift from God.

"It's okay. I'll read it."

She unfolded the letter completely and began to read.

Dear Richard,

It pains me to write these words to you. My dear son, I am so proud of you and the man you've become. You're a good husband and father, and most important, you are a true servant of the Lord. I have been blessed to call you my son.

By the time my lawyer gives you this letter, I will already be gone. Please look after your mother for me. She is a strong woman but also a loyal and loving wife. My leaving will be difficult for her. She'll need you to support her and help her regain her spirits.

I am sorry for the secrecy, and I don't wish to cause you any further grief, but I have heard of your wife's inability to handle money with care. This land was given to me by my brother, Kevin. It is the land once owned by our mother before she became the Duchess of Granville. The house has long since burned down. I had intended to build a vacation home there and take your mother to Scotland. I never had the opportunity. I am therefore bequeathing this land to my only granddaughter, Eve.

You are the steward of this land until she comes of age. Wait until she is eighteen to show her this deed. Otherwise, I fear her mother will gain control of it.

You are the bright spot of my life. I love you, my son.
Dad

Eve dropped the letter, sobbing. A second later, two strong arms engulfed her. She shoved her face into Carter's strong shoulder and wept. The tears she'd thought had long been spent welled up inside her in a torrent of grief. The sense of time vanished. It could have been minutes or an hour before the flow stemmed to a trickle and finally ceased. Carter's cotton shirt was soaked.

She opened her mouth and began to apologize, but he placed his fingers against her lips, halting her words. "Love, don't apologize. I understand grief."

She bent her head until her forehead touched his chest. "This letter was written when I was thirteen. My grandfather was larger than life. I don't remember him being sick. He was there and then he wasn't. But my dad… To have known of his wife's weakness, even then. He carried this secret for two years until he died."

Carter stroked his fingers down her cheek. Eve lifted her head and met his concerned gaze. "This is the land my uncle mentioned. I didn't understand what he meant."

"It makes sense, doesn't it?" Carter kissed her forehead then laced his fingers with hers. "Your grandmother wouldn't want it if she had a fear of traveling by boat or airplane. They didn't want your mom getting her hands on it. I don't know if she could have done anything when your dad died."

"My dad and I used to come here together. I imagine he put it here so we could 'find' it together, never thinking he'd die before he could do it."

Sighing, she turned to face the tombstone then looked back at her dad's. "Who thinks their life will end so abruptly?"

"It's sad that he felt he had to hide it from your mom."

She shrugged. "You know my mom. I never kept a diary in my room after I discovered she'd read mine."

His eyes widened. "She didn't."

"Oh yes, she did. I love my mom, but I've known for a very long time that I can't trust her."

"That's—" He broke off, shaking his head.

"I know." A grin lit her face. "She's making changes though. I might get a real mom yet. Maybe she'll make a good grandma someday."

"Maybe." He ran an affectionate hand over her cheek. "So, you own land in Scotland. What will you do with it?"

She bit her lip. "I don't need land in Scotland. But I want to do something to honor my family."

"Then we will. But first, we have a wedding to plan."

Joy bubbled up inside her like a bottle of soda someone had shaken, and she laughed. The future was bright with possibilities. And all of them featured the man at her side.

CHAPTER THIRTEEN

January

"It's not too late to back out."

Eve rolled her eyes and continued adjusting her veil. "Mom, the wedding is in less than two hours. I can't back out. Even if I could, I wouldn't. I don't want to."

Mom moved to her side, and they stood together. Looking at their reflection in the full-length mirror, Eve could see a bit of resemblance in the contours of their faces and in their mouths, one smiling, the other pensive.

The rest of her coloring, from the smoky hazel eyes to the bright red hair piled in curls on top of her head, was straight from her father, a gift passed on to them both by her grandmother. The white wedding gown floated to the floor. She felt like a princess.

"Who gets married in January?" her mother groused. "Although the honeymoon in Scotland does sound lovely."

Eve didn't rise to the bait. She loved her mother, but she was done planning her life to please her. She also refused to bring her with them to Scotland. Which was another one of her complaints. She had said many times they could afford the extra ticket.

She had no idea how true that was.

Of course, there were some details her mom didn't need to know. Eve and Carter had decided that they would donate the land in

Scotland so it could be used as a site for a treatment center for cancer patients. The hospital had insisted on paying them something, although it was much less than the historic lands were worth. In exchange, Eve would remain a major shareholder and retain a principal spot on the board. It was to be called the Rory-Fiona Granville Cancer Center. The children's wing was the Kenna Granville wing. The hospital had sent them free plane tickets so they could tour the facility, and they had timed the visit with their honeymoon. Eve was excited to finally meet some of her father's family.

"Mom, are you happy for me?"

Eve's mother stopped, her blue eyes filled with tears. "Oh, honey. Forgive me. I am. I'm especially blessed you're willing to let me share your day after the way I acted. Sometimes I still don't say the right thing. But I am trying."

Eve reached out to her mom and gave her a one-armed embrace. "I love you, Mom. I'm glad you've decided to change your life. We all make mistakes. It would have killed me to get married without you here."

Nadia, however, was out of her life for now. She'd been sentenced to fifteen years in prison. Mostly for the assault on Basil Curry.

Olivia popped into the room, vibrant in her jade-green matron-of-honor dress. "It's time, girlfriend. Let's get you and my big brother hitched. I can't wait to have you as my sister."

Emotion swamped Eve. Grabbing her best friend and soon-to-be sister in a hug, she squeezed until Livvy burst out laughing.

"Enough! The limo is outside."

Eve released her. Jill and Teri, her other two bridesmaids, waited in the hall. They had become fast friends over the past few months. For the first time in years, she had women her own age to confide in.

She could hardly believe seven months ago she had returned to Gnaw Bone a stranger. Now her life was full, with a man she adored, a close group of friends, and a new pediatric practice in nearby Nashville that relit the joy in medicine her high-stress job in Pittsburgh had nearly destroyed.

Giggling, Eve entered the limo with her bridesmaids. They made the short drive to the church and parked in front. The driver hopped out and opened the door for them, assisting them from the vehicle one by one. Eve thanked him and made her way to the top of the stairs.

In the lobby, she stayed out of view of the door into the sanctuary while Olivia unbustled her train. Her bouquet, a simple arrangement of white roses tinged with green, waited for her on the counter. She drew in a deep breath and positioned the fragrant flowers in her arms, trying to settle the butterflies in her stomach. She'd attached her father's favorite cufflinks to one of his handkerchiefs and wrapped it around the base of the bouquet so he'd be with her in her thoughts.

The music began, and Olivia kissed her cheek. "Good luck."

Eve straightened her shoulders and moved to the door. She'd opted to walk alone rather than ask someone she barely knew to walk her down the aisle. No one could replace her dad. She stood alone in the entranceway until the piano played the first notes of the "Bridal Chorus," and she started her journey to her new life.

Carter couldn't take his eyes off her. Doug left his side to escort Olivia. He barely noticed. Nothing existed at that moment except the glowing redhead coming his way, her hazel eyes never leaving his face. His pulse raced.

Waiting for her to arrive nearly did him in. He bounced on his toes, forcing himself to remain in his spot when his whole being yearned to go to her and claim her hand.

She reached him and held out one hand. It trembled. In two steps, he was at her side, gathering her hand in his. Together, they turned toward the reverend. He had to clear the emotion clogging his throat before he could say his vows, he was so struck by the joy of realizing this beautiful woman would soon share his life as his wife.

When he slid the ring on her finger, peace bubbled inside.

Finally, the reverend bid him to kiss his bride. She met him halfway, and their lips met in a sweet kiss. It was a promise of love and fidelity.

"Ladies and gentlemen," the reverend announced, "I present for the first time, Carter and Eve Grant."

The congregation broke into enthusiastic applause. Carter grinned at Eve. Their new life together was about to begin. He wouldn't waste a moment of their new adventure together.

Granville Family Tree

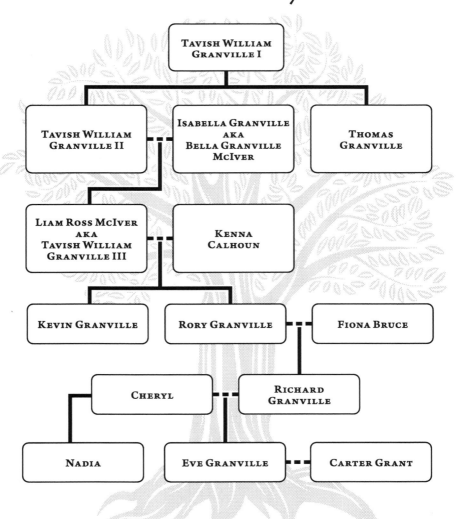

TAVISH WILLIAM GRANVILLE I

TAVISH WILLIAM GRANVILLE II

ISABELLA GRANVILLE AKA BELLA GRANVILLE MCIVER

THOMAS GRANVILLE

LIAM ROSS MCIVER AKA TAVISH WILLIAM GRANVILLE III

KENNA CALHOUN

KEVIN GRANVILLE

RORY GRANVILLE

FIONA BRUCE

CHERYL

RICHARD GRANVILLE

NADIA

EVE GRANVILLE

CARTER GRANT

▪▪▪▪▪▪ *Marriage*

Dear Reader,

We hope you enjoyed reading our stories. When we first began to brainstorm them, we needed to think of an object that would be important in both our stories. As we researched, the idea of heirloom thistle rings took hold. We especially liked the idea of a shared inscription connecting them. Alone, one ring wasn't worth much, but together, the pair was priceless. We liked the symbolism of the rings representing our souls. Alone, our souls, our lives, don't amount to much. When united with the power of Jesus's saving love, our lives are so much more.

Thank you for taking the time to read about our characters in Gnaw Bone, Indiana. We love to hear from readers.

Blessings!

Johnnie Alexander and Dana R. Lynn

About the Authors

Johnnie Alexander

Johnnie Alexander is an award-winning, best-selling novelist of more than twenty works of fiction in a variety of genres. She is on the executive boards of Serious Writer, Inc. and Mid-South Christian Writers Conference and cohosts an online show called Writers Chat. She also teaches at writers conferences and for Serious Writer Academy.

A fan of classic movies, stacks of books, and road trips, Johnnie shares a life of quiet adventure with Griff, her happy-go-lucky collie, and Rugby, her raccoon-treeing papillon.

Dana Lynn

Dana R. Lynn is an award-winning, *USA Today* and *Publishers Weekly* best-selling author of more than twenty romantic suspense and Amish romance books who believes in the power of God to touch people through stories. Although she grew up in Illinois, she met her husband at a wedding in Pennsylvania and told her parents she had met her future husband. Nineteen months later, they were married. Today, they live in rural Pennsylvania and are entering the world of empty nesters. She is a teacher of the deaf and hard of hearing by day and writes stories of romance and danger at night. Dana is an avid reader, loves cats, and thinks chocolate should be a food group.

Story Behind the Name

Gnaw Bone, Indiana

Gnaw Bone is a village of only a few hundred residents located between the Indiana towns of Nashville and Columbus (not to be confused with Nashville, Tennessee, and Columbus, Ohio).

The first settlers moved into what is now Brown County, Indiana, to escape malaria. Sometime later, many folks left to escape poverty brought on by soil erosion and economic isolation.

Gnaw Bone is famous for its three flea markets. The area, sometimes referred to as "The Little Smokies," is a popular tourist destination for its scenic views, historic attractions, and thriving art community, which dates back to the artist colony founded there in the early 1900s.

We've put "Visit Brown County" on our bucket lists and hope our stories encourage you to do the same.

Scottish Orange Marmalade Cake

Ingredients:

1½ cups butter, softened, plus
  ½ tablespoon for glaze
¾ cup granulated sugar
½ teaspoon grated orange zest
3 large eggs
⅔ cup orange marmalade,
  divided

2 tablespoons orange juice
1½ cups all-purpose flour
1½ teaspoons baking powder
¼ teaspoon salt
4 tablespoons confectioners'
  sugar

Directions:

Preheat oven to 350 degrees.

Grease 9×5-inch loaf pan.

With electric mixer, beat together softened butter, granulated sugar, and orange zest until light and fluffy, about 5 minutes. Beat in eggs, one at a time, until incorporated. Beat in ⅓ cup marmalade and orange juice.

In separate bowl, whisk together flour, baking powder, and salt. Fold dry ingredients into wet until just combined.

Pour batter into prepared pan. Bake until surface of cake is golden brown and toothpick inserted in the center comes out clean, about 50 to 55 minutes. Remove from oven and transfer pan to a wire rack. Cool 10 minutes; turn cake out of pan and place on rack right-side up. Place a rimmed baking sheet under rack to catch the glaze.

Heat remaining ⅓ cup marmalade in small pot over low heat until melted; whisk in confectioners' sugar and ½ tablespoon butter until smooth. Pour warm glaze over top of cake, allowing some to drizzle down the sides. Cool completely before slicing.

Read on for a sneak peek of another exciting book
in the Love's a Mystery series!

Love's a Mystery *in*
Tombstone, Arizona
by Bethany John & Gail Kirkpatrick

Rebuilding Love

By Bethany John

"In their hearts humans plan their course,
but the Lord establishes their steps."
—Proverbs 16:9

Tombstone, Arizona
1976

"You summoned me, counselor?"

Wyatt Clark looked over his shoulder to see his best friend's kid sister, Wilhelmina—Billie—Keenan walk through the door of the Rusty Spur, his family's Old West-themed restaurant that had recently shut its doors.

"Summoned?" he questioned as he took a good look at her. He shouldn't think of her as a kid anymore. She was twenty-seven now. All physical traces of the girl she had been faded away. Her braces were gone. Her frizzy red hair had magically transformed into shiny auburn curls. She wasn't dressed like she was as a child. Long gone were the smock dresses her grandmother had sewn by hand. They had been replaced by a fashionable pair of bell-bottom jeans and the kind of blouse his sister called a "peasant top." He could see that her time away from Tombstone had altered her a little. There was a sophistication to her, a confidence that he hadn't known her to have when they were growing up. If she weren't his best friend's annoying little sister, Wyatt might even call her beautiful. "I didn't 'summon' you. I simply called and asked if you would meet me here."

"You didn't call me. You called my brother, who called my mother, who told me to get myself to the Rusty Spur because you wanted to see me. If that's not summoning, I don't know what is."

"I didn't have your phone number," he said lamely. He could have asked Randy for it, but he felt weird doing that.

"I'll give it to you today. Although it might change soon," she said proudly. "I'm considering a job in New York. One of the biggest banks in the world offered me a position."

"New York?" He was alarmed to hear that. That would take her all the way to the other side of the country. They were both born and raised in Tombstone. New York would be another world for her. "Are you sure you want to move there? You've seen the news. It's not exactly a safe city. It's also thousands of miles away. What if something happened? It would be hard for anyone to get to you."

Billie narrowed her eyes at him, annoyance creeping across her face. "How about a congratulations? This a big deal. They don't take just anyone, you know."

"I'm happy that you were offered such a great opportunity. You deserve it. I was just in New York for a work trip. It was an experience. Stay out of Times Square." He couldn't see her there. He couldn't picture her so far away.

He didn't want her so far away.

"Aren't you being hypocritical? You took a job in San Francisco. It's not the safest city in the world either. There's crime everywhere. How can you give me grief for it?"

"I'm not giving you grief. I'm just concerned. You also can't compare us. I'm a six-foot-one 200-pound former football player. People tend not to mess with me, and if they did, I can handle myself."

"And I'm a five-foot-seven former math club champ who grew up with a six-foot-three brother and his annoying six-foot-one best friend who used to put me in headlocks every chance he got. I'm not fragile."

"I wasn't trying to hurt you then," he blurted out, feeling exasperated by how she couldn't see the difference. "I care about you. I would worry about you by yourself in New York." He hadn't meant to say it, but he had, and it was the truth.

The annoyance melted from her face, and she blinked at him for a long moment. "I said I've been offered a job. I didn't say I'd taken it. I've also interviewed for a job in Phoenix. It's a state job, not as fast paced, good benefits. I'm waiting to hear back."

Phoenix was still a good three hours away, but it wasn't New York.

"You'll get it." He motioned to a table, inviting her to sit. "You're in demand. You're the smartest person I know when it comes to numbers, and now you have an MBA to go with your accounting degree. There's no reason not to hire you."

"Why are you being so nice to me?" She looked around the empty restaurant suspiciously. "And why are we here? I thought your uncle put the place on the market."

He frowned at her. "What do you mean, why am I being so nice to you? I'm always nice to you."

"Oh, forgive me, I must have been imagining all the headlocks, hairpulling, and general teasing when we were kids."

"*Kids.* I'm thirty now. When's the last time I put you in a headlock? In fact, when was the last time I saw you? I've haven't been home in two years, and the last time I was, you were away at school."

"Has it been that long?" She looked thoughtful for a moment. "I guess it has. You wrote to me, so maybe that's why it doesn't feel as long."

He had sent her letters. On her birthday and on holidays and whenever he thought about her. Once in a while he'd included little gifts. Sometimes he sent her chocolate, other times he sent her a book he thought she would like. He got her parents and Randy gifts as well, but she was the only one he wrote to.

He clearly remembered the last time he did. It was her birthday, a little over a month ago, when he decided to leave his job and come back home. He sent her a pair of earrings, which were in her ears right now. It made him feel good to see them there.

"I'm home for good, Billie. I've quit my job."

Her mouth dropped open, a gasp escaping. "You're home for good? There can't be many corporate law jobs here in Tombstone.

Are you going to switch specialties? I guess if you open a small practice in town, you might be able to generate enough business. People always seem to need lawyers nowadays."

"I don't want to be a lawyer any longer. I came home to reopen the restaurant."

"What? You're going to reopen this place? But your uncle wants to retire, spend his golden years on a beach somewhere."

"He can do that. And I can do this. I've got some ideas on how to make it bigger and better than before. There's a new resort opening in town, and there's going to be a ton of tourists looking for a good place to eat. This can be that place."

"But you really want to run a restaurant? You haven't worked in here since you went to law school. There's so much that goes into it. Don't you know that 80 percent of restaurants fail within their first five years? It's a very risky business to get into."

Always practical. Always armed with facts. It was one of the reasons he needed her.

"But this restaurant isn't new. My great-grandfather started it over sixty years ago. People came then. They'll come again."

She looked at him and then around the empty restaurant. All that was left were some tables and chairs that had seen better days. Otherwise, his uncle had cleaned the place out completely. Tossed everything. Wyatt didn't even get a chance to save the old photograph of Wyatt Earp that used to hang on the wall over the register.

The emptiness of it all made him sad. Some of his best memories were here.

"I can't sit by and allow this place to close. It's where we both earned our first paycheck. It's where I learned how to work hard. I've done every job you could possibly do here, down to cleaning the toilets. I know I can run this place. Besides, legally, it's half mine. My father's share passed to me when he died. I can't let go of it."

She reached across the table and set her hand over his. Only she knew how hard the loss of his father was on him. It wasn't something he could share with Randy. He even had a hard time talking about it with his mother, but for some reason, he could talk to Billie. It was why he had asked to see her. He needed her to start this journey with him.

Billie looked at Wyatt for a long moment. He was no longer the silly boy who used to be at her house so often that she almost thought he lived there. He had matured. He had always been handsome. Every girl in her grade had a crush on him, but the boy with the good looks had morphed into a man that was ruggedly handsome. It was so odd to her that he had chosen to become a corporate lawyer when he looked more like a cowboy. He had dark hair, dark eyes, and broad shoulders. It was hard to imagine him stuck behind a desk all day, wearing a suit that he must have felt like he was suffocating in.

He had never told her he was unhappy with his chosen career. But she suspected he was by the tone of his last few letters.

He was more than her brother's friend. He was like family and, even though they hadn't seen much of each other these past five years, she knew him better than she had ever known anyone else.

"What do you need from me? My blessing? You have it. If you've got your heart set on doing something, how could I not support it?"

"I do need your blessing. No one else in my family is on board with this."

"Really? Not even your mother?"

"My mother loves to tell people that her son is an attorney living in California. Owning an Old West-themed restaurant wasn't in her plans for me."

"I'll support you. What does Randy think of it?"

"He doesn't know. I haven't told him yet."

"Why not?" She was surprised that Wyatt had decided to tell her first. "I'm sure he'll support you too."

"I didn't want to tell him until I had spoken to you first."

"But why?" She frowned in confusion.

"I need your help."

"Me?"

"Yes, you. Why do you seem so shocked? You're the most organized person I know. You have degrees in accounting and business, and you're the only one who's honest enough to tell me if I'm being ridiculous. Please, don't say no. I need you."

I need you.

His words, the way he said them, struck her right in the chest. He had never asked her for anything.

"How long would I be helping you?"

His eyes widened with excitement, and a boyish grin crept over his face. "You'll do it?"

"Answer my question first."

"Just the summer. Until we open. And I'll pay you a fair rate."

"Of course you will. Do you think I work for free?"

He stood up, grabbed her hand, and yanked her out of her chair and into a hug. "Thank you, Billie," he said in her ear. She shut her eyes and leaned into him for a moment. But it was only a moment, because he twisted her around and put her in a headlock.

"You're never too old for this."

"Let go of me, you big oaf!"

He did, still grinning at her. "Got to keep you on your toes." He surprised her again by smoothing her hair. It was a gentle touch that jolted her much more than the headlock. "Can't let you leave with your hair standing up all over your head."

She lightly slapped his hand away. "Don't touch me, goof."

"I promise I'll try to refrain from doing that while we're working together. Can you meet me back here around six? I want to show you the plans I drew up and see what you think."

"That's dinnertime."

"Don't worry. I'll feed you."

He took a key out of his pocket and handed it to her. "This is for you. It opens both the front and the back doors so you can come and go whenever you need to."

"You have a key for me already?" she asked as she stared down at it.

"Yeah. I picked up the copy this morning."

"How were you so sure I would say yes?"

"I had faith." He grinned at her again and set off toward the door. "Lock up when you go. I need to take care of some things before tonight."

He left her alone in the restaurant. He seemed deliriously happy, but Billie wondered if she was getting in over her head.

A Note from the Editors

We hope you enjoyed another volume in the Love's a Mystery series, created by Guideposts. For over seventy-five years, Guideposts, a nonprofit organization, has been driven by a vision of a world filled with hope. We aspire to be the voice of a trusted friend, a friend who makes you feel more hopeful and connected.

By making a purchase from Guideposts, you join our community in touching millions of lives, inspiring them to believe that all things are possible through faith, hope, and prayer. Your continued support allows us to provide uplifting resources to those in need. Whether through our communities, websites, apps, or publications, we inspire our audiences, bring them together, and comfort, uplift, entertain, and guide them. Visit us at guideposts.org to learn more.

We would love to hear from you. Write us at Guideposts, P.O. Box 5815, Harlan, Iowa 51593 or call us at (800) 932-2145. Did you love *Love's a Mystery in Gnaw Bone, Indiana*? Leave a review for this product on guideposts.org/shop. Your feedback helps others in our community find relevant products.

Find inspiration, find faith, find Guideposts.

Shop our best sellers and favorites at
guideposts.org/shop

Or scan the QR code to go directly to our Shop

Find more inspiring stories in these best-loved Guideposts fiction series!

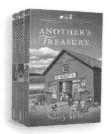

Mysteries of Lancaster County

Follow the Classen sisters as they unravel clues and uncover hidden secrets in Mysteries of Lancaster County. As you get to know these women and their friends, you'll see how God brings each of them together for a fresh start in life.

Secrets of Wayfarers Inn

Retired schoolteachers find themselves owners of an old warehouse-turned-inn that is filled with hidden passages, buried secrets, and stunning surprises that will set them on a course to puzzling mysteries from the Underground Railroad.

Tearoom Mysteries Series

Mix one stately Victorian home, a charming lakeside town in Maine, and two adventurous cousins with a passion for tea and hospitality. Add a large scoop of intriguing mystery, and sprinkle generously with faith, family, and friends, and you have the recipe for *Tearoom Mysteries*.

Ordinary Women of the Bible

Richly imagined stories—based on facts from the Bible—have all the plot twists and suspense of a great mystery, while bringing you fascinating insights on what it was like to be a woman living in the ancient world.

To learn more about these books, visit Guideposts.org/Shop